CW01642116

PEI

THE GREAT L

Rupa Gulab is a Mumbai-based freelance writer and columnist, and the author of *Girl Alone* and *Chip of the Old Blockhead*. She scribbled her first stories, *Hamlet the Cutlet* and *Nostracious Nominovich—The Commie Spy*, while in her early teens to keep her two little sisters amused. Shockingly, the stories won her two little diehard fans. She continues to write for them.

The GREAT DEPRESSION of the 40s

A Novel

Rupa Gulab

PENGUIN BOOKS

PENGUIN BOOKS
Published by the Penguin Group
Penguin Books India Pvt. Ltd, 11 Community Centre, Panchsheel Park, New Delhi 110 017, India
Penguin Group (USA) Inc., 375 Hudson Street, New York, New York 10014, USA
Penguin Group (Canada), 90 Eglinton Avenue East, Suite 700, Toronto, Ontario, M4P 2Y3, Canada (a division of Pearson Penguin Canada Inc.)
Penguin Books Ltd, 80 Strand, London WC2R 0RL, England
Penguin Ireland, 25 St Stephen's Green, Dublin 2, Ireland (a division of Penguin Books Ltd)
Penguin Group (Australia), 250 Camberwell Road, Camberwell, Victoria 3124, Australia (a division of Pearson Australia Group Pty Ltd)
Penguin Group (NZ), 67 Apollo Drive, Rosedale, North Shore 0632, New Zealand (a division of Pearson New Zealand Ltd)
Penguin Group (South Africa) (Pty) Ltd, 24 Sturdee Avenue, Rosebank, Johannesburg 2196, South Africa

Penguin Books Ltd, Registered Offices: 80 Strand, London WC2R 0RL, England

First published by Penguin Books India 2010

Copyright © Rupa Gulab 2010

All rights reserved

10 9 8 7 6 5 4 3 2 1

This is a work of fiction. Names, characters, places and incidents are either the product of the author's imagination or are used fictitiously, and any resemblance to any actual person, living or dead, events or locales is entirely coincidental.

ISBN 9780143067801

Typeset in Joanna MT Std by InoSoft Systems, Noida
Printed at Thomson Press India Ltd, New Delhi

This book is sold subject to the condition that it shall not, by way of trade or otherwise, be lent, resold, hired out, or otherwise circulated without the publisher's prior written consent in any form of binding or cover other than that in which it is published and without a similar condition including this condition being imposed on the subsequent purchaser and without limiting the rights under copyright reserved above, no part of this publication may be reproduced, stored in or introduced into a retrieval system, or transmitted in any form or by any means (electronic, mechanical, photocopying, recording or otherwise), without the prior written permission of both the copyright owner and the above-mentioned publisher of this book.

To my parents,
Jyoti and Vashu Gulab:
The two most special people in my life;
The two most charming unpublished writers I've ever read;
The two reasons why I was inspired to become a writer.
Love always.

Because I do not hope to turn again
Because I do not hope
Because I do not hope to turn
Desiring this man's gift and that man's scope
I no longer strive to strive towards such things
(Why should the agèd eagle stretch its wings?)

—T.S. Eliot, Ash Wednesday

1

The newspaper's food critic was really to blame. If he hadn't got Delhi Belly, the rest of Mantra's life may well have taken a different course. She'd have been too busy earning a salary to lose her mind, for starters. But the fact remains that the ailing food critic had been condemned to a month-long diet of boiled vegetables and chewable antacids. Mantra had been asked to fill in for him and review a new, dreadfully pretentious restobar. Four short, snappy lines of her review went down in history as the epitaph of her career:

'While the spaghetti was a bit of okay,
The meatballs stubbornly bounced.
They're only fit to be served at squash courts,
And deserve to be severely trounced.'

Now, how was she to know that Ye Ed's best buddy's brother-in-law's Armenian boyfriend owned the restobar? And why should that have stopped her anyway? Hell broke loose the day the review was published. She was summoned to her editor Partho's plush cabin and he thrust the offending article at her in a fierce, stabbing gesture.

'Explain this,' he stuttered in a wild-eyed way, dramatically rubbing the left side of his chest with his free hand.

Mantra cleared her throat nervously and replied, hoping she wouldn't be held responsible for his imminent cardiac arrest on grounds of culpable homicide. 'It's self-explanatory really.

The food sucked big time, and I was being honest like an ethical reviewer should be.' She pursed her lips primly when she said that, an invisible halo not just hovering virtuously over her head but recklessly kicking out its legs and dancing like a shameless exhibitionist. In shocking pink stockings at that.

'Ethics be damned,' he bellowed. 'That man has screamed my ear off on the phone all morning. My bloody blood pressure has shot up and it's all *your* fault!' An irate lecture followed on how diplomacy was more important than 'crappy ethics'.

'Excuse me,' Mantra cut in sarcastically, 'but haven't you forgotten our newspaper's motto—the inspiring line below our masthead that reads: *Amicus Plato, sed magis amica veritas?*'

'Yes, yes, Plato is my friend, but a greater friend is truth. Who gives a fuck about that?' Partho roared. 'Like hell anyone knows what it means!'

'I do,' Mantra muttered staunchly, prompting Partho to look a tad defensive.

'It's just some rubbish about the truth, Mantra. It sounds pompous, that's the only reason why it's there! I'll bet you the great unwashed have no clue. For all they care, it could well mean "Plato is a dickhead!"'

Silly ass, Mantra raved internally in the midst of his rant. He's just upset because he hates being ticked off by page 3 regulars.

The lecture was rounded off with the demand that Mantra fall in line with the newspaper's corporate culture. 'You've been here three years and you still haven't tuned into it. Worse still, your frequent oddball remarks are vitiating the atmosphere—the bloody juniors have started emulating you, and you're no bloody role model heroine, not by a long shot!'

Years of experience had taught Mantra that 'Conform to our corporate culture' also meant 'Kiss my ass and look like you're loving it, slave!' Her blood pressure shot up too, whizzing way past Partho's current high mark. She dug her nails sharply into her denim-clad thighs to stop herself from telling him exactly what she was thinking: that there was no way in hell she'd conform to the culture of an organization so steeped in hypocrisy and mediocrity that it didn't have the balls to take a stand on anything, not even undeniably lousy meatballs.

Partho read her momentary silence as a welcome sign of capitulation, and he encouragingly barked, 'Shape up!' for good measure.

Oh please say you'd much rather ship out, a tantalizing voice in Mantra's head pleaded with her. Who knows, maybe bungee jumping is your true calling? Hey, take a sabbatical at the very least, dammit! You're forty-three, you prefer yolks to whites, you smoke, you give veggies a wide berth, osteoporosis and quite possibly a hip-bone replacement are on their way, and you may never find out what it feels like to be truly free. Go on, tell him to go fly a kite!

Mantra did just that, and a surge of relief coursed through her body as the words tumbled out, tripping over each other in their urgent rush to be heard. She felt like she'd been instantly exorcized. It was not as though this particular organization was bad news—it was about the same as all the others. Besides, Partho wasn't really a nasty evil boss —in fact Mantra rather enjoyed his eccentricity and egotism. They gave her lots to giggle about. She was just bored of doing the same job year after year after year after year. She wanted a break. A clean break. Heaven knows, she needed a break! She suppressed an overpowering urge to leap up and envelope Partho in a warm bear hug for helping her take the liberating decision—the egotist may have thought she was making a pass at him.

Partho's jaw dropped and he began to stutter again. Not because he loved Mantra dearly, but because a lot of people were quitting the paper to join a new rag that was offering obscene salaries. He assumed that Mantra had been made an offer too. Corporate ego was at stake and he was its designated champion.

'Think about it, don't be hasty. No need for immature knee-jerk reactions,' he barked in as reasonable a manner as he could manage.

'My resignation letter will be on your desk in five minutes,' Mantra replied woodenly. 'I'd keyed it in months ago in a fit of frustration. I merely have to change the date and get a printout. Oh and, by the way, I don't have even a day's notice to serve; I've got loads of leave. I depart with my personal motto: *Veritas vos liberabit.*'

Partho scoffed. 'Utter tosh! The truth may set you free, Mantra, but, mark my words, your bills will tie you down!'

Mantra kicked his door open like she'd seen John Wayne do it in classic Westerns and strode out, ignoring Partho's anguished, 'Mantra, wait!' Her grand exit was mildly marred by the fact that she accidentally stubbed her toe in the process, but she bravely quelled the primeval urge to scream in acute pain. She knew better than to completely ruin her otherwise dignified exit. When you say something lofty in Latin, it's best to ensure that you don't screw it up.

Mantra sailed out of the office at 6.30 p.m., hoping to leave without a backward glance—the way it should always be done. Typically, however, her driver foiled her plans. Makarand gave her a filthy look for interrupting his chat with his tea-shop buddies, and held up his cup of tea triumphantly. Mantra nodded resignedly and was left to cool her heels outside the office building, while Makarand made a huge pretence of blowing on the dregs of his tea to cool it. Lording it over Mantra was a big part of his dignity. Yelling 'chutiya' and/or 'bhonsri ke' to other motorists while Mantra was in the car was another part. Oddly enough, he never swore when Vir was in the car, even if the provocation was extreme.

While waiting, Mantra debated whether she should call Vir and tell him her big news but prudently decided against it. She'd do it at home after his restorative glass of fresh lime, when he was safely sitting down. A mischievous gust of sea breeze lifted her hair and playfully whipped her face with it. Mantra's frown lines vanished instantly—the sea always improved her mood. This was the only perk of working at

Nariman Point. Watching the orange sun dunk itself into the sea like a giant biscuit from her cabin window had always helped to restore her equanimity.

About twenty minutes later, Makarand insolently swaggered towards the car in a deliberately unhurried manner, and Mantra was finally on the road to freedom. Once again, she exhaled with relief at having escaped the corporate world. The cherry on the cake was she would never have to suffer the indignity of faking laughter at puerile jokes made by egomaniacs who had the final word on her salary. Never again, she swore to herself—there were things she'd never do again for money! And just why is it, she idly wondered, that once people become head honchos, they start believing it's part of their job responsibility to act like stand-up comics? And can't they get better material to work with if that's the case?

'Please stop at the bakery first, Makarand,' were her terse instructions.

An unpleasant altercation ensued outside the bakery when Makarand aggressively stole the parking space that a pretty, young female driver was attempting to reverse into. Mantra should have guessed that the rabid male chauvinist would do that; he always got ridiculously competitive with female drivers to literally drive home the point that it was a man's world. He was made to eat crow this time—the young woman was not as delicate as she looked and viciously attempted to ram her gigantic SUV into Mantra's dinky car in a revenge quest. A motley crowd gathered and sympathies were clearly with the attractive young driver since she was in the right and, besides, she *was* a deliciously pretty, young thing. Mantra debated whether to let Makarand be lynched by the mob—the testosterone-enhanced ass deserved it—but sanity prevailed and she made him return the parking space forthwith. Even more humiliating (as far as Makarand was concerned) Mantra wrung a public apology out of him. She knew she'd have to pay for it—he was quite capable of getting her bumped off by his political connections. Really, she *must* make Vir speak to him about his brash behaviour, she promised herself. More importantly, they had to find out for sure if he was a member of the dreaded SNM party. I wonder if they're aware that their initials have another meaning that suits them far better, Mantra thought with a giggle and then became sober again when she realized that proof of Makarand's party membership would be of no help. Sacking him was out of the question—his fellow hooligans would probably rough them up and ransack the house as punishment.

Back in the car with a celebratory chocolate pastry for herself and a loaf of high-fibre multi-grain bread for Vir, Mantra ignored Makarand's filthy looks and muttered imprecations. Instead, she eyed the high-fibre multi-grain loaf with revulsion and recalled the astonishment Kaushalya (Cook the First) had displayed the very first time Vir had brought this variety of bread home.

'How peculiar, didi. This is the rubbish granaries throw out when they make flour. We feed it to cattle in our village.'

Mantra smiled fondly at the memory and thought affectionately of fat and jolly Kaushalya and greedily of her divine food. Life had been dreadful since she'd left for a more lucrative post in Dubai. A distressed Mantra had eagerly offered to match the salary, but Kaushalya had had other considerations too.

'Tankoo, didi, but I've always wanted to fly in an aeroplane and live in foreign and this is my only opportunity. And such good marriage prospects I'll get now, wait and see—boys will line up, begging to marry ugly, fat old me,' she had chuckled merrily.

So Mantra reluctantly sent her off with a hug and wished her the best. Kaushalya deserved it—she was lovely!

Vir's cholesterol was solely to blame for Kaushalya's pathetic successor. If Mantra had known about twenty-odd years ago that Vir would become a control-freakish hypochondriac when he hit middle age, she'd *never* have agreed to attach the ball and chain to her then-slender and non-water-retentive ankle. He Who'd Scowl Ferociously When Dragged To Grocery Stores now insisted that they spend practically every waking moment of their weekends there, stocking up on extra virgin olive oil, whole wheat pasta, high-fibre multi-grain bread and distasteful greens they didn't even know the names of. If that weren't bad enough, Vir had insisted that wonderful, wonderful Kaushalya's replacement would be dour Reshma, a 'jewel' their family doctor had prescribed along with his cholesterol medication. Reshma had worked at a cardiac hospital earlier and had a talent for creating meals with practically zero oil and absolutely zero imagination.

After Mantra's first bite of Reshma's first meal, she had assertively clanged her fork on her plate for Vir's attention. 'Vir, her food's awful!' she'd bravely declared.

'Yup, it's the worst I've ever had,' he'd nodded, chewing doggedly.

'So let's wish her goodbye and good luck and get someone with a little more talent,' she had exhaled, hugely relieved.

'No way!' Vir had protested. 'Her food sucks so bad, it's got to be good for our health. I say she stays.'

'And I say she goes!' Mantra had said firmly. 'The only way I can ingest this is intravenously. My taste buds find it offensive.'

Unfortunately for Mantra, Reshma had been hovering around during this exchange and the look she'd directed at Mantra could have killed a virile adult elephant.

'Excuse me for butting in,' she had said haughtily in flawless English, 'but I'm not going to stand around here being insulted. Since you think my cooking is not up to par, I'd much rather go elsewhere.'

Both Mantra and Vir had been equally stunned. While Mantra had opened and closed her mouth wordlessly like a goldfish, Vir had made a swift recovery and stepped in.

'Reshma, I must congratulate you on your command over the English language. I'm curious though, why didn't you speak to us in English from the start since you're obviously comfortable with it?'

'Because employers expect servants to speak the native language. It keeps us firmly in our place,' had been the glacial rejoinder.

'As your evil oppressive employer then, I insist that you communicate with us in English,' Vir had said, unscathed by her sarcasm. 'That is, of course, if you'd like to work with us. I for one have no problem with your cooking skills.'

'And I,' Mantra had added, after her composure returned, 'would like to sincerely apologize for my criticism. Though Reshma, I cannot deny that while it was healthy and wholesome, it could have been tastier.'

'Sorry, but that's the best I can do, so I'd better leave.'

'Oh please do stay,' Vir had exhorted with a warm engaging smile. 'I like your spunk and my cholesterol needs you!'

'Very well then, but I stay on the condition that you will not deviate from the diet while I'm in this house. Is that understood?'

Vir had nodded his assent, but Mantra had returned to performing her goldfish imitation. Reshma had cast a look of utmost scorn in her direction, and sailed away to the kitchen.

From that moment onwards, her back had been up. Reshma silently declared herself Mantra's sworn enemy and made it very clear that she was determined to give Mantra a hard time. For starters, she addressed Vir with the friendly appellation 'bhaiyya' but, despite Mantra's fervent requests to address her as 'didi', Reshma insisted on calling her 'madam'. This was an exceptionally bad word in Mantra's opinion—it made her feel like a brothel owner. And the very first thing Reshma did after the plates of the very first meal had been cleared was to imperiously toss all the delicious chocolates, cheeses and pâtés from the fridge into the bin without consulting Mantra. When questioned, she had defiantly said that she could not be expected to cure a patient with temptation lying around and if Mantra objected, she would surrender her post forthwith. Vir had looked at Mantra so beseechingly, she'd had to give in. She loved the stupid ass, after all! But she was left with the depressing realization that if Vir was an annoying health nut, Reshma was a terrifying health Nazi.

When Mantra arrived home that evening, Reshma greeted her with her usual fierce living-with-the-enemy scowl, but when she saw Makarand standing behind Mantra to hand over the packages and the car keys, her expression changed dramatically. She smiled coyly at him, and Mantra wasn't really sure but she thought she saw Makarand give Reshma a broad wink. This startling discovery led to a disturbing thought: Bloody hell! Doesn't Reshma know he's married? Gosh, I must bring up his marital status in a subtle manner.

2

Anjali sat in the large veranda shrouded in darkness, the twinkling lights of Marine Drive spread beneath her, and sighed appreciatively at the view. Mumbai looked drop dead gorgeous when it put on its evening sparkles. Well, her posh part of Mumbai, at any rate. The bottle of wine she was attempting to uncork was gripped tightly between her thighs and giggles involuntarily escaped from her lips as she remembered a similar wrestling match a few months ago: her sister-in-law Mantra watching her struggle with amusement and wickedly urging her to plunge the corkscrew right in and give it a fantastic screw. That time too, she had been unsuccessful and Karan had had to take over. Mantra had obligingly proffered a tea strainer when the deed was done. 'Wine is bad enough without bits of cork floating around in it,' she had astutely remarked.

Anjali gave up and poured herself a stiff shot of Tequila sans the tedious lime wedge and salt charade. She needed it desperately. Shiv's bolt-from-the-blue text message had thrown her off-balance, and she'd been looking forward to time alone to think back on the past with the specific intention of evicting the demons raging inside her head.

She'd had crushes and boyfriends before Shiv. Surreptitious hand holding and the usual innocuous necking had been indulged in, but no one had really touched the core of her being. After all, she'd always known that her parents would choose her husband. It was something she'd tacitly accepted, the way she acknowledged that things that taste like garbage are usually good for you. Take that ghastly Waterbury's Compound, for example. She had just been biding time till a suitable boy was unearthed for her. Then came college and Shiv, the junkie from the political science department. The fuck-you expression in his eyes, his fierce intensity and radical anti-establishment statements had turned her knees to jelly—she'd never met anyone that dangerously exciting before. Being a coward, rebels turned her on tremendously. The most special thing about Shiv, however, had been the fact that he made her feel as though she was the only person in the world who mattered to him. So much so that Anjali had been fairly certain that even if Botticelli's voluptuous Venus came to life and attempted to lure Shiv to bed, he'd disinterestedly tell her to go fuck herself. After a year of dating, things had heated up on the physical front and Anjali had been too attracted to Shiv to coyly fob him off with the good Indian girl sex holdback line. Hell, she had been as turned on as he was but there was still one little matter she had to air before she gave the all-clear signal.

'We will get married someday, won't we? We'll have to elope, of course; my parents would never agree,' she had said matter-of-factly, absolutely certain that the answer would be on the lines of 'Yes! Yes! Oh yes!'

The recollection of Shiv sharply recoiling still had the power, after almost thirty long years, to make Anjali's cheeks burn. 'What the fuck?' he had demanded. 'Are you using sex to blackmail me into marriage?'

Anjali had been caught on the backfoot. She had made her protests in a small voice, assuring him that she wasn't blackmailing, merely asking and his answer wouldn't have made a difference anyway. That had been the honest truth really. But Shiv had buttoned up and headed out of their love nest—the dank basement in the college where dusty old files were stored. His parting shot had been, 'I don't pay a price for action, geddit?'

After that Anjali had been stonewalled like never before. He'd looked through her at college, her phone calls weren't returned and her letters, smudged with tears, went unanswered too. The one time Anjali had managed to get him alone in college and begged him to take her back, he'd pushed her away with a sneer.

'Oh fuck off,' he'd jeered. 'I'm not into ruining good Indian girls. I have principles too, strange but true. But one of my chums really fancies you. I'll give him your number and tell him you're willing to put out, if you like.'

More burning hot tears had followed, and her anger towards her parents had grown with every drop. She had blamed them in her head for her love life being in tatters. If it hadn't been for their strict upbringing, she'd probably never have been:

(a) Perversely attracted to rebellious Shiv.
(b) Gauche and brought up the 'M' word at a moment considered inappropriate by someone as cool as him.

Anjali had only given up hope, however, when Shiv had started dating someone else (a slut, in her jaundiced opinion). Thereafter, she had had no choice but to watch him silently from the sidelines, digging her nails into her palms, downing bottles of vile-tasting antacids to stop the bile from rising in her throat, determinedly quelling the jealousy that welled up inside her. After they finished college, she hadn't known where he'd gone and told herself sternly that she didn't care. Time had helped her wrap him up into a tiny parcel labelled 'Caution: 100,000 Volts' and push him into the deepest, furthest recesses of her mind.

A few months after she'd graduated, her parents introduced her to a 'multinational' banker, a prize catch in their social milieu. She didn't really care who they chose for her. As far as she was concerned, the great love of her life was over and done with; no one else would ever matter. She had been as willing to stay single as she was to marry any old stranger.

She'd met Karan a couple of times for coffee. He was floored by her, despite the fact that she'd been reticent and hadn't revealed anything significant about herself during the parentally orchestrated 'get-to-know-each-other' sessions. The only personal admission she'd made was that she preferred sickly sweet white chocolate over the dark variety he'd given her in a pretty box. She hadn't bothered to be remotely gracious. Nonetheless, Karan had wanted her. Fortunately for him, their horoscopes had matched perfectly and the usual noisy, showy, no-holds-barred Indian wedding was held. The morning after, she thought she liked Karan, he thought he loved her, and, happily deluded, they never looked back, content to live like their squeaky clean parents in a squeaky clean world.

And now this text message that said, 'Hey stranger, got your number from Anisha. BTW, I've moved to your adopted city. Drink to catch up? Do save my number—waiting for your call—Shiv.' Bile rose in her throat again in a Pavlovian reaction, this time not accompanied by tears. How dare the arrogant sod assume that she'd want to see him again! She resisted the temptation to tell him that of course she'd love to meet him for a drink only for the delightful opportunity to pour it over his fat head.

The shrill ringing of the phone rudely interrupted Anjali's reverie. She glanced impatiently at the caller ID on the glowing screen, scrunching her eyes to see the number better. Then she eagerly answered the call.

'Yes, hello, darling. Need more money or have you sold your toiletries and textbooks yet again to pay for your lavish lifestyle?' she teased warmly.

'You have become senile, haven't you, Mother?' he teased back.

'Rubbish! My brain is as sprightly as it used to be.'

'On the contrary, aged parent, you've forgotten something rather important.'

'Forgotten what? Oh good grief, Rohan,' Anjali gasped, 'it's not your birthday, is it?'

'Nope, nothing as unforgivable as that. You were supposed to mail my driving license. I told you I've seen this second-hand bike I want to buy.'

'Oh that. Please, I hadn't forgotten. I just don't like the idea of you on a bike. Wait till you start earning and buy a car instead,' she pleaded.

'Back off, Mother. Father's already agreed. Now please send it ASAP.'

'Only if you promise *never* to drink and drive,' she warned, wryly conceding to herself that he'd won the battle anyway.

'Ya, ya!'

'"Ya, ya" means you're hearing what I'm saying but not listening! Rohan, I want a solemn promise, okay?'

'Ya, ya, Mother,' came the standard, disinterested response.

After Anjali spoke to her son, her mood changed. She was her old self again, besotted mother and amiable wife. Enough of this ghost-of-boyfriend-past moment, she thought. Shiv is just a rotter and I have no room for those in my warm and cosy life. I won't waste a precious second thinking about him, she decided.

3

'Honestly, I cannot understand why laptop bags are designed to sling on one shoulder. A backpack format would evenly distribute the weight and bring down the share price of stinky balms,' Mantra complained as she tenderly massaged Vir's sore laptop shoulder.

'Maybe you can get into the laptop bag business now that you're jobless,' Vir retorted sharply. 'Or do you have other concrete plans in mind?'

'Nope,' she replied brightly.

'And what does that mean? You're not going to work again?' he exclaimed, horror and disbelief etched on his face.

'Not for a bit, at any rate. I'm going to flake out for a while, just do some freelance writing and things.'

Mantra's phone rang at that opportune moment.

'Darling,' her mother cooed, 'your father and I are moving to an ashram.'

'Hello? Did you just say ashram?' Mantra squealed, hoping fervently that she'd misheard her mother.

'Yes, ashram,' her mother repeated calmly. 'A for Alzheimer's, S for scurvy, H for herpes . . .'

'Don't talk rubbish, Mum! Neither Dad nor you are remotely religious. What are you really going there for? Orgies?' Mantra screamed.

'You're being ridiculous now. You know very well your father and I are too old and decrepit for orgies,' her mother chided. 'We're just not interested in running the house any more, and we thought an ashram would be a little livelier than an old folks' home. Besides, your father and I have a business plan. We're seriously considering starting a brand new religion, and we're researching the idea. Also, you get to meet interesting people from so many countries at ashrams. Mantra, there's this tarot card reader from Glasgow and I just have to tell you the *disastrous* things she said about your marriage!'

'Have you, by any chance, moved in already?' Mantra said slowly and threateningly, cutting her mother short.

'Just about,' her mother conceded guiltily. 'We've been here a week now and, darling, it's so weird but charming. You *must* pay us a visit soon.'

'This is preposterous! And what have you done with the house? You appear to have been in such a tearing hurry to get away, I hope you locked it at least. Or do you imagine that God will look after it now that you're a believer?' she sneered.

'Of course we locked it,' her mother snapped, 'and don't you dare talk to me like that! When you feel like being civil, we'll resume the conversation.' She abruptly disconnected the call and Mantra was left gaping at the receiver.

Vir was watching her with a smirk. He'd heard enough of the conversation to get the gist.

'Oh good, so since you're not working any more, maybe you can finally accompany your parents to a shrink. You may get a fabulous deal: three for the price of two.'

'Oh cut it out! Don't you *dare* make fun of them. They have the right to live by their own rules, however strange it may seem to you and me!' Mantra shot back hotly, annoyed at Vir for crossing the line. She'd made it clear to him at the very outset that she was the only person on Planet Earth who had the right to criticize her parents.

After taking several deep breaths to restore her equanimity, she resumed the conversation. 'I've got a jolly good mind to courier Rachel Manija Brown's book on ashram life to them—they'll run home screaming! But now, back to me. As a matter of fact, I'm going to learn Chinese or write a book or learn to bungee jump to get over my fear of heights. Maybe all three.'

Vir was stunned. 'Why Chinese?'

'Don't you read the papers? Not only are they trying to be the world's biggest superpower, they're also shamelessly claiming chunks of India as their own.'

'And how will learning Chinese stop them in their tracks?' he asked, the sneer back in his voice.

'Know thine enemy!' Mantra retorted darkly. 'Did you know that we're losing our edge over them? I read this report in the papers that said they have more scientists and researchers than us these days! Our new generation is only interested in bloody IT and marketing. You can't rule the world with that knowledge alone, dammit! You have to learn how to kill ruthlessly with biological weapons, like those creepy sci-fi villains.'

Vir didn't like the idea one bit. Not the learning Chinese/writing book/attempting bungee jumping part, but the not working part. It meant tightening their collective belt drastically. The way it worked was, he provided the accommodation and brought home the bread and butter, while she provided the jam—well, a small economy pack of it at any rate—that went into their emergency kitty. That apart, he was going through a rough patch at work. While Mantra was aware of the fact that Uday Handa (fondly referred to as Urea Heap in private) had ingratiatingly slimed his way into the CEO's affections, she failed to understand the extent of the damage it was causing Vir. For starters, he had been given the unenviable job of firing people.

'I think the staff has a nickname for me,' Vir plaintively said, changing the subject.

'Really?' Mantra said cheerfully. 'What is it?'

'The hangman.'

Mantra ruffled his hair sympathetically, but couldn't suppress her giggles.

Vir's lips twitched for a brief second, and then he went back to being solemn. 'Hmm. Not so funny when you remember that I used to be the most popular suit around.'

He lapsed into broody silence. Should I tell Mantra that apple polishing isn't Uday's sole forte? he wondered. Hell, he's playing devious games to discredit my performance at work, too. A fallback income would come in handy. Vir was smart enough to figure out that there was a big chance he wouldn't just lose out in the game of corporate musical chairs with Uday, he could lose his job too. Naah, better save her the worry, he decided. She's a firebrand, besides. One hint of Uday doing the dirty, and she'll be at his throat, denouncing him in public, threatening to take him to court and writing incendiary articles in the pink papers about him. There's one job she'll be brilliant at though, he smirked.

Mantra caught the smirk. 'What? What ghastly things are thinking of?'

'Nothing. Well, just that you really should be a trade union leader—that's your true calling. '

'Where did that come from?' Mantra glared and playfully kicked him. Without waiting for a reply, she launched into a lengthy debate on the virtues of a break year. She was at her most persuasive.

'I'm looking at it as experiencing retirement while I can still go to the loo without a nursing attendant in tow. The good thing is, I have decent savings salted away, and I swear to God that I'll budget the household money so well you won't even notice the difference,' she said earnestly.

'Don't blame me if your brain becomes soft through disuse,' Vir said, resignedly. He secretly wished that he too had the luxury of quitting his job.

'I won't,' she reassured him. 'I'll do crosswords, Sudoku and play other mind games to keep it on the ball.'

Later, after they tucked themselves into bed, Mantra gave Vir a hug and he mumbled grudgingly that maybe her quitting work wasn't such a bad idea after all. 'And perhaps you won't be too tired for sex any more,' he added sarcastically.

'Well then, you'd better go to sleep and get some rest. I'm going to make up for my two months of celibacy soon,' she said optimistically.

'Correction! Five months, two weeks and three days,' Vir stated matter-of-factly.

'What, you've been counting?' Mantra squawked and raised her head to look at him.

He nodded. And he wasn't smiling.

The smile was back on his face a few minutes later though, when he tried to nudge her into getting naughty. Mantra half-heartedly began to give in when she was saved by screams that pierced through their ceiling from the penthouse above. It was Samira the page 3 wannabe again, the third night in a row. The first night they had heard her shriek, Mantra had jumped out of bed and insisted on calling the police but Vir had stopped her.

'Maybe they're listening to opera and trying to acquire a bit of class, God knows they badly need it,' he had argued persuasively.

Mantra's ear drums had almost been shattered during an amateur performance of *The Barber of Seville* a few years ago, so she conceded that Vir had a point and let it go. The second night, Vir had dissuaded her from calling the police station again. He firmly said it was absolutely none of their business; if Samira had a problem with her husband, she could just as well summon the police herself during the day while he was away stuffing black money into his (presumably) fat Italian leather office sofa set.

'Anyway, they're probably into whips and chains and perverted shit. Maybe even that strange vibrating ring condom that our moralistic political parties are railing over. Those could be screams of excitement too, you know,' he had mumbled and rolled over, sleeping through the din.

Tonight, Vir attempted to stop Mantra again. This time, he failed. She'd already dialled the police station and was listening to a sleepy, disinterested voice hoarsely whispering 'Hello'. Vir hastily disconnected the phone and firmly told her to keep her nose out of it. A few hours later, they were woken up by the insistent ringing of the doorbell. In a manly way Vir pushed Mantra aside to answer it. A weedy policeman stood outside, demanding to know if there was a problem.

'Good heavens, it's taken them that long to trace our number!' Mantra gasped.

It was her turn to push Vir aside. 'Yes there was a problem about three hours ago,' she informed the policeman caustically, pointing to the penthouse above. 'But now there's silence so he must be dead drunk and she must be dead.'

She said this in English, so the policeman looked clueless and Vir, in opportunistic-bastard mode, waved him away apologizing profusely for having dialled the police station by mistake. The policeman left, looking relieved. God knows he'd had a hard day, with an always-spoiling-for-fight local party going on the rampage because pigeons had foolishly assumed that the statue of one of their icons was a public lavatory. What *were* they implying? That their political rivals had trained the pigeons to shit on the statue? Many buses and cars had been burnt while TV cameras rolled. Pigeons—really, they're a bigger nuisance than plague-bearing rats! he thought to himself bitterly.

A huge row ensued after the policeman left, during which Mantra and Vir sent a lot of crystal to glass heaven. Not that they cared; it was the ugly fussy stuff Vir's dealers would force on him at Diwali, crammed to the brim with brain-activating almonds and diabetes-encouraging chocolates. Mantra had deliberately left them lying around, hoping their Maoist househelp, Shalinibai, would slapdash them to oblivion, as was her wont. This was her way of registering her protest against new India's show-offy conspicuous consumption.

The phone brought their internecine war to an abrupt end. They both stared guiltily at the ringing instrument, and finally Mantra answered it. It was the anxious voice of their neighbour, wanting to know if all was well.

'Yes, yes,' Mantra reassured her, 'a rat got in and I was chasing it with Vir's squash racquet. No, I didn't manage to kill it. It escaped in the direction of your flat I think,' she added helpfully.

By the time she hung up, Vir was in bed, his eyelids tightly screwed in pretend sleep, a don't-you-dare-disturb-me scowl on his face.

Mantra knew she was in the doghouse, a place she was sort of used to. It was warm and cosy in its own way. It felt like home.

4

The next morning Mantra hovered around Vir while he ate his breakfast, despite the fact that he made her feel as welcome as a pesky housefly scattering filthy germs. She persisted in the hovering, trying hard to make her brand new humble housewife self helpful. When he left she followed him to the front door, trilled goodbye and attempted to peck his cheek in the charming, old-fashioned US sitcom manner. He ducked in time and sarcastically inquired if she was going to squander his hard-earned salary on lavish Martini lunches with other harpies who sponged off their husbands. Mantra ignored his barb and swatted his retreating rear with a rolled up newspaper. She managed to get in a solid stinging whack, she noted with deep satisfaction.

The very first thing she did after he left was to enthusiastically dial a helpline to find out about Chinese lessons. The recorded message that greeted her was delivered in the husky voice of a strumpet who was evidently on the brink of multiple orgasms.

'Please jerk off, our customer care executive will be with you shortly,' the voice throatily moaned between gasps of unconcealed pleasure. Mantra was startled. Odd, she can't really be saying that, she thought. She jammed her ear against the telephone receiver to hear better. Hell, it still sounds a lot like 'jerk off'. Ah well, maybe that fake American accent is to blame.

She dutifully held on for about an hour, suffering loop after loop of the orgasmic plea and the treacly intervening music. Finally she disconnected, fuming.

Mantra had never imagined that being unemployed also meant feeling aimless. After making a few phone calls as feelers for freelance assignments, she took a walk around the house to see if there was anything that needed doing, plumped up a cushion or two during her perambulation, ran a finger along a bookshelf checking for dust like she'd seen Anjali the super-housewife do, but everything was in order. Shalinibai was so thorough and efficient at her job, she made Mantra's new housewife persona redundant. Reshma the cook, of course, was an entirely different matter and definitely needed to be taken in hand, but she would glare and start mentally sharpening knives whenever Mantra dared to enter the kitchen in her presence. The nicer Mantra was to her, the nastier Reshma became. Mantra had eventually given up trying altogether and pined for her predecessor Kaushalya even more intensely. The kitchen had been such a happy, welcoming place when Kaushalya was in charge. Wafts of delicious aromas would carry with them snatches of tuneless but cheerful folk songs, and bubbles of laughter always accompanied bubbling pots. Ooh luverly, Mantra thought, missing those happy days.

She flung herself on the bed and attempted to exercise her brain. She decided that she'd think of songs with numbers in their titles and then sort them out sequentially. A two-month project, she sternly told herself. It has to be time bound.

She already had a few titles in her head: *Love me two times*, *Six-blade knife* and *When I'm sixty-four*. She was pushing her brain to release a few more from its archives when Anjali called.

'So what's it like being home-bound?' Anjali inquired.

'Deathly dull. Boring. I don't know how you do it,' Mantra said, guiltily reminding herself that Anjali always kept herself busy learning something interesting to stimulate herself and advance her husband's career. Whenever a new cuisine was in, Anjali immediately signed up for cooking lessons. After the conclusion of the classes, a grand party would be thrown for Karan's colleagues, and their wives would gnash their teeth at being upped and beaten to it yet again. Thai, Mediterranean, Japanese—whatever the flavour of the month, Anjali could dish it out and dish it out well too. She had even been among the first to ring out the Melba toast and ring in the bruschetta. At the moment, she was riding the crest of India's wine craze and inventing ingenious snacks that were smothered in or served with the currently oh-so-fashionable wasabi sauce.

'So would you be interested in a Martini lunch?' Mantra asked just to spite Vir, looking forward to seeing his face in the evening when she told him she'd actually been for one, screw you and all that.

'Oh not Martini, darling!' Mantra could visualize Anjali shuddering as she contemplated it. 'Please, the world isn't into liquor these days, but a couple of glasses of fine wine sounds good to me.'

Fine wine, my foot! thought Mantra as she bit back the urge to remind her that in the good old days (as far back as five years ago) the only wines Anjali could tell the difference between were red and white. Ever since India's new upper crust magazines had started waxing eloquent about wine, Anjali had begun waffling a lot about it. One would think Bordeaux was the first word she'd uttered as a baby.

The real tragedy, according to Mantra, was that instead of just enjoying her alcohol, Anjali seriously believed that drinking wine was a cultural accomplishment, on par with playing Mozart on the violin. Mantra had playfully parodied her once at a party: she dramatically held up her glass to the light to inspect the colour, and after giving it a ceremonious swirl she sniffed it, imitating Anjali's I-so-know-my-wine actions, took a critical sip and finally moaned, 'Ah, larkspur undertones with a hint of feline wee'—she had pronounced it as 'oui' to throw people off the scent—'and crushed cyclotrop berries.' Her pièce de résistance, however, had been her act of fussily sniffing the wine cork before she even deigned to pour the contents into her glass. Those of Anjali's upwardly mobile guests who witnessed her actions were deeply impressed. Word spread in awestruck tones, and Mantra had been the star of the party, relegating Anjali with her perfectly honed snobbery skills to second place.

'If that hasn't taught my pretentious sister a lesson, I don't know what will!' Vir had sniggered on the way back home.

'Oh come on, Anjali, slum it just for once!' Mantra urged. 'You know I hate wine with a passion. It doesn't agree with me at all, it gives me a mother of a hangover. Vir says it's because I have peasant genes—not French peasant, of course! I don't even know if I like Martinis either—never had one. But I do want to drink one today to teach your bloody brother a lesson.'

'Why? What did Vir say?' The silly squabbles between Mantra and Vir made Anjali double up with laughter. Except, of course, when her mother was the subject of the altercation.

'He said, and I quote, "So will you be splurging my hard-earned money on Martini lunches with other harpies who sponge off their husbands?"' Mantra smugly knew that sentence would hit home. Hard.

'Hmm. So my precious little brother thinks I'm a pile-on harpy, huh? I'm in on this too, Mantra! Come right over. I'll consult my trusty little cocktail book and mix us the best Martinis in the universe! Be here as soon as poss, I'm bored to tears.'

'On my way,' Mantra agreed.

Despite the fact that Mantra and Anjali were like chalk and cheese and dreaded sisters-in-law to boot, they'd struck up a warm friendship. Vir's parents had been formidably against him marrying Mantra. She was, 'Not that pretty really, and too Westernized besides,' his mother had said with a contemptuous sniff, implying that Mantra's morals were suspect and that it was quite possible she would run away with a tourist taxi driver someday. They'd identified a lovely convent-educated girl for him in their posh Delhi neighbourhood—she had a respectable background and, better still, was likely to come in for a windfall when Daddy's company went public.

A pitched battle had ensued. Vir's parents had impatiently tossed aside the argument that he was an adult of sound mind and independent means and therefore had the right to choose his own wife. Vir had had to fight them tooth and nail and Anjali had backed him all the way. Not just for Vir's sake, but to extract her revenge. She loved her parents (she couldn't help that), but she secretly resented them for controlling her life since she'd been born. Vir hadn't been around to support her; he had always been away—boarding school, engineering college, B-school and then a job in Mumbai, only home for the holidays. He'd been freed of their tight supervision and tight-arsed upbringing from age nine because he was a boy. As a girl, she'd suffered. She'd wanted to go to boarding school too, just to taste freedom, but they'd firmly refused.

'That's not fair,' she'd wailed. 'You give him so much more than you give me!' Nonsense, her parents had pooh-poohed, they were being scrupulously fair while planning their children's futures. Vir was a boy, so an investment had to be made in his education. She was a girl, so her share of their income would go into wedding arrangements: silk sarees, gold, diamonds, rubies, pearls, sapphires, things fit for a princess. She would appreciate it when she was older, they'd assured her, smug smiles playing on their lips.

Admittedly, Anjali had secretly been wary of Mantra, though Karan had liked her well enough. They had no common reference points in their upbringing, and Mantra's wacky, politically incorrect sense of humour often threw Anjali off balance. She had been pleasant to her for Vir's sake, but the turning point in her feelings towards Mantra had occurred many years later, after Rohan was born. Mantra loved him almost as much as Anjali did. That was the cement that held them together.

Vir and Mantra's wedding, when it eventually took place, had been different from Anjali and Karan's for two reasons:

The bride's and groom's parents were introduced to each other for the very first time at the mandap itself. That had been Mantra's idea: 'If they meet my parents before we marry, your parents will need pacemakers.' Vir, much as he adored Mantra's parents, had heartily agreed.

The bride hadn't wailed piteously with the shehnais during the bidai, but her mother-in-law had. That had made the guests very happy—they'd felt they'd got great entertainment *and* value for the presents they'd splurged on.

Over time, Vir's father had caved in to Mantra's charms. Truth be told, he had been proud of her. He'd subscribed to the Mumbai paper she wrote for, and whenever her byline appeared, he'd carry the paper to Lodi Gardens and thrust it under the noses of his evening constitutional cronies to prove that the family name was alive and kicking, despite the fact that no grandchild appeared to be forthcoming. Vir's mother, however, had never capitulated. She had been glacially polite to Mantra but exceedingly distant, trying very hard to forget that she was part of the extended family. Mantra had always secretly suspected that most of the hate mails she had received in her career as a journalist were from her mother-in-law (written under a pseudonym, of course). Mantra's reasoning had been: who gets hate mails for articles on airy-fairy lifestyle subjects like the latest trends in home décor? And was it just a coincidence that the hate mails stopped abruptly after her mother-in-law died?

5

The liquid lunch was pleasant, to begin with. Anjali had, in her inimitable hostess-with-the-mostest way, rustled up exquisite hors d'oeuvres (wasabi featured in one, but of course), and made Mantra gasp when she created perfect Martinis and even garnished them with olives, which tasted so much better because they were soaked in vodka.

'Gosh, your kitchen is probably better stocked than the best five star hotel pantry in this city,' Mantra applauded.

They enjoyed a lazy, chatty afternoon as Mantra revelled in her new-found freedom when suddenly a dark threatening shadow was cast. Anjali's cell phone rang as she took the last sip of her second Martini. She recognized his voice instantly.

Left to herself she'd perhaps have said, 'Oh go away and stop bothering me,' but the alcohol spoke instead, and it spoke *very* recklessly indeed.

'Oh *hi*, Shiv, how *are* you?' it gushed. 'So sorry, I've been meaning to call but I've been *so* busy lately. Yes, of course we *must* meet. Can I call you back tomorrow? Rot, of course I'll call you back. I'm not hedging, hey why should I hedge—I'd really love to meet,' the alcohol gaily continued. 'What, you still don't believe me? This weekend you say? Let me think about it. Oh okay, Friday night it is then, yes I promise,' the alcohol conceded, sounding a trifle unsure suddenly. 'No, no, forget a restaurant, come over to my place for dinner instead,

I'd like you to meet my husband, and, um, bring your wife along too,' the alcohol ventured cautiously.

'Oh, you're divorced? So sorry. Yes, you always maintained that you weren't the marrying kind.' The alcohol gave a fake understanding laugh as bile rose to Anjali's throat.

'Right then, Friday night it is. I'll text my address. Goodbye.' Anjali hung up curtly. She'd swiftly taken over from the alcohol after the word marriage had entered the conversation.

'The rotter!' Anjali spat out and slammed her fists on the table. Mantra sat up with a start. She'd been too lost in her daydreams to catch a word of Anjali's telephone conversation.

'What happened?' she asked, alarmed.

Anjali gave her the gist of the conversation, two red spots of rage glowing angrily on her cheeks. 'My nasty ex-boyfriend slimed a meeting out of me even when it was so darn obvious that I didn't want to see his slimy face again!' she fumed.

'So you should have stuck to your guns then and screamed at him, the way you do when those persistent telemarketing guys bug you.' Mantra shrugged. 'Anyway what's the big deal? You're just meeting an ex for a drink or a meal, right? What's there to get so excited about?'

'He treated me like dirt and now I'm going to treat him to dinner, that's how big an ass I am,' Anjali scowled.

'You don't have to give him your address, and if he calls again you can hang up,' Mantra suggested wisely.

'No, I can't now! I've already made a commitment—you know how particular I am about these things. See, this is why I hate liquor!' she raged. 'Wine has never made me do anything this foolish. Bloody Martinis can go to bloody hell! I'm having another. You want one?'

'Thanks, but no. Much as I'd love to live the life of a lush, I don't want to wind up mumbling, "My name is Mantra, and I'm an alcoholic," to a bunch of strangers at AA meetings. I need a clear head to figure out what I want to do in life. I'm anxious to start something new; I'm really, seriously excited.'

'May the force be with you,' Anjali said mock-solemnly, raising her glass and downing the contents in one giant gulp. 'And may the force be with you too,' Mantra raised her glass of water.

'You guys have to be there for dinner on Friday night too, understand? I want my family on my side,' Anjali pleaded.

'Of course I will be there but I'm coming solo—Vir's going to be in Bangkok, remember? Don't worry, I'll make your ex weep if you want, and—hey! Don't you *dare* touch that bottle!' Mantra attempted to wrestle the vodka bottle out of Anjali's hands but Anjali won and defiantly knocked the contents of the bottle directly down her throat. Then she spluttered and threw up violently. The bile finally gushed to freedom.

As Mantra cleaned up Anjali and helped her to bed, she heard the full story of Shiv's betrayal between anguished sobs.

The man sounds like a nasty piece of goods, she mused. Too bad dear old Ma-in-law had never been introduced to him—she would have fixed him good and proper, just like the bitch continues to fix me, even though she's currently making God miserable.

Vir's mother had sold the family house in Delhi and moved in with them after her husband died, determined to make Mantra's life a living hell. Her glacial silence had been replaced by relentless needling. Nothing Mantra did was right, according to her. After listening to Mantra's tired defeated voice on the phone for months on end, her mother had suddenly landed up uninvited at their doorstep.

'Just flew in for the weekend, darling,' she had hissed in her astonished daughter's ear. 'I'm here to fix that nasty old curmudgeon good and proper.'

It had been mission unaccomplished. She'd only succeeded in getting Vir's mother to stop harassing Mantra about her lack of offspring.

'My daughter,' she sternly told Vir's mother, 'is yearning to have children—half a dozen of them at the very least. It's your son who pushes the pill down her throat every day—he doesn't want any. So if you must attack someone about it, go for *his* throat!'

Both Mantra and Vir were present when she'd delivered this statement. Mantra drew in a sharp breath and shot an alarmed look at an equally startled Vir. She's gone and put her foot in it this time, Mantra had groaned inwardly. Vir may be offended by this shameless outright lie, and I'll have to pay for it.

'Vir, is this true?' his mother had imperiously demanded.

'Absolutely. And now if you'll excuse me, I have to force the pill down Mantra's throat right away. I forgot it this morning. Come along, darling, there's a good girl,' he had ordered.

Mantra had followed him like a lamb to slaughter, her knees knocking against each other the moment Vir firmly shut the bedroom door behind them.

'Just as well we've made a pact never to have children, Mantra—what if they turned out to be like your insane mother?' he'd admonished with a wide grin.

She'd hugged him fiercely, and both their bodies had shuddered with silent laughter.

But there had been thorny patches too, when a weary Vir, tired of taking sides, had shut Mantra out for long periods of time. His mental lockouts triggered Mantra's physical lockouts. Vir's attractiveness had diminished in his nasty mother's presence and, besides, sex had no appeal without companionship. Random excuses like 'Stop that! What if she hears us?' had frequently been trotted out.

Three unbearably long years later, Vir's mother's love of stuffed parathas with dollops of ghee proved to be her death weapon. But she made sure her evil presence still lingered. Some Indian mothers-in-law try to kill you when they're alive. This one never stopped trying even after she was dead. Mantra was too frightened to enter the bedroom her mother-in-law had lived and died in. The first time she'd entered it, she'd stubbed her toe against the bedpost and fractured it. The second time, the ceiling fan had fallen down and missed her by a mere whisker. There had been no third time. Nor would there be. Because Mantra was determined never to enter that room again.

She was working on Vir to give up the lease on this flat and buy one of their own. A few years earlier he'd been as keen on it as her, but after their first encounter with the broker, Vir had absolutely refused to even contemplate owning a flat in the city.

His turnaround occurred when the broker waxed eloquent on all the wonderful luxuries the flat they were considering came with—playground for children, surveillance cameras, swimming pool, gym—the whole caboodle. As the final push in his enthusiastic sales pitch, the broker had added with a beaming smile, 'The best thing, sir, is that non-Hindus are not permitted to own or rent flats in this building society.' Mantra's body had stiffened.

'In which case we're not interested,' Vir had said coolly but abruptly and yanked Mantra's arm, tugging her away from the scene of the crime.

The puzzled broker's voice had followed them. 'But you are Hindus! Your names are Hindu names!'

Mantra had turned back and shot him a fiery look. 'We're Indians, not bloody bigots like you!'

Vir had jerked her arm harder and practically dragged her to the car. They'd driven back home in silence.

6

When Vir returned home the next evening, Mantra knew something was horribly, terribly wrong. His face was ashen and he looked tired and defeated. Fear didn't just grip her heart—it gave it a life-threatening squeeze.

'What happened?' she whispered anxiously.

'The worst,' Vir groaned. 'Screw the fresh lime and get me a vodka on the rocks. No, not vodka, make it Scotch. Extra large. Patiala peg.'

Mantra moved like greased lightning to fix Vir's drink and got one for herself too, just in case. She waited for Vir to take his first sip, and then rushed her question in again.

'*What* happened, Vir? What? Tell me!' She had her hand on his thigh when she said that. Not just to be reassuring but to check if he was still breathing normally.

'Great Revolutionary Leader has summoned us to his palace for dinner tonight.'

'Oh hell no!' Mantra moaned, and sank her face into her palms.

'Oh hell yes,' Vir echoed her hollowly. 'Please, I hate the idea more than you do; I suffer the sod all day at work, dammit!'

They both downed their drinks in one giant gulp. God knew, they needed it.

On the drive to Sanjay Sharma's house, Vir tersely briefed Mantra on the code of conduct. He needn't have bothered;

she'd been through this monologue so often she knew it as well as she knew the safety demo spiel on flights. At the end of it all, she agreed wearily not to drink alcohol, to spit it out even if the host or hostess forcefully poured it down her throat and to be seen and not heard. Vir generously added that she could eat as much as she wanted however, then quickly retracted his statement, reminding her about the dangers of middle-aged spread. Not because Mantra could die of a heart attack, he said, but because he might be attracted to a thinner woman if she burst at the seams. Mantra ignored his insensitive remark and meekly asked if she was meant to fawn over Sanjay Sharma's wife to help further his career. Now that she wasn't earning any more, she'd decided to do an Anjali to make their bank balance boom.

Vir looked revolted. 'That's an utterly despicable thing to do,' he said. "I'll divorce you without alimony if you even dare mention that her flower arrangement is charming!'

Mantra felt a warm glow spread through her body. She was proud to be married to a man with integrity, and swore to herself that she would not let such an honourable person down. She was hugely relieved too, since apple polishing was not one of her God-given talents.

Just before entering Sanjay's grand awe-inspiring bungalow gates, Mantra shrieked. 'Turn back, Vir! I've just realized that I'm not wearing any jewellery apart from this lurid pomegranate coloured glass-beaded bracelet Rohan gave me for my birthday! I need to wear the Indian wife's mandatory gold bangle, at the very least.'

Vir refused to turn back. 'Stop making such a fuss over nothing,' he snorted. 'Anyway, it's a good thing you're not wearing jewellery. It may drive home the fact that I'm grossly underpaid,' he wisely added, urging Mantra to flaunt the lurid glass-beaded bracelet under Sanjay's nose.

They entered Sanjay's plush house feeling like martyrs being led to the gallows. Sanjay enveloped Mantra in an effusive bear hug as though they were long lost family members from either side of the Indo-Pak border. He ruined it by addressing her by the wrong name. Mantra didn't correct him. She was too well brought up to embarrass her host, especially such a highly placed one who had the power to control their lifestyle. Anyway, it's not such a big mistake, she reasoned to herself, 'Mamta' is pretty close to 'Mantra'.

Her cheeks began to burn, however, when treacherous Vir went a step further and covered up for Sanjay's mistake by introducing her to all and sundry as Mamta. So much for his integrity, Mantra thought furiously. She caught his eye and glared at him, and though she got a quizzical innocent look in response, she detected a faint smirk playing on his lips.

Payback time came when Sanjay jovially steered her towards the bar and offered her a drink. Spite made her ask the bar attendant for a large vodka with tonic and a dash of lime and she gleefully watched Vir's smirk instantaneously transform into a dark scowl. Her cell phone beeped a second later to announce a text message from him: 'Bitch!' it tersely said. She contemplated taking a sip to make Vir sweat further but her conscience pricked and Mantra lovingly handed over her glass to him. Vir practically snatched it out of her hand and knocked back the contents in one giant gulp—knowing his wife, there was always the chance that she'd make a sneaky attempt to regain control of the glass for the pleasure of teasing him. Then he tenderly put his arm around Mantra's waist and shoved her into the drop-dead boring zenana room, ignoring Mantra's whispered 'Lead on, Macduffer' jibe.

Mrs Sharma sailed up to graciously greet them. She was playing Lady of the Manor to the hilt. Mantra was sorely tempted to doff an imaginary cap, tug her forelock or execute a deep curtsey. She exercised admirable restraint and did not give in, consoling herself by remembering that just six months ago, before Mrs Sharma's husband rose to the position of CEO, she had been just another ordinary downtrodden corporate wife—she must have suffered too. Instead, Mantra responded to her gracious smile with an even more gracious one, her flawless imitation of the late Princess Di accepting a bouquet at a children's hospital. Mrs Sharma looked terribly put out at that and caused Mantra momentary panic: Shit! Have I ruined Vir's career by upstaging Great Revolutionary Leader's missus?

After flashing forced smiles at other visibly traumatized corporate wives, Mantra slumped into a chair and let her mind wander. Her cell phone suddenly beeped, announcing an irate text message from Vir: 'You could at least attempt to look interested in the conversation or people may think you're a taxidermist's creation.'

Mantra leaned forward and tried to tune in to an animated debate on whether the Atkins diet was more effective than the South Beach diet. She stayed silent—she had nothing to contribute to this conversation. Mrs Sharma arrived with a tray of greasy, deep-fried cocktail samosas stuffed with potatoes and said that as far as she was concerned, the Atkins diet was the best. The debate was instantly resolved even though Mrs Sharma was stiff competition for Obelix. Everyone effusively agreed with her, even creepy Uday Handa's wife Pinky who had hitherto been propagating the South Beach diet with the fervour of a TV evangelist. Mantra decided that she disliked her intensely—she had a low-grade plastic smile.

Typically, offspring were discussed and Mantra tuned out again. She was brought back to earth by Mrs Sharma. 'And how many children do you have, Mamta?'

'None,' was the blithe reply.

'Why? Are you infertile?'

'Actually, I have the fertility genes of a rabbit but I don't want offspring, thank you very much,' Mantra politely informed her, fighting back the desire to physically assault her.

When she noticed that everyone looked shocked, she gave them the country's latest population statistics and virtuously said she was doing her bit to ensure that India beat China in the race to superpower status. Their eyes glazed over and

Mantra was ignored thereafter. They started showing off about the schools their children went to.

Mantra was appalled to discover that the oneupmanship game here was not about educational standards or even whether the school's extra-curricular activities included polo, fencing or fox hunting. The definitive factor was the lunch the school provided. A heated debate ensued about whether schools that served Mediterranean and Continental cuisine were better than schools that offered nouvelle Pan-Asian fare.

Mrs Sharma regally sailed in with a tray of cocktail idlis and put everyone in their place. 'Only patriotic schools that serve pure vegetarian Indian food are good enough for my children,' she proclaimed grandly. She then named a Hindi-medium school that her children went to and everyone's hands flew involuntarily to their lips to cover their shock at the utter down-marketness of it all. Pinky Handa, who was vociferously for Mediterranean and Continental cuisine in school lunch rooms, heaved a ragged sigh and clutched her bosom dramatically.

'Why,' she sighed, 'that's just the school I wanted to send my son to, but, alas, they weren't accepting new students.'

Mrs Sharma nodded kindly at her and said that she was on the board of directors and would ensure that Handa junior was registered for the next term. For a moment there, Pinky looked like she was going to regurgitate the cocktail samosas and idlis, but she swiftly regained her composure and managed to gush profuse thanks. All the other corporate wives made valiant attempts to conceal their smirks. Mantra could have butted in and told them what she knew for a fact: that the Hindi-medium school in question had very high educational standards—one of the best in the country in fact, but she held her tongue. They would have thought that she, too, was shamelessly sucking up to Mrs Sharma.

Then Mrs Sharma generously offered to accept everybody's children in the daal-rice-serving Hindi-medium school but all the corporate wives were suddenly punching texts on their cell phones in a distracted way. When Mrs Sharma finally got the message, she pointedly ignored them and showered attention on Pinky instead who positively basked under her tender loving care. Like a blooming idiot flower, Mantra thought disgustedly. She sighed inwardly to see the other corporate wives wilt suddenly—they were, she gathered, having life changing debates with their consciences: husband's future over children's future?

The senior office canteen boy moonlighting as a butler appeared and announced that dinner was served. The men arrived from the bar with alcohol-flushed cheeks and seemed in high spirits. Mantra raised her eyebrows questioningly at Vir when she noticed that Uday had a hirsute arm around his shoulder. Vir rolled his eyes heavenwards and beckoned her towards him.

'It's been a long time, Mamta,' Uday pronounced genially while pumping her hand with a sweaty palm. 'So what have you girls been gossiping about?' he continued, as Pinky joined them.

Noticing that Pinky's cheeks were rosy with triumph, Mantra couldn't quell the urge to bring her down to reality with a resounding thud. 'I *must* tell you that I'm oh so glad your son will soon study in the Hindi-medium school of your dreams,' she gushed warmly.

Pinky glared at her and pulled her astonished looking husband away. Vir sniggered when Mantra told him all in whispers. 'See, that's why I gave you strict instructions not to compliment the hostess on anything,' he gloated, in a bragging man-of-the-world way.

Thankfully, soon after the dessert plates were scraped clean, Mrs Sharma let out an exaggerated tonsil-exposing yawn—a regal signal that the party was over—and everyone dutifully leapt up to depart. There was, as always, a stampede to the door.

While Vir was brushing his teeth vigorously before bed, Mantra dropped a bombshell. 'Vir, we *must* have a baby!'

'Huh? Why?' he sounded startled.

'Because Great Revolutionary Leader's wife practically ordered me to have one.'

Vir lost interest. 'Oh, fuck her.'

'I most certainly may do just that. Here, take a look at this.' Mantra showed him a photograph on her cell phone.

'Why in God's name did you take a photograph of her tricoloured rice?' he asked bemused.

'Please note that the saffron layer is right at the bottom. Shocking! Now if those right wing moral police mobs ever get wind of this . . .'

Vir let out a low whistle of appreciation. 'Mantra you're a goddamn bitch!'

'Thanks, darling, I love you too,' she smirked and then stiffened as Vir's embrace became more urgent. Her response was the usual—less than enthusiastic.

As Mantra was drifting off to sleep later, she promised herself that she'd meet her gynaecologist soon to sort out her problems. Hell, what on earth are they? I still love Vir with every fibre of my being, I'm absolutely certain of that. No other man turns me on—not even celebs. And all the rock stars I used to fantasize about in college now look like doddering grandfathers, more genial than cool. Shit! I need help! There was no question about it: she just had to get herself sorted out.

7

'Thai spicy and sour salad wi pan-grilled beef. Grilled salmon steak served wi papaya salad. Khao niew ma muang—that's coconut sticky rice wi mango, you ignoramus—for dessert.'

Mantra received Vir's gloating text message from Bangkok while she was making an effort to eat bland steamed vegetables and watery daal. The trick, she decided, was to swallow Reshma's food whole the way boa constrictors do—not bite into it or let it come anywhere near her taste buds. When she read the message, her fingers itched to slap Vir—getting this apology for a cook was *his* idea and the sod was stuffing his face with fantastic food while she was stuck with pig swill!

'I have one word for you—cholesterol!' was her vindictive reply.

She shovelled the barely touched contents of her plate into the bin (she could do it bravely and openly since Reshma had retired to her quarters for her afternoon nap), and sneakily crumpled the property supplement of the newspaper over it to hide the evidence. Then she defiantly selected a Thai takeaway menu from her in-case-of-emergency menus folder.

'I'll have what *he's* having,' she muttered peevishly to herself as she browsed through the menu. 'Good heavens, all the dishes sound like bad words!'

Prik nam pla
Nam prik kah
Nam prik ga bi

Nam prik num
Plah raht prik

She had absolutely no idea what any of the dishes included, since the tacky takeaway menu didn't come with English explanations, so she exerted herself and Google-searched a Thai phrase book. *Prik*, she discovered, was chilli. Sometimes pronounced as *phrig*. An equally wash-your-mouth-out-with-soap-young-lady word.

Just what is it about Thailand? she wondered. The next time anyone throws a 'What's in a name?' line at me, I'll toss Thailand right back at them. Freud would go ballistic, dammit. Practically everything in the country reeks of sex and sleaze. Starting with the suggestive name Thailand itself. Bangkok, well no explanation required. Phuket sounds remarkably like 'Fuck it'. And then dishes called prik or phrig! And the most damning evidence is that the country is universally regarded as the whore house of the world. Rather embarrassing for the upright citizens of the country, though. What they need to do to save face is to hire a good Indian politician who'll promptly change the country's name back to the original (and more respectable) Siam. Look how effortlessly Bombay switched to Mumbai, Madras to Chennai, Bangalore to Bengaluru and Calcutta to Kolkata. And, of course, everyday all over India, the names of streets are changed to honour dead politicians or their wives, perhaps even dearly beloved pets. She was certain of one thing—if she lived in Thailand, she'd organize fiery demonstrations to change the country's name!

By the time she got a rough translation of the menu on the Internet it was past 3 p.m. and only fast food restaurants would deliver. Mantra called for a pizza instead, and then dialled a helpline for Chinese lessons, listened with growing impatience to the same recorded voice orgasm for about twenty minutes and finally gave up. Maybe learning Chinese wasn't part of the plan God had for her, she shrugged. Time to put Plan B into operation—write that book! She stared at the blank laptop screen, willing ideas for a book to come into her head. If she was going to write a novel, she was determined to do it properly.

Maybe I could do a great Indian novel type, she mused. The sort that Western agents would moan passionately about like recorded voices on the telephone, and tout excitedly to publishers as 'the next prize winner'.

Mantra's understanding of a prize-winning novel by an Indian author was that it should be about terrorism; that was a current hot topic with a ready market—bewildered Westerners yearning to know why the races they'd always regarded, and often treated, as inferior disliked them and their meddling governments' ways. The old-fashioned pre-9/11 prize-winning novels were more interesting, though. The ones about abject poverty or excruciating misery or utter exotica usually made it to the coveted shortlists. Not opulently exotic like going to school on caparisoned elephant-back, but miserably exotic like being trampled to death by an elephant on a sugarcane high. All she had to do was work it out scientifically. She'd attempt a parody of that, she decided, and have some fun while she was about it. Her eureka moment occurred soon after, and she keyed in the plot while inspiration was still busily hovering around her.

A poverty-stricken unmarried village belle giving birth in a paddy field without a midwife or anyone in attendance. The birthing village belle has concealed her pregnancy from all to avoid shame and banishment. She cannot marry her lover because he is from a lower caste and she knows that the village panchayat will brutally hack them to death. Her lover too is not keen on marriage—not because of fear of death or because he's a rabid commitment-phobe; he just isn't interested in soiled goods despite the fact that he soiled the goods himself. Her father does not notice her burgeoning belly because he is blind (that's another reason why they are poor). Her mother thinks her daughter's big belly is a paunch, due to the fact that she eats only starchy food like rice (veggies too expensive). The village belle never steps out of the house so no one in the drought-stricken village notices. She cuts the umbilical cord herself with a rusted sickle and leaves the baby in a field, gets lockjaw and dies of tetanus. The rest of the story is about the abandoned baby's life, how she is adopted by a Hollywood star who is also mother to an Eskimo baby. The Indian baby is given all the good things in life, becomes a junkie out of boredom and joins an ashram in India to discover her roots. She ODs one night after an ashram orgy and dies appropriately where she was born: in a paddy field.

Note: Call book *Full Circle*—irony never goes out of fashion.

Mantra re-read the plot outline several times with satisfaction. This should work, she thought cynically. It's just the sort of weepy stuff they love to read about India. And I'll make one of the characters do disgusting things like dig for earwax with a matchstick and then use the same matchstick as a toothpick. They'll enjoy that! Oh, and I should trash the country mercilessly too while I'm about it, and come across as brave, honest and all that rot. Mum and Dad can clue me in on ashram life—hey, maybe they were meant to go there because of my novel. Perhaps everything that happens in life happens for a purpose after all.

The peal of the doorbell reminded her that she was starving. 'Pizza time,' she sang out loud as she raced to the door, picking up a couple of notes from the desk drawer. She opened the door with a wide welcoming smile, but it wasn't the pizza delivery boy who politely smiled back—it was Samira, the page 3 wannabe.

'Hey, come on in. Wassup?' Mantra made an attempt to sound warm and inviting while groaning inside. This was the very first time Samira had ever dropped by and Mantra fervently hoped it wouldn't become standard practice—she had nothing to *say* to the woman!

'Oh lots of exciting things are happening to me, Mantra.' Samira rolled her eyes dramatically as she made her way inside. 'I've just been offered this fantastic role in a Bhojpuri music video, you know.'

Mantra sighed inwardly. Ever since Samira had discovered that Mantra worked for a newspaper she'd been hounding her with snippets of her life, hoping against hope that Mantra would find them riveting enough to publish.

'Wow fantastic, good for you! But tell me, how are you? You okay?' Mantra responded, giving Samira a searching look. No bruises were visible on her face, but maybe they were buried under layers of hide-the-blemish foundation.

'Oh I'm doing great,' Samira assured her breezily. 'But you don't look so good, Mantra. Your frown lines have deepened and you have dark circles too. Have you been stressed out lately?' she continued, peering at Mantra's face curiously.

Mantra felt indignant, but fought back the urge to inform Samira that *she* was the person solely responsible for her sleepless nights. If Samira didn't want to confide in her about domestic violence, well that was her problem. She shrugged instead. 'Naah, on the contrary. I have nothing really to be stressed about. I'm not working any more, see? I'm happy and carefree these days.'

'Oh is that why . . .' Samira began, and then squeezed Mantra's arm sympathetically. 'That's too bad. My husband can get you a job in his office you know, if you need the money.'

'Thanks.' Mantra grinned and motioned Samira towards the sofa. 'But I don't want to work any more, period. I'm writing a book.'

'Oh?' Samira said, looking disinterested. Her face lit up a brief second later. 'So which celebrity are you going to get to launch your book?'

'The Union minister for women and child development,' Mantra retorted, smugly secure that that would make Samira's eyes glaze over with boredom again. She'd hit the bullseye she noted, and made a valiant attempt to stifle a giggle.

Instead of taking the armchair opposite Samira, Mantra deliberately parked herself on the sofa next to her and turned towards her, their faces only inches away. She just had to see for herself if Samira was being used as a punching bag. But no signs were evident, even this close. That was terrific foundation!

'So, are you into opera?' Mantra asked innocently.

'Opera? No, why? And what's that got to do with the Bhojpuri music video?' Samira asked, looking puzzled.

'No, um, I thought maybe you'd like to listen to some music,' Mantra lied, her voice trailing away.

'I didn't come here to listen to music,' Samira said firmly. 'I've come to talk!'

Mantra nodded in a resigned way. She decided she may as well make herself comfortable and had just got up to switch seats to the armchair when Samira caught hold of her hand and squeezed it surprisingly hard. Tears of pain sprang to Mantra's eyes.

'You've got to help me, Mantra, you really have! Even if you're not with the papers any more, you still have contacts there. Mantra, I have to be on page 3, I just have to! And you're the only person I know who can help me. Please, please, please help me! Please!'

Samira's intensity shocked Mantra. She didn't quite know what to say, and fortunately the doorbell came to her rescue. 'Ah, the pizza,' Mantra mumbled and rushed to the door.

Disappointment yet again. It was Reshma who refused to make eye contact with her and was about to haughtily make her way in when the pizza delivery boy arrived.

Reshma raised her eyebrows at Mantra, in a what-is-the-meaning-of-this-you-cheat manner.

'I've, um, got a guest,' Mantra mumbled guiltily, but Reshma had already walked away in a huff.

Bloody pizza man, Mantra thought murderously, glaring at him as she fished the now crumpled notes out of her pocket.

'Sorry, ma'am, terrible traffic jam,' he apologized. 'Some SNM party workers are on the streets burning effigies because the President of a European country committed an immoral act by kissing an eighty-year-old social worker on the cheek. They saw it on TV.'

'Ridiculous!' Mantra giggled, and gave him a fatter tip than usual as reward for the entertaining nugget of information.

'Coffee, tea, fresh lime or perhaps you'd prefer something a little more spirited?' Mantra inquired as she laid the pizza box on the coffee table.

'Nothing please, really. I've already told you that I just want to talk to you, Mantra. I need help,' Samira said. Without warning her eyes suddenly filled with tears—a cloudburst seemed imminent.

Mantra hastily put her arm around Samira and led her to the bedroom, clutching the pizza box to her chest. She didn't want Reshma to see Samira crying and come to her own conclusions. News like this got top billing on the servants' quarters' notice board and then crept swiftly and insidiously into every flat in the building in hushed whispers.

She sat Samira down on the bed and gave her shoulders a tight squeeze. 'Tell me,' she urged warmly, while opening the pizza box with fumbling, trembling fingers; she was so hungry, she could happily eat the cardboard box it came in too.

She got shuddering sobs in response.

'I *hate* you, Mantra! I've been begging you to write about me, but you've done nothing about it! Nothing! And now you've gone and quit that paper and I'll get *nowhere* in life! No bloody where!'

Mantra was so stunned she almost dropped the pizza box. 'Hello? You wanted to talk to me about giving you plugs in the papers? That's ridiculous and nothing to make a fuss over. For heaven's sake, you haven't done anything that merits mention!'

Samira's sobs grew louder. 'Then tell me what I have to do to be on page 3. Please. I'll do anything! Anything! You have to help me! If you don't I'll be out on the streets. The bastard's threatening to divorce me; he has no more use for me. I need him to see that I have value.'

'Here, blow into this first,' Mantra urged sympathetically, handing Samira the bunch of paper napkins that came with the pizza. 'The bin is at your feet. Calm down, then we'll talk.'

After Samira's sobs subsided into occasional sniffs, Mantra began. 'For starters, dump that Bhojpuri music video. Once you get famous, it may be an embarrassment. Then, if you have oodles of cash to spare, invest in a good PR agency. They'll get you invites to flashy dos and push your photographs in the papers. If you don't have much money however, befriend a rich industrialist's wife and let her do the talking—that works pretty well too.'

Samira nodded compliantly as an animated Mantra continued. She was in a better mood now—the pizza had released her happy hormones. 'Mmm. This is super yum! Sure you don't want a slice?' she offered, but Samira shook her head firmly.

'Do you know that one slice, just *one* slice is loaded with five hundred calories!' she said, wrinkling her nose.

'I don't give a rodent's posterior!' Mantra said cheerfully. 'Now, back to your problem. See, if I were you, I'd develop a skill before hiring the PR chaps. Do a short course abroad in something arty that's in. Some years ago, stained glass was all the rage, and a lot of people got mentions for that. So choose something wisely: mosaic, pebbles, shells, anything. Go on the net and look for courses on the latest trends. Choose Europe as your destination—that has gravitas as far as art is concerned. Especially France or Italy.'

'But I'm no good at art,' Samira started wailing again. 'I can't draw a straight line even with a ruler!'

'Wonderful! Fantastic! Better still!' Mantra said enthusiastically. 'See, the worse you draw, the more talented people will see you as. Haven't you seen Picasso's stuff? Pick up that pen from the bedside table and sketch a horse right away! Go on—do it!'

Mantra experienced a frisson of excitement when Samira tentatively showed her the sketch of the horse—it looked like a bedraggled crow. 'A star is born!' she sang spontaneously. 'Get ready for fame, darling, this is bloody marvellous! Let the games begin. Come on, we'll scour the net together for some art courses in Europe, that should do the trick!'

Samira stared at her sketch of the horse dubiously. 'You sure it will work, Mantra?'

'Like bloody hell it won't!'

'But are you telling me that *all* the artists who make it on page 3 draw as badly as this?' Samira looked shocked.

'Of course not, not all,' Mantra said scornfully. 'Just a few. Those who can, get by on talent, and those who can't get by on the stupidity of the public. Works all the time. Honestly, I'd never choose one of that lot to be on my Pictionary team!'

'What the hell, I'll give it a shot, though I think I'll go with pebbles or mosaic—I'm not comfortable with drawing,' Samira agreed, while still looking unconvinced. 'I have nothing to lose anyway. All he has is money. Once I get on page 3, something he's always hankered after, he'll be my slave for life! Or maybe I'll dump him then, perhaps even get myself a super model toy boy.'

'Acquiring a toy boy is the height of your ambition?' Mantra squawked. 'How crappy is that? How on earth would you explain him to your house help? As a long lost shipwrecked son who's scared to sleep alone in the dark?'

'One does not have to explain anything to the house help,' was Samira's imperious response.

'Fair enough, but get this,' Mantra persisted, her imagination running wild, 'it's all very wild and sexy I guess to expect him to massage sun tan oil on your back, but would a stinky Iodex rub keep the passion burning? Come on, Samira, aging bones have to be factored into relationships.'

'Oh shut up, Mantra! And anyway, a toy boy is just a fashion accessory. Page 3 is my main ambition—it's total class!'

Mantra shuddered inwardly at the thought that page 3 was class, but let it go. To each his own, she silently conceded, and threw herself into the task at hand, feeling a lot like Henry Higgins in *My Fair Lady*. The phone rang at 6 p.m., 6.05 p.m., 6.10 p.m., 6.11 p.m., 6.12 p.m. and 6.13 p.m. but both Mantra and Samira ignored it. Finally, a very annoyed Reshma answered it at 6.14 p.m. and pounded on Mantra's door. 'Pick up the phone—it's bhaiyya's sister,' she snarled, darting a how-dare-you-make-me-do-things-above-and-beyond-the-call-of-duty look at Mantra.

'Oh hell!' Mantra leapt up stricken with guilt. 'I promised to be at her place by six to help with the dinner party tonight. She'll bloody kill me!'

Samira left reluctantly, extracting the promise that Mantra was not to let her husband know about her visit. 'He doesn't like me to have friends in the building. He says you people are not the sort we should socialize with.'

'What a jerk!' Mantra's lips curled with contempt.

'You don't know the half of it,' Samira said darkly and left.

'You bet I do,' Mantra muttered as she shut the front door.

8

Anjali examined herself critically in the mirror and gnashed her teeth when she saw a harried borderline matronly housewife instead of her usual cool self. She had changed six outfits, agitatedly discarding each on different grounds: too casual, too wannabe hip, too unflattering to the hips, too over-the-top for the occasion, neck too high to be sexy, neck sluttishly low—the usual trauma most women go through when they're dressing to impress. She rummaged through her wardrobe once again, found nothing that pleased her and sank on to the bed defeated, pressing her palms to her cheeks—they were hot enough to toast bread on. This was it—the moment of reckoning. She hoped, as Mantra had predicted, that age had battered the rock star out of Shiv. A fat, paunchy, reassuringly balding middle-aged Shiv with tufts of hair growing out of his ears and nose would definitely bring comic relief; that was what was urgently required to ease the tension in her tummy. She heard the click of the bathroom door and Karan walked out, clouds of steam following in his wake.

'Hmm, someone's looking real hot,' he leered appreciatively.

'Well it's not me,' Anjali snapped. 'I look like Shrek's aunt in this.'

'An aunt I'd like to do naughty things with, nonetheless,' Karan growled suggestively and wound his arms around her waist, pulling her to him. 'How much time before they arrive?'

'Oh stop it and help me find something decent to wear,' Anjali said irritably, pushing him away.

Karan gave her a quizzical look and then set to work, singing, 'Bet you wish your boyfriend was hot like me,' to annoy her. He made her change back into the low-necked T-shirt she had rejected, draped a scarf around her neck and modestly pinned it with a chunky brooch—the effect was pleasing. He was rewarded with a hasty peck on the cheek.

'Really, you should have fought with your parents and gone to fashion school. You're fantastic with clothes!'

'Hello, every time I brought it up my mother would sob uncontrollably, accusing me of being gloriously gay. I had to do my MBA to prove that I was as geometrically straight as they come!'

'As bad as my parents,' Anjali bit out vehemently, 'always poking their noses into my business, thinking because they made me they owned me. I hate the way they controlled my life!'

'Hey relax.' Karan stopped in the act of pulling on his T-shirt. 'Is that really you or is it your PMS talking?'

'Please, sometimes I have perfectly reasonable, non-hormonal reasons to be upset. Men are so pathetic!' Anjali shot him a withering look over her shoulder as she strode out of the bedroom to check on the preparations.

The living room looked warm and inviting with the lamps softly glowing. The table was set and the cook was adding the final prettying touches to the hors d'oeuvres, laying some on beds of fresh green lettuce, garnishing some with sprigs of herbs, artistically adding olives and splashes of sauces for colour. Anjali effusively congratulated the cook on her flair and then poured herself a splash of Scotch. She took a large gulp and enjoyed the feeling of its warmth seeping through her body. Her nerves were evidently mollified too, because they'd stopped jangling.

She turned the music on—world music stuff that was terribly in—and sank into a comfortable old armchair, gathering herself together. Then the doorbell rang and her hands shook so much she almost spilt the drink on her clothes. She rose, wiping her clammy hands on her trousers, and went to the front door, plastering a smile on her face. As the door swung open, she came face to face with Rohan, looking horrifically scruffy with fuzz on his cheeks and no hair on his head. Anjali screamed like she'd seen Banquo's ghost and Karan and the cook came racing out, alarmed.

'What are you doing here? Have you killed someone? Why are you looking like this?' she wailed, clutching him to her fiercely, practically squeezing the breath out of him.

'Please, Mother,' came Rohan's muffled voice as he made futile attempts to wriggle out of her grasp. 'You could say hello and look happy to see me. I've just got off a train—an unreserved compartment at that, in my haste to be with you guys.'

'Welcome home, son,' Karan said warmly, and extracted him out of Anjali's tight grasp. 'I see you've gone in for the hip hop look.'

Rohan grinned and ran a hand over his shaved head. 'Yeah, looks hot, doesn't it, Father?'

'Well, being a tight-arsed wanker-banker as your Aunty Mantra affectionately calls me, I'll just say that it makes you look neater than before. So tell us what brings you here immediately, before your mother bursts any more blood vessels. Food or money or both?'

'Both, of course, and lust too,' Rohan sighed. 'I met this real cool chick from Mumbai at the college fest last month and decided to check in on her before she forgets about me. You know how fickle women are; they don't see you for a few days and they're off with someone else.'

Karan laughed and relaxed, while Anjali was still wound up. 'And what about your attendance? Couldn't you have waited another two months? Your hols are coming up, or have you forgotten?' she barked.

'Oh stop being so stuffy, Mother, and besides I missed you terribly too. Heck, I thought you'd be over the moon to see your only child.' He smiled engagingly and gave her a hug, winking at Karan simultaneously.

'Yeah right!' Anjali grinned despite herself. 'Now it's off to the cleaners with you. We're expecting company and I want you to look like a human being at the very least. Get rid of that ghastly face fuzz pronto.'

'Yes, you'd better look good, Rohan. Your mother's ex-boyfriend is our guest of honour—you have to do her proud,' Karan said with a faint smile.

Anjali almost fainted with embarrassment.

'Mother has an ex? *Mother?* I don't believe it,' Rohan shook his head disbelievingly. 'She's too starchy for stuff like that, she must have been saving her, um, love for her wedding night.'

'Excuse me, once upon a time, before you were born, I was dead cool too!' Anjali retorted, stung. Then she marched him off to his bedroom and violently flung a towel at him, viciously hoping he'd get whiplash.

Rohan lifted the telephone receiver and Anjali slapped it back down. 'Not now. *First* a bath and a shave, then you'll come out and say hello politely. Once the bloody niceties are over, your time is your own.'

'Tsk. Your language, Mother. Shocking,' Rohan clucked cheekily.

The doorbell rang again while Anjali was busy laying out clothes for Rohan. Her heart hammered in her chest and she had to quell an insane urge to jump out of the window. Why oh why did she agree to meet him? She stared at the pair of clean jeans in her hands and almost twisted them into a knot. Bloody, bloody Shiv. The doorbell rang yet again, a series of short sharp beeps—Mantra's usual hurry-up-and-open-the-door-gotta-pee-despo SOS. Anjali became calmer now that her ally had arrived.

When Anjali finally emerged from the bedroom pushing an unusually neat Rohan ahead of her she tried to look casual, and tried harder to stop her eyes from scanning the room for Shiv, but she needn't have bothered. No one paid any attention to her because Rohan took centre stage. He hurled himself into Mantra's arms for a bear hug and swept off the contents of the coffee table in the process. Crystal bowls tinkled and crashed to the ground.

'Oops, sorry!'Rohan exclaimed.

'And this is our well brought up son Rohan, doing his impersonation of an exuberant bushy tailed beast to perfection,' Karan proclaimed heartily to Shiv.

Mantra ignored the mess and held Rohan in a warm embrace.

'Santa bovina, it's Ro the Hun! What a lovely surprise!' she exclaimed. 'Hey, if I'd known you were going to be here, I'd have brushed up on my Latin. All I can remember unaided are *spucatum tauri* and *vacca stulta*.'

'Oh I remember those too,' Rohan laughed appreciatively. 'That's bullshit and stupid cow, right?'

Rohan adored his batty aunt. When he was a child, Mantra would use only Latin expletives in his presence if she was in a foul mood. That way, she kept her conscience clear and his vocabulary clean while getting her emotional release. Anjali had protested in vain that even if Rohan didn't understand what she was saying, he was smart enough to understand the emotion behind them, and what if he used them at school?

'Oh don't be silly. As if anyone will understand a word of what he says! I bet even his teachers won't. *Quod erat demonstrandum* and *veni vidi vici* are about as far as they go,' Mantra had retorted impatiently.

When Rohan had turned fifteen, he'd Googled one of Mantra's expletives. It led him to a Latin swear words website and he had even more reason to be her most ardent fan. She was his buddy, his confidante and his weapon against his stodgy propah mother.

'I must tell you Aunty M that thanks to you, all the chicks in college think I'm the ultimate in cool. By the way my favourite phrase now is one of your old favourites—*crapulam terriblis habeo.*'

'Oh, I remember that one fondly—I have a terrible hangover.' Mantra had the grace to grimace. 'But it's not a good idea to drink now that you have a licence to kill, hmm? Put this down in the minutes of our meeting; I will sternly discuss it with you at length later.' Mantra gave him a steely appraising look.

'Don't get all sainted aunt on me,' Rohan pleaded. 'I know my limits.'

'Cool. And don't expect me to accompany your weeping parents to Arthur Road jail, smuggling slices of pepperoni pizza in my socks. Actually, they'll probably send you to Tihar, since you're in Delhi—you won't get to meet us that often in that case. Trust me, Rohan, they're coming down heavily on driving under the influence cases. And I'm on their side. One hundred per cent.' Mantra wagged a finger under Rohan's nose as she delivered her speech.

'Point noted,' he said wryly. Aged people, really!

Karan was fixing the drinks and laughing at Mantra and Rohan's exchange, while Anjali was left to deal with Operation Clean Up with the house help and Shiv. He'd pitched in as soon as the accident occurred, so they met again after almost three decades without a formal hello but with 'Watch out for that shard of glass there'. Their fingers touched briefly every now and then as they picked up the pieces, and Anjali experienced bolts of electricity shooting through her body. Despite her protestations, Shiv accompanied her to the kitchen, dumping his collection of glass bits into the thick plastic bin liner she held out.

'Sorry about this,' Anjali mumbled, blushing. Never in her years of hostessing had anything so dreadfully embarrassing occurred.

'No big deal. These things happen,' Shiv said, and his voice suddenly dropped to a whisper. 'You haven't changed one bit. You're as gorgeous as ever.'

Anjali blushed furiously and mumbled a thank you. She could just as easily have returned the compliment because the bastard was still maddeningly sexy—sexier than before. His voice had acquired a deep rich chocolaty timbre that went so well with his chocolaty skin. He made Karan, her sweet, gentle, traditionally good looking, good natured husband, appear about as appealing as a glass of pale homogenized milk. She felt shy and confused, and was hugely relieved when Mantra stepped into the kitchen with an, 'Ah, there you are, Anjali! I'm changing the music. Can't stand this Buddha Bar shit. Want to help me choose something, Shiv?'

Anjali hovered busily near the music cabinet while Mantra and Shiv browsed through the CDs. Shiv picked out one and handed it to Mantra.

'UB40?' he asked.

'Hey, you be forty too,' Mantra teased, but Shiv didn't get it at first. He looked puzzled and then acknowledged her pun with a polite weak laugh that wasn't reflected in his eyes.

Anjali noted Mantra's mildly disappointed expression with mixed feelings. She'd wanted Mantra to hate him, but suddenly she wasn't sure. When she managed to get Mantra to herself in the kitchen later she hissed, 'So what do you think of him?'

Mantra shrugged dismissively. 'He's okay, I guess. Proper, polite, painfully formal and eminently forgettable.'

'He's not forgettable!' Anjali surprised herself by the violence of her reaction.

'Look, he's not my type, okay? Frankly, he bores me.'

'In which case I probably bore you too, because you've often accused me of being painfully formal!' Anjali glared combatively.

Mantra's antennae shot up and she scanned Anjali's face briefly. Hmm, interesting development, she thought.

Anjali shrank from Mantra's frank stare and turned away, pretending to look for something in the fridge. She was grateful for the cool blast that fanned her hot cheeks.

Mantra squeezed her hand. 'That's bullshit, Anjali, stop being hyper sensitive. You both say the right things perhaps, but you still come across as warm and compassionate whereas he seems cold and indifferent. So there!'

All evening Mantra was on high alert, watching Shiv surreptitiously, and she didn't like what she saw. Though Shiv spent most of the evening chatting with Karan, his eyes strayed towards Anjali more often than was acceptable, and he made several attempts to involve Anjali in the discussions. Too bad Rohan left—he would have kept Anjali much too frazzled in anxious mother hen mode to pay attention to anyone else, Mantra mused.

Over dessert, Shiv politely complimented Anjali on her superb spread and asked if she would accept the odd catering assignment for cosy at-home parties his PR company hosted.

'I, um, really, um, I don't know,' was Anjali's feeble response.

Mantra frantically leapt to her rescue. After all, she'd promised to help her bat Shiv off. 'That wouldn't be possible, would it, Anjali?' she asked. 'You've so much on your plate already, entertaining Karan's clients and colleagues.'

Anjali nodded enthusiastically and the matter may have ended there if Karan hadn't stepped in. 'This will be good for you, darling. You've been suffering from empty nest syndrome ever since Rohan left for college and this should keep you busy and happy. Maybe you can take me on a nice holiday with some of your earnings, huh?' he teased.

Idiot, Mantra thought, with a flash of annoyance. Lovable, but an idiot. The ass has no idea what he's consenting to.

'Seems like a nice chap,' Karan remarked affably after Shiv had left. Fortunately Mantra wasn't around to hear him say, 'We must have him around again sometime.'

Anjali couldn't sleep that night. She lay wide awake in bed playing mental goalkeeper, energetically kicking thoughts of

Shiv out of her head. But they rushed in fast and furious again and again; she was no match for them. Finally, she wound her arms around Karan and clung to him like he was a lifesaving log in choppy seas, hoping that the warmth of his physical presence would overpower the spirit in her head. It helped—just a bit.

9

Mantra woke up to a text message from Vir—it was his breakfast menu: 'Awesome bfast. Orange juice. Exotic fruit platter including kiwi etc. Bowl of oats wi nuts. Omelette wi cheese and bacon. Whole wheat bread slices. Blueberry jam and marmalade. Roast turkey pastrami. Smoked salmon. MASSIVE waffle drowned half in honey and half in maple syrup. Washed down wi cup of tea. Can't get up now.'

She glared at it and flung the phone down. Her throat ached so. She was shamelessly taking advantage of Vir's absence by smoking furiously. Of course, she still had to do it surreptitiously on the balcony while Reshma was out, lest she found out and spitefully ratted on her. Smoking was another dirty disgusting indulgence Vir had quit after he got on his new health trip and he was on Mantra's case to kick the habit too. She swore that she'd do her best, cut it down to two a day at least, do it the slow halal way instead of the insta-shock jhatka method, but her good intentions were foiled by the lousy cooking at home. She needed oral gratification from *something*. Besides, it dulled her taste buds too, so there was no way in hell she was going to give it up.

She shampooed her hair to remove every last trace of nicotine before she went to the airport on chauffeur duty. Vir was winging his way back and Makarand had taken the day off to accompany his heavily pregnant wife to the doctor. At least that's what he'd said, but Mantra suspected he was at the SNM political rally she'd read about in the papers. While surfing through the news channels she'd caught a glimpse of someone who looked rather like him enthusiastically hurling stones at a bus.

Waiting for Vir to emerge from the arrivals section, Mantra had the misfortune of walking slap bang into Great Revolutionary Leader's wife who dragged her off to the coffee shop. Mrs Sharma informed her that she'd been summoned to the airport by her husband to carry cash for duty fees on the electronic gadgets he'd bought.

'He's a crazy gizmo freak,' she confessed, grimacing.

Mantra gave her the standard girlie eye-ball rolling 'Aren't all men?' response, and thought maybe she wasn't so unbearable in a one-on-one when Mrs Sharma suddenly got into I-am-your-husband's-boss's-wife mode again. She steered the conversation around to babies yet again, in a queenly manner.

'You're being very inconsiderate, Mamta. What if Vir is secretly yearning for a child? All men,' she grandly proclaimed, 'are genetically programmed to hand over their family name like a baton before they die.'

Mantra firmly shook her head. 'Not Vir,' she said. 'He has a prized collection of dinky cars and threatens to horsewhip any visiting child who tampers with them,' she exaggerated wildly. Mantra managed to say that convincingly because part of the story was true. Shalinibai had once dusted frenetically in a fit of conscience during the auspicious Navratras and had broken the steering wheel of a two-inch Ferrari. Vir had gone into a state of shock and Mantra had had to console him for the rest of the week, reminding him that it was not as expensive as a real car, and that Santa could well give him another one at Christmas if he were a good boy that year.

Mrs Sharma got up abruptly mumbling a vague excuse and left Mantra to pay the bill. Mantra realized with a sinking feeling that she shouldn't have told her about Vir's weird obsession with dinky cars. Please God, I hope this idiotic conversation won't affect his appraisal, she silently prayed. Maybe I should have blamed myself, and told her that it is all my fault; that I don't want children because my maths is very bad and I will not be able to help my offspring with homework. The offspring will then grow up and write a vituperative tell-all best-seller about how he/she could have won the Nobel Prize in astrophysics if it weren't for his/her ignorant mother. Oh well, what's done can't be undone.

She continued to stay morosely slumped over the table till Vir called on her cell phone and said he was at the exit. On her way there, she saw Uday Handa on all fours near the cab stand, cramming things into an overnight case: the zipper had obviously given way. Mantra was astonished that the contents were mainly hotel-branded bath salts, bottles of moisturizer, razors, shower caps and tiny soaps. Loads of them. Considering that they had been there for just three days, he must have pinched the lot from unattended housekeeping trolleys. Mantra suspected that they would be flaunted in his guest bathroom, particularly if they had the Raffles or Banyan Tree logos. It must have been his wife's idea—it was just the sort of thing Pinky would do to let her guests know she had arrived—first class, at that. Her obituary definitely wouldn't include the statement that she was well-versed in the art of subtlety. Mantra smirked, and since Uday thankfully hadn't noticed her, crept away. She wasn't in the mood to make any more polite conversation. However, she did wonder if the hotel's housekeeping staff was still giggling over the weirdo who nicked pink disposable ladies' razors.

Vir was in a surprisingly good mood and chatted cheerfully all the way home, giving Mantra the highlights of his trip.

'The very first evening, a voluptuous transvestite accosted me outside the hotel and said that I look exactly like Harrison Ford,' Vir said in a pleased manner. He still sounded terribly flattered.

'Hello, everyone knows that Harrison Ford is over sixty! It was in the papers about a decade ago. I bet your transvestite just wanted easy money!' Mantra pointed out waspishly.

That didn't chase the flush away from Vir's face, however. Mantra caught him checking himself out in the rear-view mirror, sucking in his cheeks. Heavens, he was clearly going through a mid-life crisis!

They met Samira and her husband in the lift. The four of them exchanged polite, distant smiles and rode silently up, gazing into space. All of a sudden, Mantra felt rage towards the evil husband building up inside her and she deliberately lurched towards him, swinging Vir's camera tripod in his direction. She got him smack on the left cheek.

'Oops sorry, clumsy me,' she gushed apologetically, then pretended to lose her balance and did it again. Vir hastily took the tripod out of her grasp and apologized on Mantra's behalf. The evil husband rubbed his cheek and muttered epithets under his breath. Maybe Mantra imagined it, but she thought she saw Samira wink at her. That encouraged Mantra and made her wish she'd been carrying a garden rake instead, with the prongs aimed at Samira's evil husband's face. Vir nastily asked her if she'd been drinking when they got off at their floor.

'Naah—did it purposely. But it's a long story, and not a pleasant bedtime one at that!'

'You stay the hell out of their business, understand?' he growled warningly.

Mantra was in seventh heaven when she helped Vir unpack. He'd brought back stacks of chocolates—macadamia and hazelnut ones for them (since nuts were healthy), packs of mini chocolate bars for the office staff and peons—and umpteen bottles of Thai fish sauce and other ingredients that were on Anjali's list. She was a stickler for authentic ingredients.

'I got a nice tee for you too,' Vir grinned, tossing it at Mantra. 'It's a French Connection rip off—I thought it was so apt.'

Mantra shook the T-shirt out. It read: Too tired to fcuk.

The message was loud and clear.

'And what have you bought for yourself, since I'm too tired to F-C-U-K? Herpes?' she inquired sarcastically.

'Nope, no hookers for me—don't have to pay for sex. I'm the spitting image of Harrison Ford, remember?'

Mantra was truly shattered about the T-shirt, too shattered to cut him down to size. After giving her a significantly deep and meaningful look, Vir went to the bathroom with the latest issue of *Fortune*, his head held high. Mantra noticed a well-thumbed back issue of a steamy *Cosmo* tucked not so surreptitiously inside but refrained from commenting. She did not wish to be coldly reminded of her 'Not tonight, darling, my make-believe dog ate my diaphragm' excuses. Keeping his reading material in mind, Mantra knew that Vir would be in there for an hour at the very least. She snuck out to the balcony and lit up, not caring whether she'd be caught in the act any more, contemplating her bleak life as an aged and frigid divorcee. All those girlie mag articles about sex that she'd dismissed contemptuously as bullshit ('Sex: The Bedrock of Marriage', 'Sex: The Glue that Holds Marriages Together' and the like) laughed in her face now. She mentally resolved to get a female Viagra prescription from her gynaecologist. First thing tomorrow, she swore to herself.

After the restorative smoke, she spoke to Reshma to find out about village life for her novel, but Reshma coldly informed Mantra that she'd been born and bred in the city and would never visit a village because she detested the smell of cow dung.

Later that night, as Mantra snuggled up to Vir in bed, she enthusiastically told him the plot of her novel. Vir's response was 'Bollocks!'

'You're a bloody chauvinist. You scoff because you think women are only capable of writing books on cooking and knitting. Explain Jane Austen writing novels in her time!' Mantra demanded challengingly.

'Jane Austen was a man using a female pseudonym,' Vir superciliously replied, being ridiculously stubborn as always.

'Oh? And where did you get this nugget of misinformation? Your groupie chicks at office who swear that reading self-help books has changed their lives?' Mantra asked indignantly, and got an incoherent mutter in reply.

Vir switched off his bedside lamp to indicate that the conversation was over, but Mantra didn't let up. She was primed for one of their classic fights.

'You know, you're the sort who will stick to your story even if you are being ruthlessly tortured. You'd make an admirable terrorist!' she taunted.

Then Vir said something that made Mantra shut up: He was also contemplating writing a book.

'Really? What's it going to be about? One of those pseudo-inspirational corporate types like *Who Ate My Brie?*' Mantra asked, trying hard to swallow a yawn so as not to hurt Vir's feelings.

'Moved, not ate, and the bloody cheese wasn't specified,' Vir muttered. 'Anyway, my book won't be about corporate shit. I've already got the title. I'm going to call it *The Table Gets Laid More Often than I Do*.'

Vir turned his back to her and fell asleep almost immediately. Mantra didn't sleep a wink, however. For the very first time in her life, she felt frightened and insecure about the future of her marriage. Being best friends, obviously, wasn't good enough for him. Dr Mehta would have to be consulted as soon as possible!

10

Even though she wasn't working any more, Mantra looked forward to the weekends. She still had to wake up at the crack of dawn on weekdays to help Vir get ready for work by organizing his clothes, breakfast, lunch, etc. The only thing that had changed was that she could do it all without panicking about getting late for work herself.

After a leisurely brunch, she called Dr Mehta and the receptionist offered her an appointment two months later. 'That's too late—this is an emergency,' Mantra wailed. The receptionist politely but firmly fobbed her off.

Thereafter, an aggrieved Mantra parked herself at her laptop, not exactly looking forward to working on her magnum opus but sternly willing herself onwards. She keyed in a few sentences, hated them and deleted them peremptorily.

Not working, she grimaced, glaring malevolently at her laptop like this was its fault. Maybe I should witter on about the landscape for page after dreary page—most serious Indian writers in English do that. Naah—boring. Something's got to sizzle for the right exotic flavour. Wax eloquent on cooking, perhaps? Dramatic colours, textures, wafting aromas, sounds like hot oil hissing menacingly and mustard seeds spluttering furiously, the usual rubbish. Ah, got it.

Mantra typed maniacally for the next few minutes, giving her heroine's sweaty and rank-smelling birth mother the arduous task of peeling a pomegranate, her fingers incriminatingly stained with drops of ruby red blood. The entire process was described in excruciating detail. She then reread her effort and hated it. Some desperate over-writing was called for if she wanted to do a great parody. She absolutely had to get hysterical about the pomegranate in a smutty way, like mangoes were often described—pendulous breasts bursting with the promise of gratification. Big problem. Pomegranates didn't lend themselves to sexual connotations—those darned things looked like prosaic cricket balls. Mantra sighed. Bloody hell! she thought. Over-writing is hard work. Gosh, my respect for Indian writers in English has shot up considerably. Perhaps I need something to make me feel passionate, like some of that duty-free chocolate.

When she crept to the kitchen on tiptoe, hoping Reshma would not notice her sneaking out chocolate, her worst fears were confirmed: Reshma *was* having an affair with Makarand! Mantra caught them in each other's arms and she shrieked involuntarily, hitting higher window-pane-shattering notes than Bianca Castafiore. They guiltily sprang apart. Thereafter, Mantra was speechless. Vir did his usual act. He darted into the kitchen in response to her shriek and darted out just as speedily, muttering that domestic issues were Mantra's problem—he had enough on his hands at work, what with battling Uday. Mantra had absolutely no idea what to do so she attempted to direct a meaningful look at Reshma but failed miserably because Reshma's eyes were riveted to the floor. She cleared her throat meaningfully, hoping to catch her attention. Makarand responded instead and gruffly said that Mantra should give him money to buy a rat trap forthwith as there was a large rodent in kitchen, implying that was why Reshma had leapt into his arms. Makarand's gestures indicated that the rodent was just a wee bit taller than an adult Shetland pony. Mantra was still too stunned to say anything so she nodded instead and rushed to the bedroom to raid Vir's wallet. It was so much easier to give Makarand the benefit of the doubt.

Vir was sprawled on the bed with his eyes glued to the TV screen. Mantra was disturbed to see a close-up of bare ebony bosoms bouncing on the screen. And they are not even sagging, she thought enviously. She sharply told Vir to stop watching porn with the bedroom door wide open.

'Really, Vir, you're a very bad influence on our amorous cook and adulterous driver! No wonder such nonsense is happening in our house!'

'Porn my foot! It's an educational programme on African tribals and it will vastly improve my general knowledge. Do not forget that my team won at the last corpo quiz,' he proclaimed self-righteously.

Mantra snorted derisively at that and reached for his wallet on the bedside table. Vir guffawed when she told him what the money was required for. 'So he's conned you into buying a rat trap, hmm? You're being made a total ass of, aren't you? You're literally paying for Makarand's indiscretions. Smart chap, that!'

Mantra ignored him and handed over the cash to the insolent Makarand who looked extremely pleased with himself for inventing the rat lie. Reshma also looked as cool as a cucumber and equally nonchalant. This annoyed Mantra, so she witheringly told Makarand to buy a bottle of multi-vitamins for his eight-month pregnant wife with the change. She was deeply gratified to note that Reshma's face crumpled at the reminder of Makarand's marital status. Mantra caught her glaring at his retreating back and decided to lecture her on the evils of making out with married men when she felt calmer. She returned to the bedroom with the light of battle shining in her eyes.

'Do something, Vir, talk to the sod! I do not want illegitimate children conceived in my spotless kitchen! Besides his wife is such a sweet woman, we can't let him do this to her,' she pleaded.

'I have only one solution,' Vir offered. 'Get Makarand neutered.'

'Hmm. Charming though that may be—hey, it may even make him less aggressive—he's not a fool; he'd never agree. Maybe we should put Reshma on the pill instead,' she mused, but dismissed the idea herself. 'Bad idea actually—the pill may cause a hormonal imbalance and she's moody and hysterical enough as it is. Oh what do we do?' she wailed helplessly.

Vir pleaded work, turning his attention to his laptop without taking his eyes off the TV—one of his favourite wildlife programmes had just begun. Mantra switched it off defiantly.

'Disgusting! How can *you*, of all people, watch creatures eating cholesterol-rich red meat? Doesn't that make you want to throw up?'

Vir looked annoyed but didn't dare ask Mantra to turn the TV back on. He concentrated on the laptop instead, playing an infantile computer game: trying to catch eggs that animated hens on a clothes line were laying in rapid succession. Mantra rebuked him for indulging in childish pursuits in the midst of a stormy domestic calamity but he vociferously defended the brain-dead game.

'Please,' he said sniffily, 'this is no ordinary game. It improves my hand–eye coordination and I will be able to place spoonfuls of liquidized food neatly into my mouth even after I turn ninety-nine. You should play it too, Mantra, or else you'll be a messy eater in your old age.'

Makarand returned after two hours with a wooden mousetrap. It looked too flimsy and tiny to catch a soldier ant, let alone an adult Shetland pony-sized rodent. Makarand impatiently brushed Mantra's misgivings aside, saying that the rat-trap had been ingeniously designed to catch only one paw.

'It can still make good its escape with three free paws,' Mantra scoffed.

'Arrey ma'am,' Makarand drawled, 'the point of the one-paw clamping rat trap is that the rat will make a clattering noise while running for cover. You just have to follow the sound!'

Reshma cast a look of deep admiration at Makarand and staunchly stood up for him, reminding Mantra about how often she called her cell phone from the landline to locate it. Mantra gave up. She went to the bedroom with the rat trap, leaving it to Vir to deliver the final verdict on its efficacy.

'This just won't do!' he snorted, 'We'll have to send him out to buy three more wooden traps, one for each paw. Imagine, we'll have the only rat in the building who wears Dutch clogs! *Very* stylish.'

Mantra snappishly told him she was not remotely interested in playing an altruistic shoe provider to a rat and summoned Makarand to the bedroom. Really, Vir was impossible!

The change in Makarand's demeanour was remarkable. He was obsequious to Vir, and readily agreed to get a more efficient option without further argument. When Vir curtly nodded his dismissal he walked out, casting his usual look of scorn in Mantra's direction.

'See how easy that was?' Vir gloated.

'Easy for you because he only respects men,' Mantra retorted.

'Rubbish! Honestly, Mantra, the sooner you learn to play boss the better. You can't keep bothering me with trivial issues,' he muttered impatiently while concentrating deeply on the egg catching computer game. 'You should do a course in HR to learn how to manage staff. You're a soft touch—it's shameful the way you let them walk all over you. Are you a bloody wimp or what?'

Mantra was silenced. Maybe I am a wimp, after all, she reflected. But hell, I can't bring myself to hit out at people who are too weak or economically disadvantaged to hit back. The guilt would kill me. I just can't. I'm only good with equals.

Rupa Gulab

She gave up her depressing contemplation and collapsed on the bed in a lumpy heap, flipping through the pages of a DIY acupressure face-lift book Samira had sent through her house help a few days ago. All she had to do to vanquish crow's feet was apply pressure to the corner of her eyes, it blithely said. A load of crock, she snorted and flung the book down.

She prodded Vir. 'Tell me, should I get a Botox job?'

'Don't be idiotic,' he said impatiently. 'Whatever for?'

'You know, my wrinkles. Especially the one between my eyebrows. It makes me look very stern, like a moral policeman protesting against a song with indecent lyrics.'

'Hmm,' Vir mumbled, engrossed in his game.

Mantra lifted his chin and made him face her.

'For my wrinkles, Vir! Look! Do I need Botox for my wrinkles?'

'Of course not,' Vir said firmly. 'What a silly pointless idea—I don't even look at you anyway!'

'Oh screw you. Who cares about you? I mean other men,' Mantra said, raising a warning eyebrow at him.

'Don't bother—they don't look at you either! Now shut up, will you—you made me bloody lose this game!'

11

Anjali couldn't concentrate on the newspaper article she was reading: 'Wine Grapes' Genome Decoded, Flavour Genes Found'. After three attempts when she still couldn't get beyond or even comprehend the first two sentences, she gave up and rummaged in her dressing table drawer for the nail scissors. She cut it out to read later, when she was more focused.

She'd passed the last ten days in a daze, too busy to analyse her confused feelings. It was a blessing that Rohan was at home. He kept her on her feet catering to crowds of his old school chums and his new pet squeeze, Tanya. She was a sassy little thing who imperiously bossed Rohan around.

'Quite the little hussy, isn't she?' Anjali whispered disapprovingly to Karan one evening, and he ruffled her hair playfully.

'Oh come on, stop playing the possessive mum. You boss me around quite as much you know, and besides it won't last long; they're both too young, he'll probably date another twenty women before he settles down. By which time we may be dead so it won't really matter if he marries a harridan.'

'He's not *that* young,' Anjali argued. 'Vir was exactly the same age when he met Mantra. They dated each other for years and years, and they're together still, aren't they? Come on, neither has even looked at anyone else since.'

'Valid,' Karan conceded with a nod. 'Now that you mention it, we weren't that much older than Rohan when we got married, were we? And we're still together too, happily ever after and all that.' He squeezed her hand affectionately.

Anjali returned the squeeze mechanically and guiltily caught herself wondering what it would feel like if it were Shiv holding her hand. She felt a shiver run down her spine and disengaged her hand from Karan's grasp. Oh help, please, please God, get that rotter out of my mind, she silently implored.

'Vir and Mantra like Tanya, though,' Karan continued, 'and she's not a bad sort really.'

'Oh please. Vir and Mantra don't count!' Anjali stamped her foot. 'They're both weirdos, you know that, Karan! Look at the way they talk to each other, they say rude things and insult each other—and that's when they're being affectionate. I've always told Rohan, "Love your uncle and aunt by all means but never ever appropriate them as role models."'

'I thought you liked them,' was Karan's puzzled response.

'*Of course* I like them! I adore them too, but I want Rohan to be more like us. To be proper, respectable and polite in society; to fit in seamlessly and not stand out like a sore thumb.'

The fact of the matter was, Anjali had become a little jealous of the hold Mantra had over Rohan. She had dropped by with Vir one evening to spend time with Rohan and had given him a few books. One had been a collection of modern verse which had made Rohan retch.

'A poetry book? Ew. Come on, Aunty M, I'm not wet!'

'You may not be wet but you're certainly wet behind the ears if you think all poetry sucks. Listen to this without making hasty judgements, you silly ass!' Mantra had read out her favourite poem, clearing her throat as preamble.

'*This Be the Verse* by Philip Larkin. Okay, here goes, Ro the Hun. This ought to appeal to your teen angst.

"They fuck you up, your mum and dad
They may not mean to, but they do.
They fill you with the faults they had
And add some extra, just for you . . ."'

Rohan had listened spellbound, and sighed appreciatively at the end of the poem. 'Man, I know exactly what that guy means. I feel *exactly* the same way!'

'How dare you?' Anjali had squawked indignantly. 'Your father and I have never, um, messed with you!'

'Oh but you have, Mother dear, you both have. One day, when I'm in a lunatic asylum, my shrink will tell you exactly what you put me through!'

'Impudent little sod,' Vir had reprimanded, his shoulders shaking with laughter.

'Listen, Vir, both you and I can identify with the poem—our parents gave us a rough time. But this boy had it easy. Hey, Karan and I are cool parents!'

'Not as cool as Aunt M and Uncle Vir,' Rohan had shot back, 'not even close! They even like the same music I do, you just don't get it.'

'And if you don't shut up, *you'll* get it,' Anjali had muttered under her breath. Comparisons stank. She longed to protest that Mantra had the freedom to be a buddy goddess because she didn't have the same responsibilities as Anjali had—she could enjoy play time while Anjali was bogged down by her maternal duties of which discipline played a very important part. Anjali had held her tongue though, feeling like a martyr.

After Rohan went back to Delhi and college, Shiv lived in her mind 24x7. She thought of him first thing when she woke up, last thing before she went to bed, and practically every waking moment in between. Sometimes he was the object of her anger, sometimes lust. It was so irrational, Anjali seriously wondered if she were suffering from an obsessive compulsive disorder. She felt her heart lurch every time her cell phone rang, but was always disappointed. So many days had passed and not a squeak out of him.

She even held imaginary phone conversations with him in her head. On her sane days, she'd tell him sharply that she wasn't interested in communicating with a filthy slime ball like him and how dared he break off with her in such a shabby manner, goodbye and good riddance. On bad longing-filled days, she'd yearn to be in a position to breathlessly whisper, 'Oh Shiv, I feel the same way about you, but we should stop communicating with each other. It's not right.'

Every now and then, she'd mentally reprimand herself: Stupid! Stupid! Stupid! I don't even know if he feels anything for me. I must stop foolishly imagining that he offered that catering assignment because he wanted to see me again. He was probably just being polite—painfully polite, as Mantra puts it. How dare he drive me crazy—and for the second time in my life too. Oh God, I'm aching to hear his voice—why can't he bloody call?

Time for her head-to-toe 'Mirror, mirror, on the wall' reality check again: a practice she had started after the dinner party.

Crow's feet: Yuck, yes!
Wrinkles: A few, but not deeply etched yet.
Jawline: Not yet saggy, whew!
Bosom: Will do.
Upper arms: Still taut.
Lower arms: Okayish.
Waistline: Dreadful! Vast-line would be a more appropriate description.
Hips: Ouch!
Thighs: Thin line between firmish and jellyish.
Calves: Okayish.
Ankles: Okayish.

No wonder Shiv wasn't interested. A relief really, she could do without problems in her life, but meeting him again was a wake up call to get herself in shape. It was just not right for a forty-six year old to look like a fifty-year-old pop diva's mother! Yes, it was time to join a gym and visit a cosmetologist. To make it more interesting, she'd ask Mantra to join with her. Not ask—force her, drag her screaming and kicking if need be.

Mantra hated exercise. She'd told Anjali once that she frequently had to emotionally blackmail herself to bend down and pick up something that she'd dropped: 'I tell myself rubbish like, if I don't pick it up right away, Mum will get a painful urinary infection or Dad will get lumbago or Vir will get a burning ulcer. Just stupid garbage, but it terrifies me and makes me bend down real fast!'

Anjali was a woman of action—she dialled Mantra's number and got a very curt Mantra on the phone. An icy 'Yes?' was Mantra's version of 'Hello'.

'Sorry, are you busy?' Anjali apologized. 'I just needed to talk. It's okay, call when you're free.'

'Two minutes. That's all you have,' was the terse reply.

Mantra wasn't just annoyed, she was hair-tearingly frustrated. She was just getting into the feel of her story and she *hated* interruptions; they broke her chain of thought.

'Everything in the village was barren: the fields, the granaries, the cooking pots. Everything, except unmarried Savitri's womb. The locusts, unfortunately, had spared that.'

She reread it several times with deep satisfaction and a glowing sense of pride at her ability for shameless parody. Besides, it was so heavily laced with irony, it was certain to inspire the prize-giving short-list team to sob heartbroken into their hankies. Thereafter, her inspiration dried up like the rivers and streams in her heroine's barren village during summer. Mantra strongly suspected that one of her favourite childhood authors, Enid Blyton, was misquoted about writing 10,000 words a day. It wasn't humanly possible. Not without steroids, at any rate.

'And please, if this call has anything to do with your idiotic ex, I'm hanging up right now,' Mantra added curtly. She'd had quite enough of Anjali's confidences about her confused state of mind. The woman had started calling her several times a day for emotional release, like a giddy teenager. Mantra didn't quite know how to deal with this, considering that they had never confided in each other on intensely personal matters before. Mantra deliberately hadn't because Anjali was Vir's sister—that would have been foolish, while Anjali had never seemed to have a personal crisis before, apart from upsets in Rohan's behaviour and Karan's career issues.

'Good news for you then—he still hasn't called and probably won't. He must have forgotten about his offer. It's been over ten days since dinner, remember?' Anjali glumly informed her.

'Ten interminably long days, huh? If you were a dog, you'd have aged considerably by now! Been put down, most probably.'

'Bitch!' Anjali shocked herself by using a really filthy word. She blushed.

'Darling, I said if *you* were a dog, not me. And stop thinking about that arsehole. You're married to a far better person.'

'Oh shut up, Mantra, I *know* that I'm married to a lovely man—the best there is! Want to join a gym with me? You know, to take my mind off my problems and all that.' Anjali slyly put it that way, banking on the fact that Mantra was a sucker for emotional trauma.

'You want to lose weight? Can I exchange my cook with yours? This woman has made me lose about eight kilos in less than six months. I look like I've just been released from prison. Take her, Anjali, with my blessings! I'll pay you mucho dinero under the dining table.'

Anjali shuddered. She'd had the misfortune of sampling Reshma's food, an experience she was determined never to repeat. Not even if she started resembling the Fat Lady from the circus.

'I mean toning, not slimming,' she hastily clarified. 'Our upper arms are soon going to flap unbecomingly. No more collagen production in our saggy-baggy bodies.'

'Like I care about flapping upper arms! All I think of, dream of, yearn for, is butter. Real bloody butter! Butter that seductively melts into the porous crevices of crisp white bread, and satiates my soul with the reassuring taste of saltiness and comfort. I would fucking *kill* for butter!'

When Mantra threw one of her rare tantrums, retreat was the best course of action. Anjali hastily hung up after a polite, 'I know exactly what you mean,' and got back to her tortured thoughts.

Mantra, meanwhile, was waxing hysterical. She switched off her laptop. Her novel was forgotten—there was no way she could think of anything but butter!

Had there been a stone in the vicinity, Mantra would have been kicking it moodily. To calm herself down, she picked up a glossy Vir had brought home because it had one of his company's ads on dog food and read a life-changing article on the importance of junking old things because they radiated bad vibes. The article energized her. She leapt off the sofa and rushed to evict the contents of the dressing room that served as her attic. Her fervent hope was that the municipal garbage truck would carry away all the bad vibes between Vir and herself in one clean sweep. The brutal remark he'd made over breakfast was still hurting. The exchange they'd had was over yet another alarming sign that Reshma and Makarand's relationship was growing even stronger. She played the conversation back in her head in an attempt to analyse it.

All she had said was an innocuous, 'Vir, you'd better step in since both of them appear to have more respect for you. I refuse to allow any goings-on in my house.'

Vir's response, while delivered in quiet measured tones, had shocked her into silence. 'It's not your house, Mantra. It's mine. I pay the rent.'

What exactly did he mean by that? she wondered. Is he upset because I'm not earning money? Am I being undervalued because I'm jobless and therefore worthless, or is he just sick of me and the sexless marriage? If Mantra hadn't been educated, she'd have perhaps also considered the possibility that Vir was possessed by his evil mother's spirit.

Sighing deeply, she got back to the junk in the dressing room and, typically, got involved in it. She discovered a treasure trove in an old battered-tattered suitcase: termite-ridden letters from exes and angst-ridden poems she'd written when the relationships had ended. She picked up the poems first with narcissistic interest, but was shattered when she read them; they were embarrassingly shallow, ghastly and whiny. She ripped her puke-inducing poems to shreds with her bare hands and was about to do likewise with the letters from the exes, but suddenly changed her mind. Maybe it would help her understand exactly what Anjali was going through. It might make her more sympathetic. She picked up the bundle, leaned back against the wall and wriggled into a comfortable position. Then she unfolded the first letter in a resigned, let's-get-this-crap-over-and-done-with way, and winced (justifiably) when she saw a heart scribbled on it with her initials and the loser's. Thereafter she lost track of time and when the very last letter had been folded and put away she noticed that about an hour had passed. The letters were as trashy as her poems, she had to concede, but they made her feel all warm and fuzzy. Time changes perspectives, she reminded herself. The letters made her forget how much she'd violently disliked or been indifferent to her exes after the break-ups and she started romanticizing them in her head, glossing over their glaring character flaws and annoying habits. She even laughed (albeit mirthlessly) at a very funny, rude card from her last ex-boyfriend on her seventeenth birthday. The cover copy said, 'The old gray mare ain't what she used to be.'

Mantra sighed. Hah! Thank God he can't see me now that I'm forty-three. He'll probably give me a card that reads, 'The old gray mare ain't worth the price of this card.' I desperately need to get my face starched and ironed but lack the funds. The only natural way I can get it to stop looking like a crumpled bedsheet is by using both hands to lift my cheeks. This is not a better option: it makes my eyes slanty and I look like my name is Ho Lee Shit. Wouldn't have minded if it made me look like sexy Lucy Liu instead. Heck, I may as well resign myself to the fact that I'm ageing disgracefully.

She found a bundle of letters from Vir too, written in the good old days when they were dating each other. She skimmed through one but couldn't bring herself to read the rest. The letter made her feel dreadfully empty. The person who had written that wasn't the cold person she was living with now. His remark still rankled.

She was too depressed to sort out junk any more so she tossed everything back into the battered-tattered suitcase and buried her head in her hands, feeling sorry for herself. She could feel the beginnings of a new shallow and ridiculously horrible pain-of-rejection poem coming into her head so she hastily got up and splashed reviving water on her face. The water did its job well—a charitable thought suddenly found its way into her muddled head and Mantra helplessly held on to it like a drowning man clutching at a straw: Maybe the poor chap is just stressed out at work and frustration drives him to use me as his personal whipping boy. I have to buck up and give his bad moods a lot of leeway—that's what couples do for each other; they double up as stress absorbers. I'll ask Vir nicely when he's in a better mood if things are okay at work; we'll sort it out.

Mantra bolstered her defence of Vir with the reminder that he hadn't ever been a sensitive tender loving sort of chap—hell, that was what she enjoyed about him, anyway. The last time he had displayed any human emotion was when crocodile man Steve Irwin had died. Vir had taken it badly. He'd worshipped that man, and he was in the doldrums for a week, a lot like how everyone in the UK was when Princess Diana had died.

She fervently hoped lunch would be edible, but doubted it since Reshma had been displaying alarming signs of PMS since the last evening. Mantra thanked her lucky stars that they'd never experienced PMS at the same time. The riot police may have been required. The idea of a tasteless lunch at home was junked. She decided to treat herself to comfort food at a pizza joint and then she'd pop in to the gynaecologist's and do her bit to get the marriage back in order. She absolutely couldn't wait for two long months to meet Dr Mehta—her marriage may have ended by then, going by the way Vir was behaving. Mantra decided that she would grimly sit in the waiting room and bar Dr Mehta's exit if she refused to meet her. This was a bloody emergency after all.

Mantra's mission was accomplished. She lied to the receptionist that she was bleeding profusely and possibly going through a miscarriage to gain entry. Once in, she confessed to Dr Mehta and told her the real problem.

'Please, Dr Mehta, if you can't solve my frigidity problems, my marriage will be over. I need help now!' Mantra pleaded.

Dr Mehta refused to examine her, though. 'Look, Mantra, I have all your reports from last year with me and physically you're fine. But I do remember thinking even while examining you in the last few years that you need a shrink. You yell blue murder and behave like I'm raping you when I do a simple Pap smear examination. Your problem is that you've become ridiculously inhibited—no wonder your sex life is suffering.'

'I'm not leaving this room till you give me a prescription for something like Viagra for females,' Mantra said stubbornly.

Dr Mehta sighed. 'Sorry, Mantra, till I examine you and put you on hormonal tests, I'm not giving you a prescription for anything—forget it! I'm just going to give you some advice, okay? Now listen carefully.'

Mantra's jaw dropped to her knees as Dr Mehta said the most outrageous things with clinical precision. 'Get drunk or stoned before making out. And watch hardcore porn, lots of it.'

'Porn? You've got to be joking, doctor!' she exclaimed.

'On the contrary, I'm absolutely serious,' Dr Mehta said solemnly. 'You need to sort your inhibitions out. And don't be so prudish about it, Mantra—pandas watch porn too in Thailand and China. It *does* help. Now goodbye, and fix an appointment for an examination on your way out. Meanwhile follow my advice, there's a good girl.'

Mantra stormed out of Dr Mehta's room in a murderous frame of mind and walked slap bang into Uday Handa's wife in the waiting room.

'Well, well, you finally here for fertility treatment?' Pinky drawled.

'Please! I'm just here to renew my prescription for industrial-strength birth control pills,' was Mantra's glacial rejoinder.

Pinky was not to be fobbed off. She caught Mantra's arm in a vice-like grip and took off on Mrs Sharma's pet subject. 'Come on, tell me the real reason why you don't want babies. Out with it!'

'Okay,' Mantra readily dished out nonsense, 'the real reason why we don't want babies is that, as you may have noticed, both Vir and I are not very tall. If we procreate we may create a midget and I cannot bear the idea of being mother to a child who can only earn his or her livelihood as a dwarf in a Snow White pantomime. Happy now? Goodbye!'

'Scum!' Mantra muttered under her breath. She wished she'd actually told Pinky the truth about why they didn't want children. Not just because of the country's over-population—that was part of it—but because being childless gave them the delicious freedom to say fuck off to bosses and organizations they couldn't bear to suffer. They could never do that if they had children. They may have been as pathetically ingratiating as Uday and Pinky Handa.

Vir was still in a bad mood that night. Mantra kept a safe distance from him—she was too frightened to ask him to browse through a freelance article she'd written. His scowls had deepened considerably the next morning because the screams from the penthouse above had been louder.

12

A few days later, Mantra encountered Samira in the car park. 'What? Made such great progress that you're disguising yourself to escape the paparazzi?' Mantra teased, pointing to Samira's designer dark glasses.

Samira silently and unsmilingly whipped off her dark glasses for a brief second and Mantra almost keeled over with shock—proof was not a pretty sight.

'Shit. I hope you're going to do something about it?' Mantra yelped urgently.

'Of course I am!' Samira's eyes flashed fire. 'I've followed your advice and signed up for an art course in Europe, and I'm going to win him back when I'm famous.'

'What! This is not on, Samira—he'll kill you one of these days! Don't you think you should leave the bastard?'

'Are you crazy?' Samira looked shocked. 'I'm never going to leave him, not ever! Drop it, Mantra, you don't understand.'

Mantra shook her head sadly. She stopped herself from giving Samira another piece of valuable advice: Change your Botox administrator—it seems like this one has paralysed your brain too!

'Right then, if you insist on living with that brute, go to self-defence classes and beat the crap out of him.'

'Self-defence? Ew, that's so disgustingly dyke-like!' Samira exclaimed, wrinkling her nose with disgust.

'Tell me,' Mantra asked with great curiosity, 'do you really love him that much?'

'What's love got to do with it? Marriage is about convenience, period,' Samira said, and stepped into her car with a regal wave.

Mantra did not drop it, however. All the way up in the elevator her mind was working furiously, trying to find a way to get Samira out of her destructive marriage alive. The resurrection of her own sex life would have to wait. This was deadly serious stuff.

After browsing through the yellow pages, she called karate and Krav Maga classes and jotted down all the details. Then she got a list of helplines that dealt with domestic violence. She wanted to be prepared when Samira sorted out her priorities in life; the foolish woman had wasted enough time already. Mantra called the first helpline on her list.

Mantra (*cool and collected*): Hello, is this the helpline for domestic violence?

Helpline person (*bored*): Yes. Please give me your name and phone number for our records.

Mantra (*rattles off her name and number while thinking, very clever people, they do this to follow up even if the caller chickens out*)

Helpline person (*still sounding disinterested*): Are you in trouble?

Mantra (*laughing lightly*): No, no, not me. I'm calling for a friend.

Helpline person (*sounding annoyed now; she'd clearly had a hard day*): Look, this is not going to work if that's your attitude. That's what *everybody* says. I suggest you come clean and admit that your husband is thrashing the living daylights out of you.

Mantra (*shocked and annoyed. Weren't these people trained to sound sympathetic?*): Excuse me, I've just told you that I'm calling for a friend, not for myself. Can you understand English?

Helpline person (*nastily*): I'm sorry, if you refuse to cooperate

I'll have to disconnect this call. There are other victims waiting to be helped.

Mantra (*screaming*): *You* won't disconnect this call, I will. You're bloody stubborn and useless, that's what. With your kind of fucked up attitude you should join the government!

SFX: (*Mantra ringing off*): Dial tone.

She was so furious after speaking to that obstinate ass that she decided to stop playing guardian angel any more. If bloody Samira believed that ugly limited edition handbags, diamonds, chocolate spas and caviar facials were worth being beaten black and blue for, that was her problem. Different strokes for different folks. She idly wondered what she'd do if Vir ever dared to raise a hand to her but the idea was so ludicrous, she laughed it off. He was too laidback to even harm a fly. She started thinking warm and fuzzy thoughts about him—despite his foul moods, he really was better than most husbands.

The phone rang and she had her second frustrating conversation of the day:

Caller (*mature, polite voice*): Hello? May I speak to Mantra?

Mantra (*curious*): Yes? May I know who's calling?

Caller (*apologetic*): I'm calling from the domestic violence helpline. A trainee had just spoken to you and she confessed that she messed it up. Please accept my apologies and may we start this relationship on a new note?

Mantra (*mollified*): Certainly! I'd just told her that a friend is being physically assaulted by her husband. What *should* she do?

Caller (*helpfully*): Well, we could start with some counselling and then, when you're mentally ready, help you file an FIR against your husband. That's usually . . .

Mantra (*snarling*): For heaven's sake, stop accusing my husband of thrashing me! I *told* you I'm calling for a friend.

Caller (*sighing deeply in a resigned manner*): Oh I'm so sorry, that's what they *all* say . . .

SFX (*Mantra ringing off*): Dial tone.

The phone rang again, six times at least. Mantra was certain it was them. She experienced an overpowering urge to send an army of wife-beating husbands to physically assault that annoyingly obstinate helpline team.

Mantra contemplated knocking back a couple of drinks before Vir got back from work so she could be uninhibited enough to rip his clothes off when he entered, but the idea of drinking alone didn't appeal to her. There was no point asking Vir to meet her at a pub—he hadn't been near one since his health trip began. She was very clear that she wasn't going to tell Vir about Dr Mehta's recommendations. That may raise his hopes, and if it didn't work eventually, he'd be further put off. Anjali was an option as a drinking buddy, but with alcohol inside her there was a possibility that she'd sigh and moan about that dreadful Shiv, and that was too painful to suffer.

Mantra got into her comfiest pajamas and parked herself at her laptop. The book! The book! The book! She stared at the blank screen for ten minutes, willing a decent sentence or even an evocative word to stain its pristine whiteness, but none appeared. Her mind was equally blank. Maybe she had become brain dead after all—it had been at least a month since she had played any mind exercising games.

She opened a new page and keyed in 'Number-in-the-song-title game', and put down her list:

One (U2)
Love me two times (The Doors)
Five to one (The Doors)
Six-blade knife (Dire Straits)
Fifty ways to leave your lover (Paul Simon)
When I'm sixty-four (The Beatles)
99 *red balloons* (Nena)

13

When the phone call Anjali had been fantasizing about finally came, it almost killed her. Her phone rang while she was lying flat on a bench, struggling to lift a twin set of 15 pound weights. She *knew* it was him because she'd recently set distinguishing ringtones to all her saved phone numbers—a practical thing to do, since her eyesight wasn't what it used to be. It took her by surprise and she foolishly released her grasp on the bar. It was the trainer who hastily caught hold of it, successfully preventing it from crashing down and crushing her ribcage to smithereens.

She leapt up and rushed to the changing room taking her phone out of her pocket with fumbling fingers, ignoring the trainer's angry rebukes. When she eventually answered it, she was panting as heavily as an obscene caller. Not just because of the exertion, but because she was going through one of her bad, longing-filled days.

'Yes hello, who's speaking?' she wheezed, feigning ignorance. 'Oh, *hi*!' she exclaimed, sounding extremely astonished when Shiv identified himself. 'How are you? What's up?'

She sat on a bench cradling the phone to her ear, oblivious to the fact that the other people in the room were shamelessly eavesdropping. When Shiv suggested a drink to discuss a catering assignment for a small dinner party at his house, she readily accepted, hoping it would be soon, but not today, please not today; she needed at least a day's notice to look vaguely decent.

'I'll email some of the menus we've used for small gatherings before to give you a feel of what we expect, cool? And meanwhile, it would be nice if you'd browse through my company's website just to know what we're all about—not that it's necessary, of course; you can take it for granted that you will be in very good company,' he added with a little self-conscious laugh.

Anjali giggled hysterically, the way people do at ridiculously wacky Mel Brooks movies, and tucked that line away in her mind to mention it to Mantra. 'There,' she'd pull it out and say defiantly, 'and you said he has no sense of humour!'

They arranged to meet a couple of days later, and with that to look forward to, Anjali floated out of the gym and into her car. She couldn't wait to read about Shiv's company—his *own* company, created out of his sweat and blood. How sexy was that?

His client list was very impressive: theme restaurants for a few hotels, a handful of corporate biggies, a couple of international clients and a smattering of established models and hopefuls with starry ambitions. After practically memorizing every word on the website she was still greedy for more, so she Googled his name, and came up with a treat—there were many articles that quoted him, many photographs and even a few articles written by him. She didn't just read them, she drank them in. Then, she called Mantra.

God, I desperately need someone to talk to about him. I need excuses to say his name aloud. It's not enough saying it in my head. Anjali sighed to herself while waiting for Mantra to answer the phone.

Anjali coyly told Mantra all, and she got a glum '*Alea jacta est*,' in response.

'What filthy thing are you saying?' Anjali demanded.

'It's not filthy,' Mantra snapped. 'It means the die is cast—don't you remember your *Asterix*? Anyway, go to hell and do what the hell you want, okay?'

'I have no idea what you mean, Mantra,' Anjali said coldly. 'All I've agreed to do is a spot of work. What's so damning about that?'

'Oh yeah? If it's so above board, why do you whisper when you talk about him? Why can't you talk in your usual booming voice, huh? It sounds to me like you're feeling guilty, that's what!'

'I *do not* have a booming voice,' Anjali protested angrily, deviously trying to start a new argument to save herself from the previous one.

'Whatever!'

'I don't know what's with you these days. Maybe you're going through menopause!' Anjali said waspishly.

Mantra didn't rise to the bait. The word 'menopause' brought her libido problems to mind and her annoyance with Anjali's foolish little crush on Shiv vanished. She hastily apologized for her outburst and then lied through her teeth in an attempt to enlist Anjali's help. There was no way in hell she was going to tell Anjali that she couldn't put out for her brother.

'By the way, I've been given an assignment too, an article on porn flicks,' she said chattily.

'Porn?' Anjali exclaimed astonished. 'Goodness, who are you writing for these days? *Playboy*?'

'No silly,' Mantra said, frantically trying to come up with a plausible excuse. 'It's for a boring little piece called "What Men Really Want". The usual tired rubbish about male fantasies—everything from gizmos to sex. I've got to add a couple of lines on porn too, and I lack the courage to ask our DVD library chap for it.'

'So ask Vir, why are you asking me?'

'No point—I checked his DVD collection, nothing steamy there. And Vir's really busy because the Big White Chief is down from America, so I don't want to bother him.' That part is true at least, Mantra thought with relief.

'Okay, I'll look through our collection but I'm pretty certain that even if Karan does have porn, it's kept in a secret hiding place—but worry not, I know where that is!' Anjali said reassuringly.

'Check Rohan's things too,' Mantra suggested dryly. 'He's at that age.'

Anjali briefly scoured the house but came up with nothing. She made a mental note to ask Karan at night, but forgot about it mere seconds later. Her mind, after all, was occupied with weightier matters—like what to wear for her dinner with Shiv.

When Karan got back from work he cheerfully informed her that they'd been invited out for dinner a couple of days later.

'Oh dear,' she wailed, 'I just fixed a meeting with Shiv that very night for the catering thingy! I suppose I'll have to cancel it.'

Karan was very understanding. 'Oh you can't miss that, darling. It's work. No, no, don't cancel that meeting, I'll make your excuses at dinner. I'll be proud to say my wife is at a business meeting.'

'I'll join you as soon as I'm done,' she offered with relief.

'Oh don't worry about that.' He patted her hand. 'Work comes first, always remember. Concentrate on the discussion instead of worrying about how soon you can escape, okay? And try to negotiate a good deal for yourself—it's got to be worth your while too.'

Anjali gave him a spontaneous hug. For the first time since Shiv had re-entered her life, she experienced pangs of guilt mingled with irritation. Why on earth did Karan have to be *so* nice?

14

Anjali and Shiv had been taking long polite sips of their first drink to fill the gaps in their stilted conversation when Mantra called.

'Hello, this is a porn reminder!'

'Oh dear, I absolutely forgot. Promise I'll organize your porn tomorrow. I'm out right now.'

Anjali caught Shiv staring at her incredulously. 'Porn?' he repeated.

She blushed furiously. 'It's for an article Mantra's writing,' she stammered.

'That's what they all say,' Shiv grinned. 'Incidentally, I do have a few DVDs at home, if you're interested.'

Anjali's eyebrows rose.

'I watch them for the awesome lighting,' Shiv assured her virtuously.

They laughed, and suddenly the stiffness vanished and they were chatting as freely and intimately as they'd done before, leaning towards each other conspiratorially, oblivious to everyone else in the room. It was just like the way they used to be in the good old days at the college canteen.

When Anjali indulgently reviewed their conversation in her head later that night while lying in bed, she felt as flat as a cola that had lost its fizz. There were no flirtatious tones in their conversation, only reminiscences. Nothing personal at all—college days were fondly dwelt upon with excited remember thises and remember thats. Who needs time machines when conversation alone can take you back to your favourite moments in life? It had all been so marvellously chummy and boringly clean. She *liked* clean, she sternly reminded herself. Perhaps they could be friends again and construct a new platonic relationship on the cold ashes of their previous torrid one? She slept like a baby that night. Well, almost. There was a niggling feeling of deflation.

The next day she called Mantra, after Shiv's driver had delivered the goods. 'Hey, Porn Queen, I've got a steamy present for you,' she teased.

'Gosh, you've got the DVD?' Mantra gasped.

'Not one—many, from Shiv's stash.'

'Oh God!' Mantra shrieked. 'Why on earth did you ask him? Now he probably thinks I'm an aged pervert!'

'Relax—I told him it's for an article.'

'Oh no, Anjali! That's what they all say!' Mantra moaned.

'So I've heard. Anyway, are you going to buy me a meal to thank me nicely?'

'Of course,' Mantra said warmly, 'come on right over, I'll order takeaway as a gesture of heartfelt appreciation. And, um, Anjali, I would love it if you watched them with me. I'd feel less queasy, you know?'

'Done!' Anjali pronounced grandly. 'I'll be there around twelve-ish. Will do?'

Mantra had given Reshma the afternoon off so she could order the takeaway meal without being ferociously glared at. Drinks in hand, they settled down to watch porn. After the first few seconds of gross, jaw-dropping footage, they were screaming with laughter. Mantra valiantly tried to put on a straight face when the doorbell rang, but she needn't have bothered because it was Reshma. Just a glimpse of her icy demeanour through the peep hole had the power to wipe every lingering trace of levity off Mantra's face.

'Shit! Anjali, turn it off, Reshma's here,' Mantra yelled, but the volume was too loud for her plea to register. She tentatively opened the door a crack to see what Reshma wanted, hoping to fob her off, but Reshma determinedly pushed her way in with her head held high, muttering that she'd left a book in the kitchen.

Mantra darted to the bedroom and slammed the bedroom door shut, in case Reshma caught sight of deviant sexual acts on the TV screen. Then she lurked around in the kitchen, hoping that her presence there would hasten Reshma's departure. Reshma, though, seemed to be in no hurry. She cast a scornful eye over the empty takeaway containers and the two used plates in the sink.

'Why didn't you tell me you were expecting a guest?' she grimly interrogated Mantra.

'How could I have?' Mantra lied smoothly with a shrug. 'She arrived unexpectedly.'

Of course it had to happen—just when Reshma had finally located her book and was making her way to the front door, the most awful groans and moans and, good heavens, agonized bleats and oinks too, emerged from behind the bedroom door. Reshma turned towards the bedroom alarmed and then suddenly made a dash to the front door, dropping her book to the floor in her haste.

'Bloody, bloody hell,' Mantra swore to Anjali, 'now I'm sure she thinks I was having an orgy with bestiality thrown in!'

Porn as a libido-revival remedy was definitely not working. Mantra crossed it off her list. She hadn't experienced even a hint of sexual excitement when she saw that rubbish—it was as ridiculous as cartoons for adults. After Anjali left, she browsed the net for articles on sagging libidos in desperation, and discovered to her horror that an active sex life actually helped bring down stress levels considerably—proof that it was *absolutely her fault* that Vir was acting so snappish and strange of late. She just had to get her act together, and, in the meanwhile, perhaps she'd buy him one of those squishy stress balls to vent his frustration on.

15

Vir dreamt that he'd stumbled upon a communal riot and his body was in flames. He woke up sweating to realize that his body was really on fire—he had very high fever. In his usual stubborn way, he refused to let Mantra take his temperature, but she felt his forehead and it was so hot that her hand jerked back involuntarily. After pretending to examine her palm for scorch marks to drive home the point that he was seriously ill and quite possibly dying, she did her best to push him back into bed.

'Hmm. Just as well we're too poor and pleb to own satin sheets; you'd have burnt a hole right through them. And no, there's no way you're going to office today, you stubborn ass, forget it!' she panted, sweating with the effort of keeping Vir down.

'Godda go, geddoudadaway,' Vir snuffled in a martyred voice.

'Oh, okay,' Mantra dropped her ineffectual sumo wrestler act and played along. 'If you actually are pompous enough to believe that you're a crucial pillar in your organization and it will crumble without your heartening Samson-like presence, please do go. Pompous people *deserve* to die! But I insist you have breakfast in bed first before you bathe, cool? Your tum needs to have something in it before you pop a paracetamol.'

Vir grunted his acquiescence and slumped back on the pillows with his eyes shut. After forcing half a toast down his throat, Mantra slyly made him pop two tablets—not just a paracetamol as promised, but an antihistamine too that was guaranteed to send him to the Land of Nod within seconds. Years of living with Vir had taught Mantra that she had to be devious to keep him alive.

She took his temperature in his knocked out state, but despite the combination of her reading glasses and the magnifying glass she always used to check small print in vital documents like cinema listings, she couldn't read a thing. Helpless, she went to Reshma who took charge immediately with a clinical efficiency that surprised Mantra. She glanced at the thermometer with a practised eye, pronounced '103' and asked Mantra for eau de cologne and hand towels.

'Now add this to iced water and bathe bhaiya's forehead with it,' she ordered officiously, checking Vir's pulse and nodding silently to herself as she did that.

Mantra looked on in astonishment, and then remembered that Reshma had worked in a hospital before, though as a cook. Oh well, maybe one of the staff had taught her.

After the pulse reading, Reshma muttered a mysterious 'Hmm' and made for the telephone. 'I'll call Dr Pant right away.'

'I think his number's in the phone book,' Mantra muttered distractedly, but Reshma raised a hand imperiously.

'I know his number by heart. Please do remember that the doctor had recommended me,' she stated with dignity.

Mantra had no chores left but to lovingly dab iced water and eau de cologne on Vir's forehead. Looking at him lying there vulnerable and pale made her heart lurch violently. I really do love this idiotic man, despite the fact that he's annoying, stubborn, sarcastic, rude and indifferent most times, she thought.

Vir suddenly murmured, 'Why the fuck can't you fuckers meet a simple sales target for dog food? It's not difficult considering dogs are hungry all the time and they'll eat any rubbish besides!'

Mantra panicked—he was obviously delirious. She rushed to Reshma who calmly assured her that the doctor was on his way, and meanwhile she should give Vir's entire body a rub down with iced water too.

While engaged in the act, Mantra suddenly recalled how her former colleague Shanti had found out about her husband's affair when he was down with malaria. In a delirious state, he had repeatedly mumbled the other woman's name. Shanti was smart, she'd put her hand comfortingly over his eyes and pretended to be the other woman, keeping the conversation going. She'd found out practically everything.

Vir stirred and Mantra stroked his head tenderly. He'd never have an affair, not him. He was too lazy and laid-back to bother about other women. She mentally kicked herself for being suspicious a few nights ago when he went out for dinner with a female colleague who was visiting from the Bangalore branch. He used to always beg Mantra to join him on informal nights out with colleagues to take the pressure of making tedious polite conversation off him. This time, however, he hadn't—and that had made her antennae twitch nervously. She'd caught a whiff of alcohol on Vir's breath when he'd returned late that night, and that had made her angrier. The sod categorically refused to take her out for an occasional drink, flaunting his high cholesterol statistics in a martyr-like manner, but he was okay drinking with other women? He deserved to be slapped! Mantra had barely slept a wink that night, wondering if her sex holdback had already started destroying the marriage, and, equally importantly, what his Bangalore colleague looked like. In her fevered and insecure mind, the colleague had the lithe, taut body of a pole dancer, the face of a dead sexy cover girl, and the morals of a nymphomaniac.

Mantra had woken up ridiculously early the next morning with a bad attack of acidity. While she had too much pride to air her insecurities, the atmosphere at home had been distinctly chilly. Sadly, Vir had seemed oblivious of the fact that he was in the dog house. Perhaps if he'd made any attempt to converse with her, he'd have found out.

All Mantra had got in response to her brittle, 'So how was your dinner last night?' remark was a grunt.

Now she reassured herself that she had probably over-reacted—the dinner may well have been a hard-nosed business meet and Vir could have been playing his unenviable role of hangman with the Bangalore collegue, for all Mantra knew. Damn. If only Vir would tell her what exactly was happening in his life the way he used to, she wouldn't have to deal with monstrous thoughts raging in her stupid head. Jealousy and resentment reared their heads once again, but she determinedly quelled them. Vir would not leave her for another woman—of that she was fairly certain. The only competition she had was from wild animals. If Vir had the choice of living with a monkey or Mantra, he'd take the monkey. Tigers, though, were his real passion. No matter where in India they went on holiday, one entire day would be spent at the local zoo, and Vir would linger for hours outside the tiger enclosure watching them pace up and down restlessly, shaking his head indignantly and muttering, 'It's a bloody shame to see them locked up—they should be free to roam in their native habitat. Humans are so fucking cruel!'

During their dating days, Mantra had devotedly accompanied him on camping trips in the forests, her heart pounding madly with fear—bandicoots had been the most ferocious animals she'd encountered till then. Vir invariably chose the most dangerous nature trails infested with man-eating cats or crocodiles. Despite his impatient assurances that they were safe, she couldn't sleep at all, worrying that prowling leopards bored of their staple diet of venison would effortlessly claw through their flimsy canvas tents for an exotic midnight snack.

Their honeymoon was the last time Mantra had accompanied Vir on a wildlife trip. Intrepid Vir had pulled strings and booked a room in a government rest house planted right inside Corbett National Park. There was no room service, no mints on the pillows (maybe because there weren't any pillows) and no privacy either; their guide and the jeep driver were sharing the two-bedroom rest house with them. Even worse, the solitary bathroom in the cottage reeked of a vile odour, prompting a queasy Mantra to believe that the animals used it too.

Day one had been spent driving around in an open jeep, Vir bristling with excitement as he eagerly scanned the landscape for tigers, while Mantra gloomily took in the usual suspects: monkeys, spotted deer, barking deer and nilgai. Not a single member of the cat family was in sight, but every now and then the guide excitedly commanded the driver to stop the jeep, leapt out and pointed to pug marks on the ground. Everyone scrambled out and followed the pug marks which, oddly enough, ended abruptly in the middle of an open plain. The guide always scratched his head, looking puzzled.

'Oooh, this must be a flying tiger, how wonderful! Are we in Narnia or what?' Mantra had caustically remarked, and got a ferocious glare from Vir in response.

After the fourth pug-mark inspection had proved to be fruitless, Mantra had had just about enough. They'd been driving around since sunrise, the sun had just set and she had the worst kind of headache imaginable, more shattering than a hangover brought on by mixing half a bottle of whiskey with three bottles of beer.

'Look,' Mantra had snapped at the guide, 'I have never, ever seen a tiger in the wild and, trust me, neither has Vir—and we've been to more jungles in India than anyone else in the world. Pug marks are all we have seen. Tell me the truth now—are these pug marks the handiwork of forest department rookies on pogo sticks with pug-mark stamp pads attached?'

It was the guide's turn to glare at Mantra. He'd bent down, scooped up a handful of animal poop and thrust his palm under Mantra's nose.

'Just smell this, ma'am! If this isn't tiger droppings, I'll eat it!' he had daringly offered.

Mantra had shrunk back disgusted, but Vir leaned forward and inhaled deeply. He had had a silly, happy smile on his face for hours thereafter.

Mantra had stormed back to the jeep muttering darkly under her breath, 'Bloody liar! Tigers, obviously, are mythical creatures, and the striped cats we see in zoos are leopards made over!' She shunned the dinner of baked beans and toast at night, popped a tablet and fell into a deep sleep, only to be woken a few hours later by the trumpeting of a herd of elephants on the rampage. They wildly thundered past the lodge and it had taken all of Mantra's strength to hold Vir back from racing out with his camera to photograph them. They had their first marital row that night. Had a member of the law fraternity been present, the feasibility of a mutual consent divorce would have been discussed.

On the second day, Vir had almost given Mantra a heart attack. While touring the park, a leopard had dashed in front of their jeep and Vir had leapt off and chased it, wielding his camera like a deranged Japanese tourist. Mantra had shrieked and the guide had had to forcibly drag him back. After that, Mantra stopped accompanying Vir on wildlife trips altogether—that act of his had damaged her heart for life. That never stopped him, of course—he'd go on long weekends alone or with Rohan, and once he had been devious enough to shift an office conference location from a palace hotel to a national park. Maybe that was one of the reasons why they'd drifted apart, Mantra mused. Marriage ruthlessly strips away all pretences of common interests.

The arrival of the doctor brought Mantra's not-so-fond memories to an end. Reshma ushered him into the bedroom with flushed cheeks and sparkling eyes. She stayed at his side throughout Vir's examination, and hung on to his every word, behaving like an awe-struck teenage groupie in the presence of a rock star. The doorbell rang during the examination and Reshma played deaf. Mantra had to sharply order her to get the door and was rewarded with a filthy look.

What the! Mantra thought indignantly. How dare she expect me to leave Vir's side now? She heard Makarand's voice and suppressed a smirk. Ah, now she won't be back for hours, the poor doctor has been upstaged.

The door slammed shut and Reshma was back within a split second. Mantra raised an eyebrow at Reshma, who sullenly volunteered the fact that Makarand had wanted a cup of tea.

'And?' Mantra persisted, curious about why Reshma hadn't instantly pandered to his request as was her wont.

'He can't very well get one now, I'm busy!' Reshma snapped. 'Besides, he'll be required to be on duty to get the medicines soon, isn't that so?'

Mantra nodded, very impressed. The rock star doctor was the hands-down winner.

'Nothing to worry about,' Dr Pant pronounced cheerfully. 'It's just a bad attack of the flu. A few tablets and bed rest for three days should do the trick.'

Vir groggily protested that three days away from office was absolutely out of the question, but the doctor, Reshma and Mantra shouted him down. He nodded silently, but Mantra saw his lower lip sticking out defiantly. A very bad sign. She led the doctor out of the room and urged him to prescribe medicines that induced sleep.

'I promise you, doctor, if you don't knock him out he'll stagger to office as soon as your back is turned. That man's impossible! He's always looking for ways to make me a widow—if it's not carnivorous animals, it's bloody germs!'

Dr Pant laughed and agreed, and Reshma scurried to the kitchen to make him a cup of coffee—she knew he preferred coffee—while he scribbled out the prescription. As the doctor handed the prescription to Mantra, he gave her a conspiratorial wink, and she felt her cheeks grow hot—hotter than Vir's forehead in fact. Wow! No man has winked at me since I was thirty-five, she exulted inwardly. Even cheap roadside Romeos have stopped yelling 'Hey, Item' to me. This feels strange but good, real good!

She peered at the prescription and admonished Dr Pant for the mysterious hieroglyphics. 'Is squiggly, unintelligible handwriting a special subject in medical school? I can't understand a word of what you doctors write!'

He had the grace to look embarrassed, and in a sheepish little boy's voice told her he'd write it out again, neatly and in capital letters this time, but Reshma arrived and snatched the prescription out of Mantra's hand.

'I can read this clearly,' she stated and rattled off a list of medicines. 'You don't worry, madam, I'll take care of it. This is *my* department after all!' she concluded triumphantly.

Mantra was too stunned to protest and watched as the doctor patted Reshma on the back. 'I have full faith in you, my dear,' he said heartily. Reshma glowed like she'd swallowed a 3000-watt light bulb.

After the doctor left, Makarand automatically sprang back in Reshma's favour. 'I'm going with him to get the medicines, just in case the chemist can't read Dr Pant's handwriting too,' she cannily said.

Mantra suppressed a smirk.

16

The next day Vir took a turn for the worse. His temperature shot up to 104, and he tossed and turned restlessly. Mantra never left his side for a second, her brow as feverishly furrowed as his. When Reshma popped in with the ice pack, she glanced sharply at Mantra and felt her forehead.

'Oh no, madam, you'd better lie down. You have fever too!' she exclaimed, looking delighted.

Ah, the joys of one more patient to take care of, Mantra thought sourly, and shook her head. 'No, no, it's nothing, just sympathy sickness. This always happens to me when Vir falls ill. I can't explain it really,' Mantra said, impatiently waving a thermometer-brandishing Reshma away.

'Oh that! I'm familiar with that condition. Even if he hurts his little finger, your little finger starts paining too, correct?' she pronounced triumphantly.

Mantra looked up, surprised. 'My God, yes, but how do you know?'

Reshma shrugged. 'There's a term for that condition, I used to know the name, but now I've forgotten.' Her eyes went blank and hostile again, and she walked briskly out of the room.

Vir stirred, and Mantra turned anxiously towards him again. His eyes were half shut and he was tugging Mantra's arm with an urgency, mumbling in a 'Hsst, psst' way.

'Listen, Mantra, I have about two crores in my HSBC bank account and another fifty odd lakhs in Stan Chart, okay?' he whispered hoarsely.

'Huh? Oh God, I think he's delirious again,' she muttered feeling panicky.

'I'm not fucking delirious, you stupid cow! I'm telling you this in case anything happens to me! Bloody woman! This is the thanks I get for providing for your future!' he snapped tetchily in a stronger voice.

'Ooh, thank you, kind sir, but you're not bloody dying on me till you save a couple more crores at least, got it? I can't live on a pittance, can I?' Mantra teased and lightly kissed his forehead. It was cool and damp—the fever had finally broken, she thought with relief. 'I'll take your temp,' she said getting up, but Vir pulled her down again.

'Can you be serious for one moment, dammit? Do you know how many of my colleagues have had heart attacks over the last few years?'

'Stop being foolish, Vir, you can't have a heart attack because of the flu! You're bloody *non compos mentis*. What the hell did they teach you at your fancy boarding school?' Mantra said impatiently, struggling to loosen his grip. Vir stubbornly held on to her arm in a limpet-like way.

'Not flu but stress! I'm all stressed out at work, and the bloody thing kills!'

'Look, stop worrying about when you're going to die, we're all going to the big party in the sky one of these days. We're not immortal, you ass, deal with it,' was Mantra's reasonable rejoinder.

'I don't give a fuck about dying! I'm just scared that a stroke may turn me into a vegetable.'

Mantra's heart lurched to see the naked fear in Vir's eyes. 'Okay, I swear to you, hand on heart, that if you turn into a turnip or broccoli, I'll pull the plug,' she promised solemnly. Mantra felt her heart racing madly. Good lord, now I've got sympathy stress, is it? she thought alarmed.

Vir felt a little better by lunch time and wanted to watch a movie with his soup and toast. Mantra handed him a pile of DVDs to choose from without even glancing at them, which was a big mistake—the porn films were there too. She'd forgotten all about them in her worry. A very astonished Vir asked her where they came from.

Mantra shrugged innocently.

'Oh, Anjali found them in Rohan's cupboard. She'd wanted me to give them to you to vet out, just to see if he's normal. She hasn't told Karan about them in case he blows a fuse.'

Vir laughed out loud and said, 'Of course he's normal—I mean, just look at these raunchy titles! I have always maintained that there's good in that boy. Now put one on. Immediately! Hell, it's been so long.'

Mantra acquiesced, secretly relieved that he was ill—there was no danger of him feeling like making out later. Even if the spirit was turned on by this dreadful rubbish, the body was weak. She inserted a DVD into the player, deliberately the very same one she'd been watching with Anjali when Reshma had popped in unexpectedly. She put the volume on extra loud and then stepped into the kitchen, pretending to look for something. She lingered there till the groans and moans punctuated by agonized bleats and oinks part played. Reshma gave her a startled look again, but this time Mantra looked her in the eye. Reshma knew that Vir was alone in the bedroom. Which meant she was now aware that Mantra hadn't been indulging in an orgy.

Ah, vindication. Mantra sighed with relief. I can finally hold my head up high again.

By the evening, the fever had abated but Vir was restless as the headache persisted. He was in no shape for his regular pastimes (books, TV or computer games) and Mantra grabbed the opportunity to treat him as a captive audience. She snuggled up to him in bed, idly chatting about this and that; it almost felt like old times—the only difference was, she was doing all the talking while Vir occasionally contributed a few grunts.

Very occasionally, admittedly, but Mantra put it down to him being ill. Things were going fairly pleasantly till Mantra put her foot into it by stepping into emotional terrain.

'You know, Vir, a few months ago, I saw a well-turned out old man on the road hurling obscenities and waving his walking stick at passers-by. He actually hit a woman on her head and the cops arrested him. I suspect he had Alzheimer's. And then I wondered what it would be like if you suddenly became mentally unhinged and started shooting people with an airgun and the like. I know I'd never abandon you and that I will always see the man I fell in love with instead of a crazy coot,' she said earnestly.

Ignoring the glazed expression in Vir's eyes and the faint sneer on his lips, Mantra foolishly persisted. 'Would you still love me if I had Alzheimer's?' she asked.

'How does it matter since you won't be able to recognize me in that condition anyway?' Vir scoffed impatiently and then rolled over on his side and away from her.

Mantra tried to turn him towards her again, but he kept his body rigidly in the opposite direction. On an impulse, she did an If-Muhammad-won't-go-to-the-mountain-the-mountain-will-go-to-Muhammad act. She climbed over him, and they were face to face again. Vir closed his eyes immediately and ignored her rant.

'Right. I have to deal with the fact that you'd quite possibly leave me if I had an outbreak of acne. You are a very unsympathetic man! And mentally unbalanced already. Now I'm not sure if I would still love you if you spitefully started shooting tyres of sports cars that are way bigger than your stupid dinky cars!'

She knew he was feigning sleep because his lips twitched.

Later, after gentle snores revealed that Vir had really drifted off to sleep, Mantra sat on the bed next to him, keying in her novel on her laptop. Unfortunately, she'd forgotten to unplug the landline and its shrill ringing woke him up. He answered it promptly, and to Mantra's horror, the conversation she heard went like this:

Vir (*in his usual impolite, brusque manner*): Yes?

Vir (*sounding mildly surprised*): Yes, this is her husband speaking.

Vir (*roaring*): What? What! The! Fuck! How *dare* you accuse me of beating my wife!

Mantra leaned over and snatched the phone out of his grasp. Since he was weakened by the flu, she succeeded and she gave that annoying helpline woman an earful, while Vir was gesticulating wildly, his face red with rage. Then she slammed the receiver down with a final threat that she'd complain to the police if they dared harass her again. Vir roughly turned Mantra around to face him and his expression made her knees turn to jelly.

After she explained it all, she was savagely reprimanded for sticking her nose into other people's business. 'This is what really annoys me about you! How many times have I told you to stop interfering in other people's lives? Now you've got me embroiled in this idiotic crap, like I don't have enough problems already! But do you listen? You want to get me bloody arrested?'

Vir paused briefly to refuel his breath and viciously lashed out at Mantra again, taking off on a different tack this time.

'And do stop interfering in my life too. What's with this new "How was your day?" chant when I get back from work?' he simpered in a mocking way. 'Can't you take one look at my face and gauge how the fuck my day went? Don't you fucking know that all I want, the only thing I want when I get back from work, is to flake out watching mindless shit on TV? Just because you spend the entire day sitting on your arse doing fuck all, don't you dare use me to relieve your boredom.'

'I only ask because I care,' a stunned Mantra said quietly, blinking away the tears that involuntarily sprang to her eyes. She felt like she'd just been horsewhipped.

'If you really cared you'd just leave me alone,. get it?' Vir snapped. 'And I seriously think you should get back to work. You never used to bother me with stupid, irritating questions or make attempts at polite conversation when you were gainfully employed. Fuck, it used to be so nice to come home to companionable silence. If I can't enjoy peace and quiet in my own house, where the hell else can I get it?'

Since he was ill, Mantra didn't argue or make the slightest attempt to defend herself. She merely nodded and handed him two sleeping tablets instead of one with his regular medication. She heaved a sigh of relief because they knocked him out mid-rant.

Mantra pushed her hurt feelings and whimpering thoughts deep inside and concentrated on being mad at herself for the helpline episode. Serves me right for enthusiastically hurling myself into other people's affairs like a bleeding self-appointed guardian angel. If I carry on like this an old proverb may be rewritten to commemorate my stupid impetuousness: Mantra rushes in where silly asses too fear to tread. She promised herself that she'd never do it again, not even if it killed her to stay mum.

She was in such a bitter mood the next day that the novel proceeded beautifully and effortlessly. As she reread the thousand-odd words she'd just keyed in, she suspected that Shakespeare too would have approved of the death-bed soliloquy her heroine's tetanus-infected birth mother spouted even though it didn't have any classical allusions. That would have been extremely incongruous, considering that her heroine's birth mother had studied up to class 2 in the local village school. Mantra would have loved to have put some weighty references in, not about Yamraj, the Indian God of death, but Pluto, the Greek God of the underworld—that would have struck more chords with Western readers, who were meant to be her main target audience anyway.

Art and pain clearly go well together, she mused. Maybe

it's a good thing Vir and I have relationship problems. I've always enjoyed his rudeness but, of late, he's changed. It's not what he says but how he says it. There's no laughter in his eyes when he makes nasty remarks any more. No matter. Shit happens—and I'm resilient enough to deal with it. Better still, the angst may inspire me to write a tear-jerker. And after that, if it's a success, he may consider the time I spent away from work as worthwhile, and he may respect me again, at the very least. Wishful thinking, I know, but hey, dreaming is cheaper than Prozac.

Anjali and Karan paid a visit that night to entertain the impatient patient. His headache had receded to a dull throb, his temperature was down to 100, and he was back to watching wild animals mate and eat each other on TV. In his opinion, he was, as many of Mumbai's suburban grocery shops are grandly named, A-OK.

Karan proudly informed them that Anjali's first catering assignment was scheduled to take place in a few days. 'She's doing a Mediterranean theme—Greek to be precise. And she's such a perfectionist,' he continued with pride, 'that she's even bought a dinner set in white and aquamarine to add to the ambience.'

'That's it?' Vir teased. 'I'd have thought Anjali would get cheesy mermaid-shaped swizzle sticks too and imitation vine leaves to scatter around. You're slipping up big time, sis!'

'Oh shut up, Vir,' Anjali protested. 'You know very well I'd never use imitation vine leaves—I only do authentic.'

'Hey, if you're doing authentic, be warned. The guests may get carried away by the Greek theme and ceremoniously smash your lovely new plates after the meal,' Mantra said with an evil grin.

'You guys are bloody impossible,' Anjali shook her head sadly. 'Just as well that you married each other.'

'That's because no one else would have us,' Mantra said tartly. Anjali noticed that Vir's eyes glinted with amusement at Mantra's remark, and experienced a sharp pang of envy.

What they had between them was true love—an experience she had always been denied.

The grand show of geniality Mantra and Vir put up crumbled the very second their guests left. The hostility was back in Vir's eyes, the hurt was back in Mantra's mind, and not a single word was exchanged between them. Mantra didn't bother to sneak the knockout pill in Vir's medication at night. It was pointless. He was so determined to go to work the next day, she knew he'd sleepwalk there if need be. Besides, she was looking forward to time away from him. His constant glowering was giving her a headache.

17

There were going to be four people at dinner. Anjali had worked hard on preparing the menu after carefully researching on the Internet, and consulting her well-thumbed recipe books and scrap book of dog-eared articles to match wines to the dishes. She'd quadruple-checked each selection and then e-mailed the menu and wine list to Shiv with a rough estimate. He'd approved it enthusiastically and not a single change was called for. Karan gave it the thumbs up too because his meals before the big day were fabulous—Anjali did a dress rehearsal of every dish, hors d'oeuvres included, to make sure she got them right. Her best cutlery was polished, the new dinner set was scrubbed squeaky clean and orders for the finest ingredients were placed.

Work was smoothly in process on the morning of the dinner party when Shiv called. 'By the way, it's a formal occasion since he's a prospective client, so wear something extra nice, will you?'

'Why I should I dress up? I'm not going to be there!' was Anjali's astonished reply.

'What do you mean you're not? I thought you'd be there to supervise the dinner arrangements?' Shiv said, sounding equally astonished.

'No, no, my cook will be there all evening to help your staff heat and serve the dishes. She's very accomplished at this, you needn't worry,' Anjali warmly assured him. 'And my driver will bring her back after dessert and coffee is served,' she added soothingly.

'That's not good enough!' Shiv grumbled petulantly. 'I'd assumed you'd be the hostess too. Look, I can't impress on you how important this dinner is for the company—I'm trying to reel in a new client, dammit! He's bringing his wife too, and I need someone polished like you to entertain her while we discuss business.'

'Sorry, no can do,' Anjali said firmly. This was the longest sane phase she'd had since Shiv had reappeared and it had been aided by their cool, platonic dinner. Every time she felt herself weakening, she'd remind herself of his most cutting remark after the break-up: 'Fuck off. I'm not into ruining good Indian girls. I have principles too, strange but true. But one of my chums really fancies you. I'll give him your number and tell him you're willing to put out, if you like.' She'd repeated that phrase so often in her head that she knew it by heart. It worked reasonably well as a getting-over tool.

Shiv changed tack. 'Oh please, please, please, Anjali, just this once. I can't do this without you,' he wheedled.

After five minutes of being assaulted by relentless begging, Anjali's resistance faltered and she considered giving in. Only after she spoke to Karan though, but she didn't tell Shiv that. 'I'll think about,' she promised, 'and now goodbye. I have work to do, remember?'

'Please, please, please!' was Shiv's final imploring response.

Karan was very unhelpful. After he heard a breathless Anjali out, he brusquely informed her that she'd caught him in a middle of a busy day. 'You decide whether you want to be there or not, you're a big girl now,' he said tersely.

'Oh God, call me when you're free then, Karan, and please—' A sharp click informed her that Karan had hung up.

All day she debated with herself while anxiously waiting for Karan to call. Finally, an hour before the dishes were meant to leave for Shiv's house, she frantically called Karan again but he didn't answer the phone. She punched Mantra's number in a state of agitation.

'Hmm. So you're in tortured Hamlet mode, is it? To go or not to go, that is the question?' Mantra declaimed dramatically.

'And the answer is?' Anjali snapped. She wasn't in the mood for Mantra's frivolities.

'It's obvious, isn't it? Don't go. Period. Keep your relationship with Shiv purely professional or else you'll be in deep trouble. You're already veering too close to the edge and that creep is encouraging you to take the leap,' Mantra warned.

'How dare you! I'm not remotely interested in him—not that way!' Anjali protested angrily.

All she got was an airy, 'Methinks the lady doth protest too much,' from Mantra.

'Fine, believe what you want to believe—I'm going! And thank you for helping me decide!'

Had a comic book artist been present, he would have sketched puffs of smoke billowing out of Anjali's ears.

'Right. In which case, I'll stock up on stacks of extra-absorbent tissues for when you come crying to me later,' was Mantra's terse response. She wasn't in a sympathetic mood—heck, she needed someone to sympathize with her and offer advice, for a change. She was tired and tetchy after days of doing a walking-on-eggshells act with Vir. His constant sniping and snapping was getting on her nerves.

Anjali curtly disconnected the phone and made straight for her wardrobe, her blood boiling with rage. She was very annoyed with Mantra, and not just for warning her off Shiv. The I-know-what's-best-for-you tone in her voice put her off too. It reminded her of her parents taking despotic decisions for her. She was in defiance mode. It was her life that was playing and nobody but she was allowed to tamper with the script.

The dinner went off smoothly. Shiv and the prospective client were huddled together over the early part of the evening, while Anjali and his wife made desultory conversation. It was only when they sat together at the dining table that the conversation became four-way. A minor hiccup occurred when the prospective client enthusiastically praised the dinner.

'This is far better than any meal I've had at a specialty restaurant,' he said, directing an appreciative nod at Shiv. 'Your wife is a marvellous cook!'

Anjali stepped in before Shiv could respond. 'Oh, um, we're not married to each other; we're just old friends.'

'And very close friends at that,' Shiv swiftly took over. 'I've been urging Anjali to try her hand at catering, and this is her first venture.'

The prospective client's wife oohed, earnestly stated her intention of hiring Anjali's catering services in the near future, and held out a hand for her business card.

Anjali felt gauche and hid her embarrassment by pretending to fish in her handbag for her non-existent card. 'Sorry,' she muttered when she composed herself enough to look up, 'I've forgotten to carry my cards with me. I'll give you my phone number, if you like.' She promised herself that she'd brainstorm with Mantra for a nice brand name and get business cards printed post-haste.

Anjali stood by Shiv's side at the front door while farewells, thank yous and fervent promises of staying in touch were made. When the front door finally shut, she strode to the living room and picked up her handbag, ready to make her way home.

Shiv followed her into the room, laughing. 'Well, that went off rather nicely, don't you think? I'm not sure if he'll give me his business, but you have certainly made a new client tonight! And hey, what's the hurry? I haven't had you to myself all evening. Sit,' he ordered playfully, 'I'll pour the wine.'

A quick glance at her watch revealed that it was just a few minutes past 11 p.m. A glass of wine wouldn't hurt, and anyway she was rather annoyed with Karan for not calling or even responding to her frantic text message. He'd probably be sulking, and she wasn't in the mood to deal with that right now.

'Here's to a great career in catering,' Shiv saluted her, raising his glass.

Anjali silently raised her glass too, exulting in her personal success. It felt so wonderful to be appreciated *and* to earn money for doing what she really enjoyed.

'So what do you think of my brand new apartment?' Shiv waved a hand airily around as he spoke.

Anjali critically surveyed her surroundings. She hadn't really noticed them before since she had been busy with the dinner arrangements and the polite conversation. It was decidedly masculine—dark polished wood, striped upholstery in muted shades, sophisticated but impersonal—quite like five-star hotel décor.

'Nice, but there's not even a hint of your personality here,' was her honest response.

'Thank God for that—my personality is not remotely attractive.' Shiv shrugged self-deprecatingly.

'Oh, I wouldn't say that,' Anjali said with a polite smile.

Shiv gave her a piercing look and shook his head ruefully. 'You haven't changed a bit, Anjali. As sweet and forgiving as you used to be. I was a prick. I can never forgive myself for treating you so shabbily. And you'll never know how much I wish I could turn the clock back.'

Anjali didn't quite know how to react. This was what she'd been aching to hear for months after Shiv had given her the brutal brush-off. She'd had a list of responses ready then, depending on her mood at the moment. Some weepy, some angry, some bitter, but all eventually forgiving—she'd wanted him back at any cost then. She remained silent staring at the carpet. That's what I was like then, she thought objectively, a willing doormat, begging him to wipe his muddy boots on me.

Shiv got up and held out a hand to her. 'Let's go to the balcony, shall we? The view is spectacular during high tide.'

She followed him, deliberately clutching the stem of her wine glass with both hands as an excuse to avoid physical contact. The full moon encouraged the waves to leap higher and higher as they unleashed their fury on the shore, relentlessly thrashing jagged rocks with their sheer muscle power. It was a mesmerizing sight, but Shiv's confession was even more compelling.

'It's just as well, Anjali, that our relationship ended when it did. Because the longer you'd have stuck around, the unhappier you'd have been. The fact is, I've been a prick to everyone who's loved me. I disappointed my parents, my girlfriends, my wife, oh everyone. It's like that Groucho Marx saying, "I don't want to belong to any club that will accept me as a member." I don't know, I used to feel so worthless; perhaps that's why I was contemptuous of people who cared for me.'

He paused and gazed into the distance while refuelling his breath. 'Srila—my wife,' he added as explanation, 'left me, surprise, surprise. It wasn't the other way round as you may have imagined. Why she married me in the first place, I don't know. I was a junkie when we met—hey, I was a junkie when the two of us dated too, as you may recall.'

He cocked an eyebrow at her, and Anjali nodded briefly.

'My poor father had to sweet talk one of his school chums into giving me a job after college. I graduated with a low third, I just barely scraped through. The only thing I was qualified for was being a pusher; I could tell pure Manali hash from the fakes. Srila, incidentally, was my employer's daughter, which is why I wasn't sacked though I should have been. And so we muddled along in a hazy daze till she wanted a baby. I could have dealt with that, but no, she insisted I go to rehab first—I had graduated to cokehead status by then. After I walked out of rehab for the second time without cleaning up, she walked out the door. I lost my job too, naturally.'

Anjali couldn't stop herself from gasping. How different her life with Karan had been. How gloriously pure and safe and wonderful!

The depressing story of Shiv's life took an upward swing. Shortly after his mother passed away, he resolutely checked himself into rehab again and emerged many months later, only after he was absolutely clean. Thereafter, he got his life together once and for all, starting out as a shameful thirty-one-year-old trainee in a two-bit PR firm.

'My first supervisor was five years younger than me,' he laughed bitterly, 'but I worked so hard to make up for lost time that my rise was meteoric. And then I did my usual bastard thing—I walked away with two highly prized clients and set up on my own. So here I am today, unrecognizable by all who knew me in my wild days,' he concluded.

'Well, thank heavens for that.' Anjali shook her reeling head. 'And stay clean, okay?' she muttered.

Both their glasses were empty and Shiv pleaded with her to join him for another drink, but she firmly refused. She felt claustrophobic—all she wanted was to bolt out of there and go home to Karan's safe, reliable arms. Her crush on Shiv was over. O-V-E-R!

Karan was in bed reading, when Anjali returned. 'So how did your ex-boyfriend's Rent-a-Wife scheme work out?' he inquired, looking terribly put out.

Anjali leaned over to give him a warm hug. 'You want me to tell you now, or after I make you happy?'

'After you make me happy, of course!' was Karan's instant response.

18

It was Sunday, glorious Sunday. Vir reluctantly left the house at dawn for an office cricket match and picnic, grumbling at the injustice of it all. Mutter, mutter, mutter, he went, under his breath.

'Stupid bloody HR chick and her annoying employee bonding schemes. Who the fuck wants to go for this crap? We'd be nicer to each other if we weren't forced to meet on bloody holidays too!'

He urged Mantra one last time to join him, but she flatly refused. 'Forget it! I don't love you that much.' She really didn't. Vir had been playing the Incredible Sulk since his outburst over the domestic violence helpline episode. Mantra had been too scared to utter a word to him in case he accused her of shattering his peace, while he hadn't bothered to initiate conversation at all. She'd be damned if she was going to exert herself to put on a charade of camaraderie in public.

He made such a racket getting ready, angrily slamming drawers and wardrobe doors shut, that Mantra's sleep vanished completely. Despite that, she lazed in bed till 9 a.m., tying up a few loose ends of the novel in her head. She promised herself that she'd complete at least two more chapters that day.

It was Reshma's fault that she didn't get a single word into her potential magnum opus. The doorbell had rung twice while Mantra was eating her breakfast and since Reshma seemed disinclined to answer it, Mantra scraped back her chair and made her way to the door. It was Makarand. Mantra almost keeled over with surprise because:

a) It was a holiday.
b) He was beaming at her, for a change.

'Good morning, Makarand. And what brings you here on a Sunday?'

Makarand thrust a box of mithai into Mantra's hands and proudly informed her that his wife had given birth to a bonny eight-pound boy late last night.

Mantra congratulated him with genuine warmth, feeling hugely relieved for the nation. Makarand had three daughters already, and if this new baby had also been a girl, he'd have tried for a son again and again and again till his prayers were answered. His wife would probably have died in the attempt.

Mantra gave Makarand an envelope stuffed with money and two weeks off, promising to visit his wife and baby soon. After he left, she went to the kitchen and offered the mithai to Reshma who was looking even more hostile than usual. Frightening.

'Makarand's had a baby boy,' Mantra said feebly as explanation.

Reshma snatched the proffered box and in one swift movement tossed it into the bin. 'I have said this before and I'm saying it one last time—I will *not* allow unhealthy food in this house,' she shouted, her voice shaking with anger.

Mantra shrugged and went back to her breakfast that was now stone cold and even more inedible, thinking of how mortifying it must be to be the other woman.

Barely had she taken another bite when muffled, hiccoughing sobs emanated from the kitchen. She briefly debated with herself whether to comfort Reshma or let her express her sorrow in dignified privacy, but when the sobs became even more breathless and heartbreaking, she rushed to her and gave her a comforting, 'there, there' hug.

Keeping in mind Reshma's propensity for tight-lipped silence, the matter should have ended there. After the sobs subsided, Reshma would have splashed her face with water to wash away telltale traces of tears and made for her quarters where she would perhaps have cried louder and harder and set Makarand's photographs and letters on fire like most girls her age do.

But so distraught was Reshma that she spoke through pauses in her sobs. 'Life is so unfair! I never, never get anything I really want!'

A startled Mantra patted Reshma's back even harder. 'Come now, Reshma, you knew his wife was pregnant all along. Why should this bother you?'

'Because it's a boy! He promised me that if his wife gave birth to yet another daughter, he would leave her and marry me!'

While Reshma shuddered with tears, Mantra shuddered with horror. Makarand really was a nasty piece of goods. As Reshma continued to weep, Mantra consoled her, promising her that she'd meet a much nicer man than Makarand. She fell back on her imagination to list out Reshma's sterling virtues; not a particularly easy exercise, considering their history together.

Reshma cut Mantra's excessively glowing obituary-like statements short. 'Madam, may I have access to the medical cabinet? I'm going to take the day off, and I need a sedative.'

'Of course, of course! Help yourself.'

After the front door was softly shut, Mantra felt the weight of Reshma's sorrows fall on her frail shoulders. It was just rubbishy heartbreak over an idiotic man, of course, not a truly tragic situation, but even so. She wryly reminded herself that what was really tragic was the fact that she was so old she'd forgotten how painful break-ups were. She decided that she'd have a chat with Reshma's family. The girl was twenty-seven years old now and bursting with hormones. A suitable unattached boy must be found for her or else she'd get into scrapes with the likes of Makarand and, equally possible, write a dreadful chick-lit novel about the trials and tribulations of being single, psycho and looking for love.

Maybe I should persuade her to do something else that may help her earn more money, Mantra wondered. Since her English is so good, perhaps a call centre? All she has to do is watch our old tapes of *Yes Minister* and other sitcoms to get the Brit accent right.

A phone call from Vir interrupted her plans for Reshma's future. 'Please ask Reshma to make chicken for dinner. The picnic spread is so damn greasy I refuse to touch it and I'm bloody starving to death!'

I'll make Mum's roast chicken, Mantra decided after hanging up. I'll show Vir that healthy food can be tasty too.

Rooting around in the kitchen cabinets to locate the necessary ingredients, she congratulated herself on the call centre idea. It was fantastic. Why, Reshma could pronounce Worcestershire sauce correctly too! Ingredients in place, she got down to calling the chicken shop.

'Is it fresh?' Mantra sternly inquired, making a valiant attempt to sound like a listen-buster-butter-wouldn't-melt-in-my-mouth housewife.

'Fresh?' the chicken shop man scoffed contemptuously. 'Ma'am, I will kill it the minute you get off the phone!'

Mantra gagged. Her enthusiasm for roast chicken waned considerably. She hung up and her conscience took over.

Creep! You're getting something murdered for your own pleasure, it stonily informed her. Hey, the next time you are hungry, why don't you just rip out Rohan's liver?

'Yuck! I'd better call back and cancel it right away,' Mantra muttered.

She redialled the chicken shop number with a trembling finger—there was no reply. Her heart was beating as crazily as a drummer jamming with Carlos Santana; she had to place her free hand over her chest in an attempt to calm it down.

She held on persistently. By the time the chicken shop man answered the phone, she could hear frenzied clucking.

'Fuck, too late,' she gasped in a whisper, gagged again and disconnected the phone.

Half an hour later, the doorbell rang. Mantra handed over the exact change and a tip and gingerly carried the low grade plastic packet to the kitchen sink.

You're a bloody hypocrite, aren't you? Mantra's conscience hissed as she recoiled when she opened the packet tentatively and saw raw flesh oozing blood. The overpowering stench of the freshly killed meat almost knocked her out cold. There was a strong whiff of iron, and a stray defiant thought informed her that the poor murdered chicken rather fancied spinach. She rushed to the bathroom and threw up her breakfast in bits that clogged the sink. All her plans for cooking flew out of the window. One thing she knew for certain was that she was never going to eat flesh again. Never ever. Only, perhaps, if she got a written guarantee that the animal was road kill, or that it died a natural death by pollution, a terror attack or old age. No, even that was out of the question. How do surgeons eat non-vegetarian food? she thought with a shudder. The mutilated chicken was buried in a flower pot. The very first one facing the wicker chair she always sat on, so that she would always remember why she converted to vegetarianism.

When Vir returned that night, he was silently served broccoli and pasta by a severely grim Mantra.

'I told you I was in the mood for chicken!' he whined petulantly, pushing the plate away.

There was no way Mantra was going to tell him that she'd literally chickened out. 'You know, I think we should give up meat forever. I just read an article that said that pure vegetarians have no cholesterol problems,' she informed him, congratulating herself for speedily making that up.

'An article on cholesterol, eh?' he said, his eyes lighting up. 'I hope you cut it out for me.'

'Naah.' Mantra shrugged. 'I read it on the net. I meant to

save it for you but the phone rang and then I forgot. And hey, I also read an article on how you can live longer.'

Vir gave her a quizzical look.

'According to a survey, men who kiss their wives goodbye when they go to work live five years longer!' she said cheekily and got Vir's standard 'bollocks' in response. Well, at least he hadn't snapped at her, at any rate; that was a good sign, Mantra thought with relief.

Vir ate the broccoli lustily without further complaints or conversation while Mantra pushed it around her plate guiltily. Suppose, just suppose, vegetables also felt pain?

19

Reshma turned up calm and dry-eyed the next morning, in time to prepare breakfast. She informed Mantra that she would cook the entire day's meals in the morning and take the rest of the day off.

'Well, well, good to see that you're looking more composed today,' Mantra nodded approvingly, 'and don't bother about my lunch, just cook Vir's dinner and off you go.' She didn't bring up the call centre idea yet; she thought it was wiser to give Reshma's bruised heart and distressed mind a few days to recover.

Before leaving, Reshma popped her head into Mantra's room and asked for access to the medical cabinet again. Mantra agreed in a distracted way; she was concentrating on a stubbornly perverse character in the novel who refused to toe the line and insisted on doing her own thing. Stupid annoying bitch, Mantra mentally swore. I'm going to have her brutally murdered in the next chapter if she doesn't get her act together.

It was only after the door slammed announcing Reshma's departure that Mantra experienced a niggling feeling of discomfort. Instinct made her leap up and check the medical cabinet—and instinct proved her right. Reshma had not merely taken a couple of sleeping tablets—she'd purloined two entire strips. Mantra knew this for sure because she was a control freak; she had a list of all her medicines with the expiry dates carefully noted in her diary.

With a pounding heart, she picked up the house keys and rushed out, keeping her finger pressed insistently on the elevator button. When she finally located Reshma's room in the servants' quarters with the help of the building security guard, she was huffing and puffing more violently than the predatory wolf in the story of the three little pigs. She didn't bang on Reshma's door, though, she rapped on it politely.

Don't do anything to let her know that her game's up, she warned herself.

She continued to rap on it gently, ignoring Reshma's insistent '*Kaun?*'

Finally, the door creaked open and Reshma peeked out. Mantra stuck her foot in the doorway and once she gained access, slammed it shut and confronted her. 'I think you know why I'm here,' she said coolly.

Reshma shot her an innocent look but her telltale flush gave her away.

Shaking her head, Mantra lowered her body on a large tin trunk. She was mildly astonished to note a torn up poster at her feet. She caught a glimpse of a very strong jaw line and wide lips—she was willing to bet it was George Clooney. On an impulse she bent down to pick it up but sternly stopped herself mid-act. This was not the time for trivial musings—there was a matter of life and death to deal with. Taking a deep breath, Mantra began.

'I know you know; *you* know I know, and I'm not leaving till we get it sorted out.'

Reshma remained silent, but her eyes blazed with animosity.

'Okay, since you won't talk, I will! So tell me,' Mantra said deliberately languidly, crossing her arms across her chest and leaning her back against the wall in an attempt to look nonchalant, 'do you really think a creep like Makarand is a good reason to end your life?'

Reshma glared at her wordlessly.

'And do you think it's fair to get Vir arrested for your suicide? You know very well that we will be the first suspects in your suicide case. I'm aware that you don't care about me, but Vir's always been good to you.'

She paused for a bit to let it sink in, and then continued. 'Look, maybe you should go on leave and spend some time with your family,' she said in a kinder, gentler voice. 'Be with people who care about you.'

'Everyone who cares about me is dead. They've been dead for years!' Reshma stated bitterly, her eyes welling up with tears. 'I've got no one and nothing to live for. Absolutely nothing.'

Mantra sighed. 'Perhaps if you tell me a little more about your life and yourself we can figure something out?'

'And perhaps if you'd showed any interest in my life before this dramatic moment, I'd have thought you were sincere about my well being,' Reshma countered. 'But no, why should my life interest you? I'm just a servant, a visible robot but an invisible human being. You never even asked how my English was as good as yours.'

'That's unfair, so unfair! You rejected all my friendly peace-making overtures! And did you even answer when I asked you random unimportant questions like where the salt was kept? You refused to speak to me at all. Drop the self-pity, Reshma. You're way too intelligent to act in this silly manner.'

They were silent for a while, both lost in their muddled thoughts. It was Reshma who broke the silence after what seemed like five hours. 'Okay, here it is: The story of my life. Should I go on? Are you really interested?'

'What do you think?' Mantra glared.

'Right, so. My mother was born in a village in Maharashtra. Her family lived on goodwill, not money. Her father was a practising Brahmin who conducted religious ceremonies for a living, and he was seen to be a decent man, overflowing with the milk of human kindness. On the days when he was free, he used to hold informal classes for children from the untouchable classes in the courtyard at home. My mother and her sisters attended those classes too—they didn't go to a formal school like their brothers. My mother fell in love with one of his students—they'd been in love since she was nine and he was eleven.'

'Gosh,' Mantra's eyes were shining, 'and that boy grew up to be your father, did he?'

Reshma nodded. 'They kept it a secret. But when she was sixteen, and her father started looking for a husband for her, she summoned up the courage and told him she wanted to marry this untouchable. And then his milk of human kindness curdled.'

Mantra shifted uncomfortably on her seat, and not because the tin trunk was hard and cold.

When Reshma went on to say that her parents had eloped, had been caught a week later and her father hacked to death by her mother's relatives, she felt like she was reading an article in the papers—those brief clips that appeared practically every single day. Different names, different parts of the country, same story. Result: blind spot.

'I'm a bastard. They hadn't even had time to get married in a temple before they were caught in the neighbouring village. When my mother's pregnancy became obvious, her parents sent her to a relative in Mumbai.

'"Let her give birth, then abandon the baby in a dustbin and send her back," were the instructions. That's the best place to keep the bastard child of an untouchable, isn't it?' The bitterness was back in Reshma's voice.

Instead of hotly challenging the statement, Mantra raised an eyebrow, imperiously indicating that Reshma continue without self-pitying asides.

'My mother gave birth to me in a government hospital. The regular staff was on strike, and a retired widowed doctor assisted in my birth. When my mother saw me, she burst into tears and begged the doctor to save me from her relatives. You know, tell them I was a stillborn and keep me safe, that she'd get me later. He agreed without asking her any questions—not even one.' Reshma's voice had dropped to a whisper, and Mantra pretended not to notice that Reshma was brushing away a tear with the back of her hand.

'You know what he did?' she said breathlessly after she regained her composure. 'He hired my mother as his housekeeper. We lived in a big room with an attached bath in his sprawling Juhu bungalow—not in the servants' quarters like the male house help. Oh madam, his house was so fancy,' Reshma sighed, 'not like yours.'

Mantra flinched as Reshma paused to take a deep breath, recalling that Samira had said the same thing. Just what is it about the way Vir and I live that makes other people think we're slumming it, she wondered. The chic minimalist look Vir insists on is definitely not working!

Mantra's mental meandering came to an end as Reshma resumed her confidences. 'Dadaji—that's what I used to call him—sent me to a good English medium convent school in the area, and he was so interested in my education, he used to attend all the PTA meetings. Fortunately, I was a good student and I worked extra hard to never let him down. His private chambers were in the bungalow and when I grew older, I used to assist him in the evenings. Dadaji always said I had the makings of a fantastic nurse, so that's what I planned to be when I grew up. Madam, I came first in all my science subjects till I passed out of class 12—I did him proud. I topped the state in the SSC exams, my photograph was even in the papers! It was when I was preparing for my nursing entrance exams that Dadaji had his third heart attack and died—he was in his mid-eighties then. That's when I was finally tossed into the dustbin by his real children—seventeen years after I should have been. And I deserved it—I truly deserved it! I'm rubbish!' Reshma didn't pretend to hide her tears any more—she sobbed uncontrollably.

'Hush, hush,' Mantra whispered. She was up on her feet, rocking Reshma in her arms. 'Don't be silly, no one deserves to be treated like shit.'

'But I acted like a shit!' Reshma wailed. 'I was a total shit! I wasn't much nicer than all you privileged upper class people, you know. The awful truth is, I loved him more than I loved my mother. I was ashamed of her because she was a servant. I never used to invite my classmates home because then they'd know who I really was, and once, when a class mate dropped by uninvited, I called my mother by her name and asked her to serve fresh lime! She never said a word, but I saw the hurt in her eyes. I'll never forget that look—it will haunt me till I die. And I want to die! I deserve to die!'

'Hush, you were a child then; you couldn't have known better.'

A fresh outburst followed, and after it blew over, leaving occasional sobs in its wake, Reshma wrenched herself out of Mantra's arms. 'I need to be alone. Please, please go,' she pleaded.

Mantra held out a hand meaningfully. Within a few seconds, the purloined strips of medicines were placed on her palm—exactly the same number that she had taken, Mantra swiftly noted.

'May I have one sleeping tablet? Just one for now?'

'Just one,' Mantra consented, and handed it to Reshma herself.

'I'll look in on you in a few hours,' she said calmly, and left.

20

The lone sleeping tablet was no match for Reshma's consciousness. Though it struggled gamely to do its job, her agitated brain fought back tooth and nail with memories. It was Reshma who had called Dadaji's older son in Philadelphia when his body lay like a fallen statue in the morgue. A few days later, both his sons arrived without their wives and children. After the pundits played their role in a special shortened-for-NRIs-who-can't-afford-leave ceremony, the lawyers took over. Two lakhs of his inheritance had been left to Reshma and her mother. Dadaji had always told her he was leaving her something to pay for her nursing school.

'I know you'll be a fine nurse, my dear. Better and more well informed than any of the nurses who assisted me in the hospitals I've worked at. But, if you prefer to do something else like commerce instead,' he winced, 'please still do your best. I want you to do your best. Whatever you do, be the best!'

Dadaji hadn't legally adopted Reshma, so he was made out to be of unsound mind, and Reshma and her mother got just five thousand rupees. Very reluctantly at that. Samira would have sniffed that you can't even buy a pair of decent shoes with that amount.

'Have mercy, Burra Sahib and Chotta Sahib,' her mother had pleaded. 'My daughter is bright. Doctor Sahib had wanted her to go to nursing school. Five thousand rupees won't cover anything. Don't give us any money, just pay her fees directly to the college—that's all I ask.'

Burra Sahib had remained cold and impervious, while Chotta Sahib's face registered guilt—a brief flicker only, admittedly, so it could well have been a trick of light—when Reshma's mother had pressed the newspaper clipping announcing Reshma as the state's SSC topper in their hands.

The driver, cook and gardener, all of whom had resented the favouritism meted out to Reshma and her mother had a secret celebratory party with a full bottle of Scotch pinched from Doctor Sahib's well-stocked bar. Now all of them were equal.

The bungalow was sold to a builder and Reshma and her mother were evicted. Burra Sahib flew back to his prestigious job in America while Chotta Sahib tied up loose ends. Reshma's mother made one last desperate attempt, prompted not just by love for her daughter, but anger against Doctor Sahib's sons.

'She was more of a devoted child to him than you boys ever were. You never bothered to visit him; *he* used to make annual trips to America to see you. And when he wasn't allowed to travel after his first heart attack two years ago, did you bother to come to India even once? No, no, it was the children's school, work, whatever. Every year you promised, and every year you put him off. Reshma should have lit his funeral pyre, not you boys!'

'Take all his medical books and instruments if you want,' was his gruff response. And though Reshma categorically told her mother not to touch even one object apart from Buddy, a present Dadaji had given her on her fourteenth birthday—she'd snuggled up to it every night since—her mother ignored her.

By the time the fracas had ended, the entrance exams were over. Not that it made a difference to Reshma. She couldn't afford the fees. Neither could she get in on the reservation list on her biological father's lowly status. His name didn't feature on her birth certificate—she was a bastard after all.

Doctor Sahib's stethoscope was the first to be sold. After the medical equipment, the text books followed in batches whenever money was required. The only book that Reshma hid from her mother was a Richard Gordon. Dadaji had loved Sir Lancelot Spratt. She'd hear him guffawing late into the night over the fictitious surgeon's deliciously sarcastic remarks. This was the only keepsake she wanted of Dadaji; the only one that brought him back to her.

Her mother never gave up. She got in touch with Dr Pant, one of Doctor Sahib's junior colleagues, a frequent visitor to the house in the good old days. He obligingly got her a job as a live-in maid in his neighbourhood and was instrumental in getting Reshma a job too, at a hospital. While he'd recommended her for the post of a receptionist, the sniffy personnel manager had informed her that the only vacancy available at that moment was for a cook. Take it or leave it, she'd said. Reshma took it.

Reshma's mother had urged her to get a job as a secretary or teacher somewhere else instead. 'You can read and write English. You're too educated to waste yourself on menial jobs,' she insisted in an outraged manner.

Reshma ignored her. She was too numb to care about the brilliant future prospects her mother threw at her. More importantly she was frightened of being out in the big bad world without Dadaji's influence.

Dr Pant had popped into the hospital kitchen a few weeks later to look in on her. 'Hello, hello,' he said cheerfully. 'Are you enjoying yourself?'

Reshma nodded.

'Good,' he said briskly and patted her on the back. 'I'm sure you can work your way up to being a nurse someday.'

He didn't look her directly in the eyes as he said that, but she read his apologetic thoughts: Sorry, but I've got my grandchildren to put through medical school. It's become bloody expensive these days.

He'd walked away feeling that he'd done his bit, and Reshma

didn't grudge him that. This was life and she was an adult now, capable of looking after herself. Thereafter, a stoic Reshma had met her mother every Sunday evening till she died.

Mantra's insistent knocking broke Reshma's reverie.

'I'm not hungry,' she said sulkily as Mantra proffered a flask and a box of sandwiches.

'Like I care. Consider this medicine. And if you're a good girl and leave only crumbs for the birds, I have dessert you will definitely appreciate,' Mantra said complacently, and held out two sleeping tablets. 'If this isn't incentive to a tortured soul, what is?'

Mantra stayed long after Reshma had finished the sandwiches and swallowed the tablets. She heard everything.

'Tell me, do you still dream of being a nurse?' she asked curiously.

'As if! I don't have the money, remember?'

'Suppose, just suppose, you had the money—would you try then?' Mantra prodded gently.

'In a shot! You know it's been a long time, but I can still name every bone in your body, including the finger you're pressing thoughtfully into your cheek. I could be the best nurse on Planet Earth,' was Reshma's haughty response.

Just then a gust of wind blew lustily through the open door, scattering the remnants of the torn poster. Mantra picked up the pieces closest to her and put them together. It was definitely George Clooney!

'So you're a Clooney fan, huh?'

'I used to worship him—Dadaji and I never missed a single episode of *ER*,' Reshma said flatly.

'Then why did you—' Mantra held up bits of the poster in her hand.

She got stony silence in response.

Mantra shuffled the torn bits and suddenly the penny dropped. Makarand's lips and strong jaw-line were astonishingly similar. Excellent—Reshma was making a concerted effort to get over the cretin!

21

No bells rang in Anjali's heart when Shiv called over the next few weeks. His power over her had evaporated swiftly since his confession. This time she was absolutely certain that it wasn't just another random swing of the whimsical pendulum in her attraction–revulsion feelings for Shiv. She was free now. His calls came frequently though, and his pretexts were usually flimsy:

> Thank you so much for organizing the lovely dinner.
> Congratulate me, I got the account!
> Where can I get readymade curtains?
> Your cheque is in the mail.
> Need advice on blah blah.

She was helpful and her responses were polite, but she kept the conversations brief and to the point: Sorry, got to go, someone at the door/organizing lunch/got a guest/just going out.

Emails with forwarded jokes were in her inbox daily too, as frequently as junk mails advertising penis enlargements, Viagra and Cialis, replica Rolex watches and letters from alleged lawyers of unknown philanthropic Nigerians informing her that she had inherited billions of dollars and could she just send hundred dollars for the bank clearance? Shiv's multimedia onslaught was treated with supreme indifference.

'I know you won't believe me, Mantra, but I'm definitely over him—I couldn't care less if I never heard from him again. But that idiotic Karan insisted I invite him over for dinner tonight.'

Hmm. Not idiotic Karan, clever, clever Karan! Mantra thought approvingly. The wily fox wants to see them interact with each other, just to be sure.

She didn't articulate her thoughts, however. After Anjali's explosive reaction the last time round, she'd decided to keep her lips sealed on the subject of Shiv. Just as well that Karan's antennae were twitching nervously—it was his business, after all. It would be interesting to see how Vir reacted to him too—Vir's instincts about people were surprisingly accurate.

'I didn't tell him it was my birthday, though.'

'Because you don't want him to know that you're a doddering forty-seven year old today?' Mantra teased.

Anjali grimaced. 'I've already warned Karan that if he gets a cake I'll stab him with the knife!'

'Yes, yes, no cake,' Mantra agreed. 'With so many candles, the icing will be buried under layers of wax, yuck!'

'Meanie! You have a couple of years to go before you hit the wrong side of forty-five. I'll remind you of this conversation then!'

'By the way, what's the dinner theme for tonight? Mashed old age home delicacies?' Mantra joked.

'It's Russian, Ms Mean Mouth! Karan's got some fab Beluga caviar, so I'm working around that. See you tonight, darloshka!'

It was Mantra who was threatened with the knife later in the evening, as Karan had designated her to bring the cake. She'd given the bakery detailed instructions on how to decorate it. Anjali shrieked when she opened the box: the round cake was in the shape of a face—and it had strands of white hair and granny glasses. She swore to get Botox and cosmetic surgery as a present for herself.

'I promise you, I'm going to make that Jolie woman look like my great-grandmother!'

Vir and Mantra jeered and Karan joined in cheerfully, but Shiv remained silent. When he got Anjali alone for a few minutes he whispered, 'She already does look like your great-grandmother. Well, actually, your ugly step sister.'

Anjali had ha-ha'd it off, but she felt a little pleased. God, it felt good to get compliments, even though Shiv didn't make her heart hammer against her chest any more.

'So, what did you think of your sister's ex?' Mantra casually asked Vir on the drive back home.

'Hmm, an okay sort. Too strong and silent for me, though.'

'Do you think Anjali would have been happier married to him?' Mantra persisted.

'Hey, why don't you write to an agony aunt and find out? I'm not into this girlie bull shit, okay?'

Mantra exploded. 'Can we never have a conversation about anything at all when we're together, just the two of us? Why is it that you only deign to talk to me when there are other people around?'

'And you still haven't taken the hint.' Vir muttered.

'What the hell you mean by that?' Mantra challenged him spiritedly.

'You're a smart woman—you figure it out!'

Mantra let it go for the moment—she had other issues to air too. She hated it that her voice sounded whiny and needy, even to her own ears. To think she'd imagined that her neediness would vanish after marriage!

'I only know what's happening in your life when I overhear your conversations with other people on the phone or during outings. You were never like this before; we used to spend hours chatting about anything under the sun!'

'That's because I thought I'd be getting sex afterwards,' was the insolent response.

'You're a bloody creep!'

'And you've had too much to drink!'

After Vir went to bed, Mantra crept to the veranda for a smoke. Her hands were shaking as she lit up. Not just because it had been six interminably long hours since her last cigarette. Vir's cutting remarks were still ringing in her ears.

So what exactly is he hinting at? she asked herself. That marriage without sex is not acceptable? I can just as well tell him that marriage without companionship is equally unacceptable. At least I make an effort to respond when he makes sexual overtures. He doesn't bother to respond to any conversation I make. We're not good together any more. I don't know how to deal with this—oh God, I just want to die!

Waves of self-pity washed over her. Fourty-three years old, practically half of her life over, and what had she achieved? Zilch. A career that she had quit because it didn't excite her any more; a husband who frankly wouldn't notice if she were dead—and when he did notice he'd probably be relieved; and a libido that had run away without a forwarding address. And what did she have to look forward to, anyway? Wrinkles, a scraggy chicken neck and lousy eyesight among other horrible things. The awful truth was, life didn't hold any charm for her any more. The book included—she'd lost the stomach to write it after Reshma's miserable life story. There was no way in hell she could parody other people's pain. The only book she was inspired to write now would be worthy of a title like *The Great Depression of the 40s*.

She had to find something to do—something to help kill time while waiting for death. She felt as weary as a hamster on a stationary cycle, moving constantly but getting nowhere. She'd foolishly imagined that she'd be flooded with freelance assignments after quitting her job but very few came her way—not surprising because the recession had trimmed newspapers down to less than half of their original number of pages. She had only small, fleeting joys now—winning five straight games of FreeCell or level two Spider Solitaire, her latest brain stimulating games since she really couldn't think of any more songs with numbers in their titles.

Reshma, she promised herself impulsively. I've got to do something about Reshma first. After that, I will research euthanasia. I've read somewhere that pentobarbital does the trick. It's easily available at pet shops in Mexico. Maybe I'll drop by as a euthanasia tourist. I wonder, if we'd had children, perhaps I'd have had a reason to live—to make sure that they dressed warmly in winter, ate their greens and weren't innocently fattening the bank balances of Internet service providers by chatting with paedophiles.

Mantra wasn't the only tortured soul awake at 3 a.m. Anjali was wiping away silent tears in her living room, clutching the present Shiv had given her. He'd remembered her birthday, and, even more touching, the perfume she used to wear when they'd dated. That's what he'd given her, a bottle of White Linen. She used to sneak a few drops from her mother's bottle before she'd meet him. Inhaling it now brought back the sweetest memories imaginable. Urges too. The pendulum had dangerously swung back to attraction. The good days with Shiv had been the best days of her life. That was an indisputable fact. She drifted into flashback mode, just like in the movies. Soft focus vignettes of her happy times with Shiv whirled in slow motion to the tune of the cheesy song from *Dirty Dancing—I've had the time of my life.*

This is madness, she admonished herself sternly. I'm never going to see him or have anything to do with him again. Never. It's tearing me up inside.

22

The next morning, Mantra had a brief debate with her conscience. She guiltily remembered the promise she'd made to herself about not poking her nose into other people's business—her well-meaning acts just boomeranged, flinging egg at her face, and made Vir nastier to her than usual. On the other hand though, Reshma wasn't economically empowered like Samira—the poor thing was incapable of helping herself. The decision was made and Mantra steeled herself to dial a helpline and wearily listened to loop after loop of 'Please jerk off; our customer care executive will be with you shortly.' Finally, she got the number she wanted and a short while later she was at a musty registrar's office scribbling down details.

The good thing was the common entrance test for nursing was still a couple of months away. On the flip side, she didn't know if that was time enough for Reshma to prepare for the exams. The money she could manage from her savings: the fee was sixty or seventy grand a year, and with hostel accommodation and other miscellaneous expenses it would work out to around a lakh a year. Not exactly chicken shit considering she was barely earning anything, but she badly wanted to do this.

The moment she returned, she summoned Reshma and calmly informed her that she wasn't required as a cook any more.

A stunned Reshma managed to stutter, 'Madam, I promise I won't attempt suicide again, please! I need this job, I'll do—'

Mantra cut her short. 'Look, Reshma, you're a lousy cook—face it. And I think you'd do so much better as a nurse. Please read this and revert.'

Mantra handed her the college prospectus and the admission form and sailed away into the bedroom. She needed to lie down and recuperate after meeting tedious government officials. She'd lost count of the number of counters she'd queued up at, only to be triumphantly told, when her turn finally came, that it was the wrong one.

'Why can't you people direct me to the right counter instead of always misdirecting me,' she'd screamed like a banshee after fruitlessly shuttling between counters number 1, 3, 4 and 6. 'Or is that classified information?' she had added sarcastically.

All she got in response was a bored look tinged with contempt from the official she was dealing with and sympathetic titters from equally harried citizens.

About half an hour later, Reshma knocked tentatively on her door and entered. Her expression was unreadable as she stiffly said, 'It's very kind of you to get the details for me, madam, but I can't afford it.'

'Oh, but I can. And I'm not taking no for an answer, so forget it. Now hurry up and check out the list so we can get your textbooks. I want you to start studying right away or you'll miss a year.'

'No, madam. I'm *not* doing it! Suppose you change your mind midway or die like Dadaji, then that's another dream crashed. I can't take disappointment any more. Thanks but no thanks,' Reshma said adamantly.

Mantra felt her heart sink as Reshma mentioned the possibility that she may die soon—did she look *that* old? Dismissing the morbid thought, she sat up and looked Reshma in the eye.

'I definitely won't change my mind, but yes I may die midway through your course—after all, it's for two long years,' she added wryly. 'So I'll tell you what I'm going to do—I'm going to open a joint account with you and transfer the money for the entire course there at the very outset. How about that?'

'Are you really sure you want to do this for me? Really, really sure?' Reshma said slowly, haltingly.

Mantra nodded.

'I'll pay you back—every single penny,' Reshma mumbled, her voice thick with emotion.

Then Mantra fell back as Reshma flung herself into her arms. Fortunately she was on the bed, so no bones were broken.

'Easy, Reshma, I'm at the age when osteoporosis attacks!' she admonished.

'I'll be there to take care of you when that happens, didi. Don't you worry,' Reshma giggled.

Reshma had never called her 'didi' before. Mantra felt a lump in her throat, the way mothers do when their babies utter the word 'mummy' for the first time. She felt wanted and needed and unbelievably special.

It was decided that Reshma would stay with them till she got into college. Mantra wanted her to move into the spare bedroom so she could study in quiet surroundings, but Reshma insisted on her old room in the quarters—she felt at peace there, she maintained. She also insisted on cooking while studying, despite Mantra's objections.

'Look, it takes up a little over an hour of my time a day—half an hour for breakfast, half an hour for dinner and ten minutes for your lunch. Please let me do it or else I'll feel like a total shit.'

Mantra was a little startled, at first. The formal language had gone and Reshma sounded like any old Westernized teenager. Quite like Rohan really, Mantra thought. Reshma's benefactor must have sent her to a really cool English-medium school.

She shuddered as she mentally compared Reshma's life before and after—what a shocking let down that must have been. Her resolve to help Reshma became even stronger.

After the trip to the bank and the textbook shops, Reshma invited Mantra to her room in the quarters and revealed yet another skeleton in her cupboard.

'I want you to meet Buddy—he's sort of like a cuddle bunny,' she gushed as she opened a rusted trunk—the very same one Mantra had sat on a few days before.

The lid creaked open and Reshma invited Mantra to peer into it. Mantra screamed as the skeleton folded inside leered at her.

Reshma lovingly lifted him out and held him up. 'This was a present from Dadaji. He's my best friend in the whole world! I can't sleep without him, but I have to keep him locked up during the day because people like you scream when you see him. He's lovely, really. Want to give him a hug?'

Mantra shuddered a 'No, thank you' and beat a hasty retreat home.

After Reshma cleared the dinner plates that night, she reappeared with a small bowl and placed it on Mantra's table mat.

'Bread pudding. Dadaji's favourite dessert,' she whispered in response to Mantra's quizzical look.

Vir looked at Reshma expectantly but no bowl of bread pudding was handed to him. 'Why not me, Reshma?' he whined.

'Have you forgotten about your cholesterol, bhaiyya?' Reshma said sternly and sailed away.

Mantra laughed outright, she couldn't help it; served hypochondriac Vir bloody right! It gave her great pleasure to watch Vir's expression as she took each spoonful, dramatizing her 'Ooh, it's scrum' expression like they do in TV commercials. She stretched it out for as long as she could, waiting for Vir to ask for a bite.

That wasn't Vir's style, however. He kept his eyes unblinkingly trained on her, watching wordlessly, but beseechingly, like a mournful dog.

Halfway through she gave in, pushing her bowl towards him. She'd have had a guilt-ridden sleepless night if she hadn't.

Vir walloped it up in Bowser fashion too—in less than two seconds the bowl was licked clean. Then he got up and left. No 'So long and thanks for the dessert'. As always.

There was one thing Mantra wanted to find out and she cornered Reshma in the kitchen. 'That was simply marvellous, Resh. Why didn't you ever make it before?'

'Because I totally hated you then,' Reshma said bluntly.

'Right,' Mantra replied, a trifle disconcerted. 'Now off you go and hit the books. Exams in two months, remember?'

'What exams?' Vir asked curiously. He'd popped in to the kitchen for a glass of water.

Mantra excused herself when Reshma launched into the story and beat a hasty retreat to the bedroom. She couldn't bear to hear herself being described as a cross between Mother Teresa and Wendy the Good Little Witch. Besides, she had a very strong feeling that Vir would explode and accuse her of interfering in other people's lives again.

She was in bed feigning sleep when Vir returned to the bedroom after what seemed like an eternity. 'And why didn't you tell me about this before?' he asked, nudging her awake.

'Why should I have? Do you tell me anything about your life? And it's my money anyway,' was her acid response. She was trembling inside, steeling herself for the outburst that was certain to follow.

There was no reply. Oddly enough, no outburst either. But a short while later, a cheque for three lakhs was pressed into her hand.

'Not required, Vir—I'm doing the sponsoring. I've already transferred the funds.'

'You've done your bit and now I'd like to do mine too. This is for clothes and all the foolish things that girls are into—please add it to her kitty. She mustn't ever want for anything or feel small compared to others,' he said gruffly.

Mantra cursed him in her mind as she put the cheque into her handbag. I hate you, Vir. And I particularly hate it when you remind me why I fell in love with you.

23

Anjali scrunched her eyes, straining to read the menu. The print was in stylish light italics which made it all the more difficult to read, so she gave up and feigned indecision.

'I really can't decide. Why don't you order for both of us?'

Shiv grimaced. 'I was just going to ask you to do the ordering—can't read the damn menu. I forgot my reading glasses.'

'Me too,' she confessed sheepishly.

They laughed hysterically.

Anjali's smile was wiped out a second later when Shiv said, 'Oh, it feels good to grow old together, doesn't it?'

If only it really could be that way, she thought wistfully as Shiv called the waiter over and asked for his recommendations to save them the embarrassment of squinting helplessly at the menu. A lock of hair fell on his forehead during his consultation, and she had to suppress the urge to tenderly brush it back into place. Lines could not be crossed.

Anjali hadn't been able to resist answering the phone when he called a week later, despite the stern lectures she'd been giving herself to avoid him like the plague. The perfume had made her fall in love with him again.

How can conversation hurt me? she fooled herself. A few weeks later, she accepted his invitation to lunch. How can lunch hurt me? she told herself reasonably.

She brought up the birthday present lightly, teasingly. 'So you're a man of the world, huh? Imagine knowing the name of the perfume I used to splash on. I don't recall mentioning it to you.'

'No, you didn't. I found out many years later. My wife had bought it, and I recognized the fragrance immediately. That's when I took a dekko at the name.'

A stab of jealousy smote Anjali's heart at the mention of his ex-wife but the pain was soothed away with his following remark.

'She used it just once though, because I told her I was allergic to it,' Shiv grinned. 'That perfume is special—it's meant only for you.'

He'd done it again—like he used to. He made her feel like she was the only person in the world who mattered.

Their eyes met and smouldered simultaneously. Anjali felt a fire lighting up somewhere a little below too. What she felt for him wasn't just love or lust—it was pure passion, a deadly combination of both. She wanted him now and she wanted him forever. She had an epiphany in the middle of a crowded restaurant—that what she had with Karan was camaraderie and companionship. Not this. It had never been as beautiful and exhilarating as this. If she'd been single, she'd have snapped it up. Right now, she was like a bird flinging its body repeatedly against a cage, fighting for freedom. She'd been given a second chance, and she yearned to take it. So she flirted back, first shyly and then dangerously.

How can flirting hurt me, anyway? she reasoned with herself. Karan does it in a charming, polite way. According to Mantra, Vir always has a bunch of office groupies buzzing around him like flies and giggling foolishly. Mantra says flirting at the work place is de rigueur, harmless and makes work more exciting. Who do I have to flirt with? The milkman? Why can't I just enjoy Shiv's company, hear him say lovely things to me, feel good and go home? I'm a stodgy bore—everyone but Karan calls me that. I should stop reading so much into everything and just go with the flow.

So Anjali went out with Shiv more often. Hurried lunch dates or teas were squeezed into his desperately busy work schedule. Dinners were few and far between—that would mean telling Karan, something Anjali wasn't comfortable with. But this worked well for Karan too, she would console herself. Shiv always left her in a good mood, and Karan was the beneficiary—she was sweeter to him and more attentive. It was a win-win situation, she justified to herself. Everyone was happy, and no feelings were hurt. Every time her conscience attempted to rain on her parade, she'd silence it with an excerpt from an article she'd read in the science page of the papers—'In most species, faithfulness is a fantasy.' The erudite Professor David P. Barash had said, 'Infants have their infancy; adults, adultery.' He went on to add that fidelity is best seen in *Diplozoon paradoxum*, a flatworm that lives in the gills of freshwater fish. 'That's the only species I know of in which there seems to be 100 per cent monogamy.' Heck, she wasn't a flatworm—she was a human being!

So Anjali took a detour that initially appeared to be just a small deviation from her path. However, with every step forward she grew further and further away from the reality that was her life. Spring gradually turned to summer and Anjali was in tune with the weather—the heat was on. Her body was hot too. The gym membership was paying off.

24

Makarand had been getting nastier over the last few months. Reshma's abrupt rejection of him had drastically decreased the vital supply of feel-good chemicals to his brain and released his inner evil goblin.

It had begun when he returned from his celebrating-birth-of-son leave. Instead of getting his morning cuppa from Reshma's loving hands, Mantra had given him a tenner for the tea stall below. Smouldering over his tea and mentally identifying Mantra as the obstacle in his love life, he'd waited near the lift to accost Reshma at 10 a.m. when she always retired till lunch time. To his shock, Reshma had cold-shouldered him, refusing to acknowledge his presence.

'Has ma'am been working on you?' he'd snarled, but got no reply. Makarand had suppressed the overpowering urge to shake her—there were too many saabs and memsaabs around.

When he attempted to storm the servants' quarters for an explanation, he was barred by the building security guard. 'Get out. I have strict instructions to keep you out.'

All his attempts to meet Reshma the rest of the day had been foiled, and his rage was directed at Mantra. 'Speak to me in Marathi from now onwards,' he barked at her when he went off duty that evening.

'I'm afraid I won't be speaking to you at all, Makarand,' Mantra sweetly informed him. 'From tomorrow onwards you will be working with Vir. So you will have to report for duty earlier since he leaves for work at 8.30 a.m. By the way, I said that in Hindi, one of our nation's official languages. If you've forgotten it, do let me know—I'll hire a tutor for a refresher course.'

Makarand was torn. On the one hand, sir had a dead sexy car; he'd driven it a couple of times and oh, the adrenaline rush he experienced when his foot pressed the accelerator! Given a choice between dating a buxom Bollywood beauty and driving sir's car, he'd take the car. Just sitting behind the wheel made him rise in his own esteem. On the other hand, sir's working hours were crazy. Ma'am always let him off early and she was a pushover, that one. With sir, he'd have to be careful. Very careful.

Makarand's misgivings proved right. Vir came down heavily on him for overtaking female drivers and talking on his cell phone while driving. He frequently interrupted Makarand's afternoon naps by going for meetings and didn't give him a second to finish his tea. Makarand was beginning to think of Mantra with longing. He also yearned to punish her for keeping Reshma away from him. It had been ages since he'd caught a glimpse of Reshma. Her practice of accompanying him on Saturdays for grocery shopping had been stopped too. He would, he promised himself, give Mantra 'a fitting reply', the favourite words of his fiery SNM party leader.

If he'd had a hint of the emotional trauma Mantra was going through, he may well have thrown a celebratory party. It was just as well that Reshma hadn't accepted Mantra's offer of the spare bedroom. It was occupied now—by Vir. He'd moved out ostensibly because Mantra's hair and clothes reeked of cigarette smoke. He'd become allergic to it—that's what he'd defiantly muttered, as he picked up his reading glasses and toothbrush one night. Over the next few weeks, there was no trace left of him in the master bedroom and bathroom. His possessions had gradually shifted with him.

Mantra felt like a cockroach that had been deliberately and ruthlessly crushed under an army boot. If this weren't a neon sign saying 'The marriage is over!' what was? What was she waiting for now? For Vir to give it to her in writing? How humiliating. The first night alone in the bedroom, she feverishly threw some things into a suitcase, deciding to relocate to her pink bedroom in her parents' home, and muffled her sobs into her pillow. Her sobs grew louder when she hit upon the painful realization that she had already lost Vir as her best friend a long while ago—losing him as a disinterested husband was much easier. By the time dawn broke, though, she was relatively calmer and promised herself that she'd give it one final shot. Just to be sure—she didn't want to spend the rest of her life wondering if she'd been too hasty. If it were a live-in relationship, she'd have walked out without a backward glance. Marriages demanded much more effort. Even mutual consent divorces were questioned deeply by the court. There'd be a year of separation and counselling, among other things. It made more sense to try and sort it out herself, first.

So she determinedly took Vir's feeble excuse at face value and made a concerted effort to quit smoking—despite the fact that she was certain it wasn't the real reason for the separate bedrooms. She knew in her heart that he'd really moved out that fateful night because of a disastrous attempt at sex. It was odd that he'd initiated sex in the first place—hell, they weren't even on speaking terms. Even so, Mantra had tried very hard to get into the mood; if it helped their relationship improve she was willing to give it a try. She'd resignedly put all her energy into the necking and made what she thought were the right noises, but he had seen through it all and stopped abruptly at second base, mumbling that he wasn't into necrophilia.

'I've quit smoking,' she informed him brightly some weeks later at breakfast.

'And pigs have wings,' Vir said dryly without looking up from the papers.

'No, really, it's been about a month since I had so much as a drag,' she insisted virtuously.

'Good for you then,' was the cool rejoinder. Then he muttered something about the moon being made of Cheddar.

'So,' Mantra tentatively mumbled while fiddling nervously with a fork, 'you can move back in.'

'Nope. I like my space. It's been bloody years since I had a room of my own.'

'And when we have guests?' Mantra ventured, still tentative.

'Why do women always have to go into the future?' Vir sighed, looking up finally. 'On the first date you think of nappies, on the second date you're into incontinence diapers. Just go with the flow, dammit. Tell me, honestly, isn't it better for you too, having a room of your own? You can read late into the night without me snarling at you to turn off your bedside lamp, and you can watch TV without inconveniencing me, come on!'

Mantra exploded. The nicotine withdrawal had made her excessively short-tempered. It was worse this time because she didn't have a smoker to sidle up to for the SOS purpose of inhaling second-hand smoke, the way she used to during her half-hearted attempts to quit while she was working.

'How fucking dare you? I never inconvenienced you—it wasn't *me* who kept the TV on till the crack of dawn! It was always you!'

'In which case you should thank me nicely for not inconveniencing you any more,' was the smooth rejoinder. He smugly folded the paper, scraped his chair back and left for work.

Filthy sod and bastard, Mantra seethed, glaring at his retreating figure. He'd done it again, used his sneaky strategy skills to confuse her into conceding his point. After Reshma left to study in her quarters, Mantra summoned up the courage to venture into the guest bedroom out of curiosity—just to see how he'd settled in. She tripped over a shoe, skidded on the floor and banged her face sharply against the bedpost with a sickening crunch. She felt blood trickling from her lips. Tears sprang to her eyes from the pain and were swiftly followed by a flood of emotion. She cried loudly and uncaringly since she was alone at home. Her mother-in-law was up to her old tricks again! She must be exulting, Mantra thought bitterly as she picked herself up. How odd that there aren't fragrant rose petals lovingly strewn on her precious son's newly adopted bed.

Back in the safety of her bedroom, the tears flowed unchecked as she examined her face in the mirror. The cut lip was smeared with blood and a tooth was slightly chipped—she looked like a lioness after a kill. If wildlife-crazy Vir were here to see me now, he'd probably be overcome with desire, was the random thought that ran through her head. For the first time in her life, she hated him as much as she disliked his mother. It finally hit her that maybe it wasn't just sexual frustration and work stress that had taken its toll on him—it was just his DNA, his mother's nasty genes.

'Nobody loves me,' Mantra wailed aloud inconsolably like Rohan used to when he was punished as a toddler. Her troubled thoughts gave her reason to weep even louder. The last chance is over—this marriage is dead. I absolutely must walk out before it decomposes and leaves a stench. The person I fell in love with doesn't live in Vir's body any more. That person would deepen my laugh lines; this one increases my worry lines. And where's the damn support? He's constantly deriding my efforts to find something else to do with my life instead of burying myself in corporate drudgery. Stop being in denial and stop constantly making excuses for his weird behaviour!

After the tears finally subsided, Mantra tested her voice aloud. She cleared her throat several times to get the wobbliness out of it and then called her mother. It had been ages since she'd had a decent chat with her parents, usually because they were busy. They were always at a yoga session or prayer meeting or meditation or with a tarot card reader—always something or the other. She needed to talk to them desperately right now, to be in touch with people who loved her unconditionally and for eternity. Maybe she'd invite herself over to the ashram for a while. She'd never be too old to sit on her dad's lap, bury her head into his chest and howl uncontrollably—the way she used to whenever she got injections till the age of eighteen when she left home. She needed to feel her mum lightly caressing her furrowed brow, talking to her in a tone of voice that was always tinged with love, even if Mantra had done something very, very naughty. Mantra caught herself snuffling again and blew her nose violently before dialling their number. She was warming up to the idea of visiting the ashram; maybe a spot of meditation would help—give her peace of mind to deal with this crap, at the very least.

'Darling, is this telepathy or what? I was just going to call you, I have fantastic news!' her mother gushed.

Mantra sighed. If she let her mother speak first, she'd go on for hours and Mantra wouldn't be able to get a word in edgewise. She resigned herself to being a listener. Anyway, it was painful to talk with a bust lip. 'Tell all, Mum. Go on then.'

'Guess what, Mantra?' her mother trilled in her usual bubbly way. 'Your dad and I are on a completely different trip now.' Her parents had left the ashram a couple of weeks ago and were staying at a hotel in Pune.

'Ah, so you finally came to your senses.'

'Actually, we were asked to leave,' her mother sheepishly admitted.

'You were *thrown* out?' Mantra gasped. Really, her parents were embarrassing at any age.

'Well, it was your dad's birthday, and we threw a small bash in our room. Just a few people with alcohol and music—you *know* he has to listen to Elvis Presley on his birthday, it's a ritual. Anyway, that sanctimonious widowed witch in the room adjoining ours wasn't invited and she spilled the beans to the authorities. Alcohol isn't allowed here, tragically.'

'Why on earth did you choose that ashram then?' Mantra sighed.

'Gosh, we only discovered that once we'd got here, and we thought it would be good to let our livers get some rest and rejuvenation. So would you like to hear about our new project or not?'

The resident tarot card reader at the ashram had told Mantra's mother that it was in the cards for her to do something for herself that would greatly benefit other people too. Setting up an old folks' home was the first idea that popped into her head, and whatever she decided, her husband enthusiastically supported. They'd roped in a couple of friends too.

'It's for people like us who want to have fun till we die and not age gracefully and fade weakly into the background. After we were expelled, we worked it out on paper with another couple as partners and are in the process of setting it up. We've already got a few options for the name. Now, which do you prefer? Elvis Will Never Leave This Building or Old But Not Dead Boring or Ancient But Not History?'

She carried on without waiting for an answer. 'And we're going to sell most of our assets including the house. We're thinking of pitching the idea to companies too—you know they have corporate social responsibility programmes to save on tax and look good and this is so much more meaningful than planting a few shrubs on traffic islands, isn't it? Ooh, Mantra, I'm so excited. Aren't you happy for us?'

'Very happy, Mum, congrats,' Mantra faked a cheerful voice.

'Thanks, darling. Oh and you won't get an inheritance from us, of course, since we're putting practically everything we own into this, so if you wish to poison us for our money, you have just a couple of weeks before we change the will,' her mother chuckled heartily. 'Now what was it you wanted to say, darling?'

'Nothing much, Mum, just hello. May I speak to Dad now?' Mantra couldn't bring herself to dump her problems on them. It would be cruel. They'd worry and that would make her feel worse. Better to have them happy, hell at least someone was happy!

After the conversation ended, Mantra experienced a sickening lurch in her stomach—it was the same feeling she'd had as a child when she'd lost sight of her parents in a busy, bustling fruit market. Luckily, they'd found her then. This time, she was old enough to find her own way home—if only she knew where the hell that was these days. She was well and truly abandoned. She attacked her emergency pack of cigarettes and lit up defiantly. The cigarette was stale but it felt good, and what made it better was that she was smoking it in her bedroom—a zone previously banned. What the heck, if Vir wasn't ever moving back in here, she could do whatever she wanted till she got the hell out of his life.

The act of smoking was conducive to deep contemplation, and with every thoughtful inhalation, Mantra regretted the fact that she'd lost touch with her old friends. After they'd had babies they were impossible to socialize with. After a hard day at the office, they'd play hysterical mothers in a bid to over-compensate for their absence, and weekends were spent in child-related activities. Even conversations on the phone weren't child-proof, with constant interruptions:

'Stop pulling your little sister's hair or you'll get what for!'

'No, the dog can't wear skates, darling.'

'You cannot leave the table till you finish every scrap of food on your plate even if it takes you ten years, understand?'

Wearying of this and resigned to resuming ties after their children had left the nest, Mantra had fallen back on Anjali by default. Being family had brought them together.

The drawback was at times like these she couldn't confide in Anjali—you can't very well tell your friend that you hate her brother—really, really, really hate him!

The doorbell rang and Mantra guiltily stubbed the cigarette out. Then she re-lit it, reminding herself that it was nobody's business what she did any more. She took a few puffs, hoping that if she delayed answering the door the caller would give up and go away by the time she got there.

The caller was still waiting, unfortunately. Even more unfortunate, it was Samira.

'Oh my God, Mantra! What happened?' Samira squawked.

'Fell, and I really can't talk now—it's painful,' Mantra grimaced, covering her lips with her left hand and wincing, hoping Samira would take it as a cue to depart.

Samira, however, made her way into the house and forcefully pushed Mantra down on the sofa. 'He beat you up good and proper, did he? All men are bastards!' she snorted, while peering curiously at Mantra's lips.

'He *did not* beat me,' Mantra said through gritted teeth. 'And if you don't believe me, check out the bedpost in the guest room—it still has blood on it, so there!'

Samira gave her a look that implied she didn't believe Mantra but declined to inspect the guest room. She thrust a card at her instead.

'Whatever. Anyway, my PR agent has organized an exhibition for my mosaic works of art next month, so be there, okay?'

'Congrats, will do,' Mantra said curtly, willing Samira to go away.

She did, fortunately. Her parting shot was an airy, 'You know, you really should take those self-defence classes you'd recommended to me. You look dreadful.'

When Mantra was in the act of shutting the door, Samira pushed it open and thrust another envelope in her hand. 'Oops

I almost forgot to give this to you—it's a thank you present for giving me guidance. You really need this, babe!'

The envelope had a gift coupon for twelve Botox sessions. Mantra chucked it into the bin and then retrieved it. Anjali would probably appreciate it—she'd been threatening to indulge in cosmetic surgery. 'To match my new youthful body,' she'd told a disgusted Mantra.

Anjali's body *had* become youthful. What was even more youthful were the clothes she'd started wearing. Body hugging, cleavage revealing T-shirts, and jeans that seemed to have been painted on her legs. A rather drastic change from her earlier elegant memsaab attire.

'How?' Anjali had coyly asked Mantra a week ago, as she preened outside a department store changing stall in a T-shirt three sizes too small.

'Well, um . . .' Mantra searched desperately for a euphemism when a comely teenager sporting an identical T-shirt popped out of the neighbouring stall for the approval of her friends. She definitely looked much better in it. It was obvious even to the over-confident Anjali. The teenager decided to rub Anjali's nose in it and gave her a pitying glance, whereupon all her friends giggled.

Anjali ignored her. Back in the changing room, as she peeled off the T-shirt she had muttered, 'We all grow old, darling. Someday your lovely matchstick thin arms and flat abs will be history too, yay!'

The changing stall walls were made of thin plywood. Anjali fervently hoped that the teenager had overheard her

'Let's go, Mantra, let's go,' she briskly said when she emerged. 'I'll buy you lunch as a treat for accompanying me. I've got loads to tell you about Shiv.'

Mantra hastily declined the offer, pleading work. She was horrified at the sneaky way Anjali's relationship was progressing. Even worse, she felt terribly guilty even listening to Anjali's emotional outpourings—she was *very* fond of Karan. She didn't want to be party to this and be labelled an accessory to the imminent crime. All her fervent attempts to put Anjali back on the straight and narrow had been irritably fobbed off. Even more incriminating was the fact that from her earlier, 'Oh come on, we're just good friends' excuses, Anjali had switched to a sharp, 'Stop being judgemental' statement. Shiv had not just come between Anjali and Karan, he was responsible for the decline in Mantra's easy rapport with Anjali as well.

Reluctant as she was to disturb Reshma in her examination preparations, Mantra intercommed her upstairs later that evening. The cut on her lip was hurting and the family doctor too may have thought that Vir had turned into a wife beater. After a searching examination, Reshma pronounced her okay.

'No stitches required, didi, just an antiseptic lotion and a few anti-inflammatory tablets. And try not to talk today, cool?'

'I think I'll just go to bed now. Don't mention this to bhaiyya, okay? Now get right back and hit the books!'

The phone rang soon after she popped a sleeping tablet—her feelings were hurting more than her cut lip. It was from Dr Mehta's clinic. 'This is to reconfirm your appointment for 11 a.m. tomorrow, ma'am.'

Mantra's instinct was to reschedule it—she couldn't go out in public looking like this, but better sense prevailed. A rescheduling would mean a delay for another few months.

'I'll be there,' she said curtly and hung up.

She didn't cry herself to sleep over Vir and her plan to walk out, though. It didn't merit any more tears—enough had been shed on that subject. The thought of Dr Mehta's examination took precedence in her mind instead, filling her with another kind of dread. It was more frightening than getting a tooth extracted, mainly because local anaesthesia is not administered before a Pap smear. This was the first time in her life that she wished she'd had a baby. She remembered that Anjali was never queasy about her visits to gynaecologists.

'After you get pregnant, you're stripped and poked and prodded so constantly by doctors and nurses that you lose your sense of dignity forever,' she'd once told Mantra in a matter of fact way. 'I often shamelessly breastfed Rohan in airport lounges.'

Anjali had shrugged carelessly at Mantra's horrified expression. 'Oh come on, these things are natural.'

25

Dr Mehta gasped when Mantra reluctantly shuffled into the room. 'What on earth's happened to you, Mantra?'

Mantra's hand involuntarily flew to her lips in an attempt to conceal the wound. She'd forgotten all about it. The anti-inflammatory tablets Reshma had prescribed had succeeded in dulling the pain, but the swelling hadn't subsided completely.

'My beloved mother-in-law socked me in the teeth,' was the terse reply.

'Good heavens! Is your husband aware of this?' Dr Mehta asked with concern.

'Nope,' Mantra shrugged. 'Besides, he wouldn't believe me.'

Dr Mehta shot her a strange look and then composed her face into her regular clinical mask. It was business as usual again.

Before the dreaded Pap smear and mammography, Mantra tried hard to persuade Dr Mehta that perhaps her menopause had begun.

'That's impossible, Mantra,' Dr Mehta said as she glanced through the reports of the tests Mantra had brought with her. 'Your hormonal tests are fine, your periods and oestrogen levels are normal.'

'But I've been getting those hot flushes or flashes or whatever you call them of late. It's horrible—my face sweats too!'

'Hmm. Have you considered that it may be the weather and not menopause? It's May and the temperature is soaring. Now stop with the delaying tactics and get your underwear off!' was the unsympathetic response.

As Mantra reluctantly submitted to the examination, she composed an article in her head, titling it 'SPCW—Society for Prevention of Cruelty to Women'. The Pap smear instrument was like a gigantic ice-cream scoop; it scraped her insides raw. The mammography machine was like a juicer, intent on ruthlessly squeezing her senseless. Instruments of torture, all.

'The reports will be ready next week,' the receptionist cheerily informed her, as she walked out battered and bruised, cursing Dr Mehta under her breath for molesting her.

On her way back home, the urgent feeling that her future had to be provided for prompted Mantra to instruct Makarand to take a detour to her former workplace. She almost changed her mind midway: Dr Mehta's sharp intake of breath at the sight of her swollen lip had made her wonder if she should delay the meeting, but now impatience prevailed.

Screw my bust lip! she thought. If people want to think Vir thrashed the living daylights out of me, it's their problem, not mine. Anyway, that bunch there probably won't even notice.

Her pretext would be a casual 'Oh, I was in the neighbourhood and decided to pop in to say hello.' She'd leave it to Partho to take it up from there, if he was interested—that's the way it was done. It was Makarand who was more excited. He drove like the wind in anticipatory delight of catching up with his former tea-drinking buddies and skipped a red light. He was handsomely rewarded with a ticket and a ticking off by the traffic policeman. Mantra had been looking out of her window in an abstracted way, so she wasn't aware of how the fight began. The sound of a sharp stinging slap broke her reverie and she jerked her head around to see the policeman's hand fly to his cheek in shock. The rest happened in a blur. Makarand shot into the car and sped away, leaving the outraged assaulted policeman hurling invectives and making a spirited attempt to chase the car.

'You absolute ass! How could you slap a cop? Now we're done for, aren't we? He's got your licence and our car number! Personally, I'd be delighted to hand you over when you're discovered. What the hell got into you?'

'He abused me,' Makarand roared self-righteously.

Mantra punched Vir's number into her cell phone and got a busy signal. As she looked up with a deep sigh, she noticed to her horror that Makarand was punching a number into his cell phone too.

'Put that down,' she shrieked. 'You'll get another ticket for talking while driving!'

'Arrey ma'am, I'm calling my lawyer. Everything will be okay.'

'You've got a lawyer?' Mantra gasped. This was too much. Now it was painfully clear that he was a member of the dreaded SNM party. He could do anything to anyone, policemen included, and get away with it.

Hello, Sirishji?' Makarand said in the politest tone Mantra had ever heard issuing from his lips.

Mantra leaned over and grabbed his cell phone. 'I'm keeping your phone with me till we reach the office. Call him then. I will not, absolutely not, allow you to break any more traffic rules and implicate me in the process!'

Her heart was still beating madly when she entered the office. She walked into her former department to find Partho in a paroxysm of rage, jabbing a finger at a copy of a newspaper and hurling insults at the chief copy editor.

'How the bloody hell did Trattoria become Prattoria, is what I'd like to know! That bloody restaurant has been in the bloody city for years and your subs can't bloody tell the difference? Next you guys will probably change Marine Drive to Zarine Drive. Get your bloody act together or get out!'

He stopped short when he caught sight of Mantra. 'And what brings you bloody here?' he snapped. 'Coming to gloat over our bloody low standards? And what's with your bloody lip?'

'Oooh, you noticed?' Mantra simpered mock-coyly. She grinned cheekily at him as was her wont, he glared ferociously at her in his usual fashion, and everything was reassuringly normal again. Before she could trot out her rehearsed excuse, he caught her by the arm and swung her towards his cabin.

'Honestly, Mantra, these incompetent eejits are going to kill me one of these days. Every day my bloody blood pressure hits new highs.'

Mantra meekly let herself be led away, while directing a sympathetic grimace at the chief copy editor.

'I hope you haven't come here looking for a job because I have nothing to offer,' Partho said abruptly, when they were seated.

'Not a job, no,' Mantra swiftly changed her plans. She wasn't going to beg. 'Freelance,' she added. 'I've come to offer my services as a freelancer. Anything. Subbing, edits, articles, whatever.'

'Thanks but no thanks,' Partho said dismissively. Mantra could tell that he was secretly exulting at turning her down. The grudge-holding sod was paying her back for quitting.

Neither of them noticed that the editor of the business section had popped into the room. 'Hello there, Mantra! If your services are still on offer, I'd love to have you write for us regularly. I enjoy your style. How about a weekly column?'

'Oh I'd love that, Zaheer,' Mantra bestowed a warm, genuine smile on him, 'but I'm afraid I know nothing about business.'

'I was thinking more on the lines of corporate satire —that's right up your street, isn't it? I still laugh over the stories you used to regale us with, the ones about Vir's colleagues. *Particularly* the one about meetings.'

'Ah yes,' Mantra smirked. 'The time when Great Revolutionary Leader decided that they wasted too much time on meetings and called for a series of super long meetings to discuss why they had so many.'

'Yup—that's my favourite one!' Zaheer grinned.

'Hmm. I think I'd like to do that. In fact,' she said, while directing an arch look at Partho, 'I have an idea for a column on weighty issues—the higher you go, the fatter you get!'

Mantra giggled at her own idea. Zaheer laughed at the innuendo. Partho, however, scowled and mentally trashed all those bloody page 3 dos he was forced to attend—they were to blame for his bloody weight gain.

'Love it, Mantra. You're on! Let's discuss it in my cabin right away, shall we?'

Mantra followed him without giving Partho a backward glance.

On the drive back home, she hugged the idea of the freelance assignment to herself. Zaheer had been very generous with the money and had even thrown in regular edit jobs as well.

'I'm thinking of offering you a monthly retainer deal, but don't get too excited yet. I have to get the CEO's approval, and remember he's Partho's drinking buddy.'

It was amazing, she marvelled, how just the day before she had been in the depths of despair, thinking that nothing was going right for her, and now she'd been given a chance to get at least one thing in her favour. Of course, she still had to wait for a bit before she could even look for accommodation. Zaheer had said he'd get back to her with the formal offer sometime next week. She already had the title of her column in her head: 'Up the Ladder and Around the Bend'.

She was brought back to earth by Makarand. 'We're going to a police station first, ma'am.'

'What do you mean "we"? *You* got into a fight and behaved atrociously, I didn't!'

'My lawyer's waiting for us there. He says you should accompany me as a witness.'

'Forget it. I'm not going to lie to save your skin. Drop me home and go yourself.'

Makarand stopped the car and refused to proceed further till Mantra agreed to accompany him. She tried Vir's number again and explained the situation to him. She was instructed to hand the phone over to Makarand.

She was dropped home meekly and the car keys were rudely thrust in her hand.

'Sir says that since I may take time at the police station it's better to leave the car here,' was his final, face-saving statement.

26

Every year, without fail, Anjali, Karan and Rohan went on a holiday in the summer to escape Mumbai's muggy heat—or the incredible sogginess of being, as Mantra morosely called it. This year, however, Karan had no takers. Anjali begged off on the excuse that her hands were full for a change—catering orders were sporadically coming in and she didn't want to turn anyone down till she'd firmly established herself. Rohan's refusal stemmed from the fact that this was the only quality time he had to spend with the object of his affection in Mumbai.

'And besides, Father, I'm too old for these sweet family thingies anyway. Next year I'll be working, remember? I'm a big boy now.'

'Don't bet on it!' came Anjali's sarcastic rejoinder. 'You've got to study to graduate, and all you do is listen to dreadful music when you're not worshipping at the feet of Her Hotness! And please stop playing your CDs so loudly. Believe it or not, Karan, the new cook ran out of the kitchen in panic when he played some music with frenzied screams and maniacal laughter—such rubbish!'

'Philistine!' Rohan retorted. 'Don't tell anyone that you don't appreciate Pink Floyd or they'll know for sure that you're a weirdo.'

'Don't you call me names!' Anjali snapped.

'Then don't call my girlfriend names either!' Rohan shot back.

Karan winced and buried himself deeper in the newspaper as the screaming match between Anjali and Rohan continued at increased decibel levels. This was not the time to guiltily confess that it was he who had given Rohan the Pink Floyd CD purely as a way to maintain peace at home. It had been one of his favourite bands when he was in college and he vaguely recalled that there weren't bad words in the lyrics. Anjali had been railing for weeks about the profanity in the songs Rohan listened to. It had begun when Rohan played Akon's *I want to fuck you* and gained momentum when she caught the word 'dick' in an Amy Winehouse song. Anjali had a jaundiced opinion on practically every song and every artiste that he listened to.

'I'll call Tanya whatever I want! "Junkie" is another word that comes to mind! Every time she's over, your room reeks of some suspicious odour.'

'Oh help,' Rohan moaned, 'you're so pathetically out of it, Mother, you really are. That's not dope, that's Gudang Garam, a bloody Indonesian clove cigarette! Tanya enjoys it because it has a nice biryani flavour—so there!'

Then he strode to his room, slamming the door behind him. Plaster cracked.

Anjali's shrill voice followed him. 'You're wasting your time on this harpy—people in love should look happy instead of wearing mournful hangdog expressions.'

'Take it easy, Anjali, don't get *that* personal. And you really shouldn't call Tanya "Her Hotness", you know, it's not nice,' Karan gently admonished her.

'Well, she's not nice either!' Anjali shot back. 'And I'm going to check up on that stinky Gudang Whatever cigarette too. I bet it's dope! Honestly, Karan, ever since she's come into Rohan's life, he's not been himself. He used to listen to cheerful music before, now it's only depressing drug-inspiring music like Pink Floyd.'

Karan shook his head helplessly—if she carried on like this, the only song Rohan would be allowed to listen to was the kiddie alphabet song with a missing letter 'F'. Maybe a missing 'P' too, if she was in an over-vigilant frame of mind.

'Darling, that hip hop lot does get into a lot of trouble too—they're always hipping and hopping out of jail,' he said reasonably. He gave her hand a placating squeeze. 'You've been on edge these days, is it that time of the month?'

'How dare you? How often do I have to tell you that my periods have nothing to do with my moods?' She glared and made her way to her bedroom, the sharp slam of the door echoing Rohan's earlier outstanding effort.

She locked herself in the bathroom and perched on the edge of the bathtub, her body still shaking with anger, her hands shielding her ears from the loud blast of music emanating from Rohan's room. Pink Floyd was playing defiantly despite the ban. 'Mother, will she tear your little boy apart? Mother, will she break my heart?' the singer yowled.

'Yes, yes,' Anjali waspishly hollered in response to the question posed in the song. 'Yes, Mother thinks she'll definitely tear my little boy apart and break his heart. Mother can give it to you in writing!'

Anjali had to admit to herself that much as she loved Rohan, sometimes she resented being a mother. It completely eclipsed her personality. And Karan was right—she *was* in an irritable frame of mind, but his rationale for it was way off the mark. She felt trapped with both Karan and Rohan at home. Karan had taken a week off to recharge his batteries and she had no privacy in which to conduct her daily phone calls with Shiv. Their conversations had subtly shifted from harmless flirting to out and out longing and desire. She wanted him so badly, the pain was physical and excruciating, and it took its toll not just on her but on Karan too. She started to find fault with him on the flimsiest of excuses, like leaving his towel on the floor, blamed him for everything including the lousy weather, brought up slights from the past ('On the night of 16 January 1987 at 9.52 p.m. you made a disparaging remark'), anything and everything she could hold against him, she did. Her guilt needed to be lightened and her frustration rose because Karan had been virtually blameless in his handling of her. When baser moods overtook her, she silently cursed the fact that he hadn't physically or mentally tortured her. If he beat me even once, or was nasty it would have been so easy to walk out now.

The *Mother* song was aborted abruptly and was replaced with the 'maniacal laughter' song. Anjali stamped her foot in rage when it began, but gradually the song got to her and she found herself not just sympathizing with the lyrics but identifying with them. Particularly the line, 'There's someone in my head but it's not me.' It was true—she felt like she'd been possessed. She was acting completely out of character. She was exhausted too—she hadn't been sleeping well of late; her mind was restlessly occupied with Shiv. When she did finally drift off into sleep, nightmares would plague her. Sometimes they'd begin as sweet dreams, Shiv and her happy together, and then guilt would strike her dream persona—'No I can't! What about Karan? What do we do about Karan?'—and the pleasantness would be shattered. Recently, creepier nightmares were becoming the norm. Just the night before, she had dreamt of being wordlessly ushered into a dinghy by malevolent-looking shadowy figures and being deposited in a deserted town crowded with dilapidated moss-encrusted temples and overrun by bandicoots intent on attacking her. She'd run to the waterfront screaming for help, but the dinghy and the shadowy figures manning it had deserted her—all that was left of them was a speck in the distance. That was when she'd woken up sweating and crying and Karan had cuddled and comforted her. She had no idea what Freud would have said. Mantra had been consulted instead, and her unsympathetic verdict fell on deaf ears. 'Stop communicating with Shiv. Period. You'll have wonderful dreamless sleep thereafter.'

Anjali's colourful dream had secretly stirred Mantra, though. If she'd still been writing her parody of the Great Indian Novel for Western Audiences, Anjali's elaborate dream sequence with its deserted Hindu temples would have been a nice touch. She could have tied it up with karma—readers in the West would have thirstily lapped it up.

I'm a horrible person, Anjali cursed herself. I'm cheating on Karan emotionally. I've got to stop this nonsense with Shiv right now.

Telepathy struck, because the very moment she'd firmly sworn Shiv out of her life, her cell phone beeped. It was a flirtatious text message from him. She promptly responded in like vein and a series of messages volleyed back and forth. Anjali was smiling tenderly again.

'Rescue me—Pink Floyd onslaught at home!' she messaged.

'Ah, wish u were here—dat's d name of one of their albums, u ABBA freak,' was the prompt response.

God, she loved him. It frightened her how badly she wanted him. She'd made all sorts of excuses to herself to desist from giving in completely. Gosh, she didn't want him to run screaming.

My legs are not waxed—he'll get turned off.
My water retention is so bad this week, he'll think I swallowed a beach ball.
If he gets too close, he'll notice that my roots are showing. Can't go in for a touch-up for another week or else the chemicals will make my hair fall in clumps.

Rubbishy excuses, but they worked. Vanity is a very effective deterrent.

27

Deafened by the music, Anjali didn't hear the doorbell announcing Vir's arrival.

'Where's Mantra?' Karan asked.

'Under the weather.'

'Hope it's nothing serious.' Karan's eyes reflected sincere concern.

Vir shrugged. 'If it was, would I be here? Come on, you know what Mantra the hypochondriac is like—she visits specialists for the silliest of things like paper cuts. She's got insanity in her DNA.'

As the words tumbled out, Vir experienced a fleeting feeling of guilt. The truth was, he had no idea what Mantra's problem was—all he'd heard from her was a muffled, 'You carry on, I'm not feeling so good', through the locked bedroom door. He hadn't so much as caught sight of her for the last few days. She'd kept herself locked in the bedroom whenever he was home. She was probably still sulking about the separate bedroom status, so it was just as well that there was no conversation. It was a relief, really, because Vir was in no mood for fireworks at home too. There were enough of those at work—he'd even got proof that Uday had his hand in the cookie jar. All he wished for now was a peaceful place to consider how to act on this information. Softly, softly catchee monkey. Thereafter, he would confront the board of directors with it. Maybe even leave the company. He'd got a few interesting offers, but he had to clear his name first. Then he would leave with his head held high and a squeaky clean record to boot.

'And where's my sister?' he inquired as Karan handed him a drink.

Karan shrugged. 'Sulking after a screaming match with Rohan.'

'Women!' Vir muttered shaking his head contemptuously.

'Women!' echoed Rohan, who had sneakily joined them, in a disgusted voice.

An animated discussion on the lines of Professor Higgins's 'Why can't a woman be more like a man' followed when all of a sudden Rohan got specific.

'Tanya wants a no strings attached scene,' he confided morosely.

'You lucky dog!' Vir exclaimed and Karan cheerfully added, 'Damn! I wish I'd known women like that when I was single!'

They both stopped laughing when they realized that Rohan did not look as thrilled at the prospect as they were.

'Hey.' Karan gently ruffled Rohan's hair. 'It's no big deal—you're too young for commitments anyway.'

'You know what the real problem is?' Vir added contemplatively. 'Women have changed so fast these days, men just can't keep up with them. They're leaving us behind now; they don't even need us to make babies any more. Anyway, you'll get over this shit. Everyone does.'

'I won't,' Rohan whispered. 'You have no idea how crazy I am about her. I'll *never* get over her.'

Vir and Karan laughed uproariously. 'Want to bet?' Vir challenged, but Rohan wasn't biting.

'I wish,' he sighed deeply. 'She told me she had a brief scene with someone last month after we'd had a tiff over the phone. I'm trying to forgive but I can't forget!'

'Dump her!' Karan exclaimed, looking shocked.

'Rubbish! If she was honest enough to tell you, why should you?' Vir jumped in.

'And I say dump Her Hotness!' Karan thundered. He was a sudden convert to the Anjali school of thought.

'Shh, Father, I don't want Mother to know!' Rohan hissed, glaring.

The warning was a timely one. A split second after it had been delivered, Anjali made a grand entrance into the living room. 'I'm off to meet a new client. Don't wait for me for dinner,' she announced to no one in particular.

'That's nice, especially considering that you invited me to dinner,' Vir said.

'Oops!' Anjali looked startled, and then added, 'I'm sorry, I just got a call. Where's Mantra?'

'She bailed out. Perhaps because she has ESP about rude hosts?'

Anjali stuck her tongue out at Vir before making for the door. If she hurried, she would have a whole hour with Shiv. She almost tripped over a rug in her haste and prompted Vir to make another affectionate remark. 'Good God, Anjali! Those are not heels you're wearing—they're bloody hills!'

'Oh shut up! By the way, I made your favourite tiramisu for dessert. That should more than make up for my absence,' were her parting words.

'Good she's gone,' Rohan muttered.

Karan leapt to Anjali's defence. 'Come now, the poor thing's been stressed out lately.'

'Rubbish! Must be menopause!' Vir scoffed.

Karan grinned. 'You're very fortunate she's not here to hear you say that. She gets positively livid when I lay the blame for her bad moods on hormonal imbalances.' As Vir sniggered, he continued: 'You know, sometimes I have to bite my tongue from begging her to take on less work because she looks so knackered these days. I know how important it is for her to prove herself, and I guess she'll soon figure out when to take it easy.'

'You're way too good for my sister.' Vir shook his head at Karan.

'Hey, Uncle Vir, isn't it your wedding anniversary next week?'

'So it is,' Vir said, ruffling Rohan's hair. 'Thanks for reminding me.'

Vir could feel himself unwinding after his second drink. It was good fun being with the boys and making inconsequential chatter. He felt kindly towards Mantra too. Maybe he had been too mean to her. He'd make it up and move back in to the master bedroom, but only after he sorted his office nonsense out. She'd understand—she was a good sort, not like those silly women who weep and wail if you forget their birthdays or anniversaries and spout weepy rubbish about not sending flowers any more.

While Vir was thinking affectionate thoughts about her, Mantra was at her bedroom window anxiously peering at the sky for signs of pre-monsoon showers. A couple of grey clouds drifted briskly past, but they were too wispy to provide even a drop of rain. The puffs of smoke from my cigarette are more robust, she thought scornfully, and got back to the book she was reading. To her horror she discovered that her eyesight had deteriorated further in the fifteen minutes she'd put the book aside. She had to squint desperately hard to read—a new reading lens prescription was called for. Mantra sighed. Why oh why can't the point size in reading matter for adults be as gigantic as it is in children's books? Children have better eyesight; it's us decrepit old sods who can't read! Oh I wish I could die before I grow older. I hate living!

When Vir returned, cheerfully humming a rugby song under his breath, he saw light under Mantra's bedroom door and knocked gently. No response. He knocked harder and got a terse 'What?'

'The anniversary is coming up; what do you want?' he asked in a spirit of bonhomie.

'A bloody divorce, that's what!'

Vir laughed good naturedly, and stumbled to his room. Mantra was a card!

It was just as well that the door had been shut and he hadn't seen the grim determination in her eyes and her tightened lips. Mantra badly wanted that divorce. She cursed herself for not learning life lessons in history class: Napoleon and Hitler were both short. How incredibly stupid of her to have married a short man!

She had no choice but to live in his flat till she got a job or died first. She was forced to do a shameless Samira—opt for convenience till she was capable of providing for herself.

She prayed that night—not for herself, she'd given up on herself. Her pleas were for Reshma. The exams were over and the results were awaited. Please God, let her clear the exams with flying colours. I want her to do well and get a place in the hostel, too, so I can leave here with a clear conscience. Please don't let her down again! Okay so I don't really believe in you, but if you really exist, prove it to me.

28

Mantra had already started writing her new column despite the fact that Zaheer hadn't given her the go ahead yet. Two long weeks had passed since he'd made the suggestion. She could just as easily have called him up, but what stopped her was the unwritten rule that if you sound too eager, people lose interest and undervalue you.

She reread the article she'd just keyed in, the first of the series:

UP THE LADDER AND AROUND THE BEND

The Higher You Go, the Fatter You Get

Cast your mind back to your famished days as the office rookie: starving for recognition, starving for meaty assignments and, well, starving for meatier food too. I'm sure if you think hard enough, you'll remember zillions of instances of your supe cheerily waving goodbye as he stepped out for an expense account lunch at some dead posh joint while you gloomily swallowed pig swill at the office canteen. For some, this has been a seminal moment in their lives, causing them to utter a fiery phrase that's as inspirational as the *Chariots of Fire* theme music: One day, I'll wine and dine as well as him, so there!

Flashback moment over. It's today, you're in one of the highest seats in office, and there's a distinct possibility that it's sagging under your weight. It's time to come to terms with something Confucius might well have said had he lived in our times: the higher you go, the fatter you get.

Oh, there are lots of things to blame it on. But I'd say globalization is mainly responsible for making your corpus global too. You want to be seen as a man of the world to impress your clients, so you wearily order whatever international cuisine is in, not having the foggiest what *tham ka plunk* really is or whether it will clog your arteries.

Power meals, however, aren't the only dietary pitfalls in your life. Your PR agency will insist that you make an appearance at dreadful events and page 3 bashes for the company to look good. So off you go, muttering darkly under your breath and rueing the fact that food cannot be surreptitiously tossed into potted plants the way alcohol often is.

I hate to say this, but your subordinates also have a lot to answer for, really. It's bad enough that they get married. You don't just absolutely have to be there to prove you're democratic, you have to eat there as well—and face it, the two wedding staples, paneer makhni and butter chicken, are equally bad for your waistline. It doesn't end there—the amorous sods shamelessly have babies soon after, even if you make them work 24x7! So you're back at their family celebrations again, condemned to eat your heart out of your body and into the hospital incinerator. What's worse is, you may be bored enough to write a puke-inducing book called *I Am Bunty's Heart* while recuperating post your transplant.

When you go on official tours, you'd think you could order a simple low-cal room service brekker at least, right? No way, José. Your branch head would have vindictively fixed up breakfast meetings with key customers to punish you for thinking that branches are places where people swing from trees, so it's off to the buffet with you. You may sanctimoniously place a bowl of muesli on your plate, but before you know it, some devil in you adds just a spot of baked beans and bacon, a cheese omelette (it smells so darn good) and a muffin because, heck, it goes so well with coffee.

It's infinitely worse for your waistline if you're married to someone who works from home. On those rare non-touring weekends when all you're fantasizing about food-wise is home-made creamy lentil soup delicately flavoured with sautéed garlic flakes and sprigs of cilantro, otherwise known as daal, your home-rooted spouse will speak wistfully about how long it's been since she's eaten out. Oh come on—it would be churlish to refuse!

It's a hard life, but you needn't let that harden your arteries too. There are ways to get around it. To ensure that you don't give in to high calorie temptation, consume a bowl of oats before a corporate do. Trust me, you'll be way too stuffed to consider eating even that olive in your Martini.

Better still, if you want to kill two birds with one stone, give away the yummies that inevitably arrive during festivals, publication launches, media anniversaries, whatever. You could offload them on to your personal assistant who has not just served you but your family well by fixing all their dental appointments and travel arrangements—that would be a lovely gesture. If you get almond rocks, however, don't give your loyal helpful personal assistant a second thought—hand them over pronto to subordinates who are in dire need of brain food. Now, that may do wonders for your bottom line and the company's bottom line as well.

The article seemed to be working, but her heart wasn't in it yet. Mantra's frustration levels had hit a new high. Perhaps once Zaheer calls—if he calls at all—I may feel more inspired, she reasoned wryly. And, more importantly, be economically empowered to move out. Damn Vir for turning out to be a big disappointment! Damn Mum and Dad for selling the home I could have moved into! Damn myself for not staying in touch with my friends after I got married—they may have provided succour and shelter from my current storm. And damn Zaheer too, for bringing up the freelance assignment in front of Partho—just when he'd joyfully turned me down. There's no way in hell Partho will let it happen now—his pathetic ego is at stake. Perhaps I should start looking for a full time job elsewhere. Not easy in the time of global recession. But, hey, sex is up in these hard times. Those Viagra, Cialis and penis enlargement vendors seem to be minting money. Maybe I could write the subject heads for their spam emails. I quite enjoyed the last few I read:

> Women will stare at your member like at a museum.
> You will love to measure your tremendous treasure.
> Say no to tiny-sized losers.
> A bigger baby maker is not a dream any more.
> Ten things to tell a naked woman.

Hello, I can churn out ridiculous stuff like that too and at least I'll be laughing while writing that crap!

She logged on to a job hunt site when the landline rang—it was Dr Mehta's receptionist.

'You still haven't collected your report, ma'am. Dr Mehta wants to discuss it with you. Would 4 p.m. today be all right?'

'Nope. I'm busy.' Mantra wasn't remotely interested in meeting Dr Mehta any more. Now that she was leaving Vir what was the point in reactivating her libido anyway?

'Tomorrow morning then?'

'No. I'm busy for the next few months.'

'I'm going to connect you to Dr Mehta.' The receptionist sighed. Patients could be so difficult and annoying.

Mantra didn't hold on. She hung up instead. The phone rang a few more times, and it was ignored. Mantra was busy, *very* busy, identifying job opportunities and browsing through company websites. Too busy for lunch too, despite Reshma's fervent entreaties.

A couple of hours later the phone rang again and Mantra sprang to answer it, hoping against hope that it was in response to one of her job application emails.

'Mantra, get your body to my clinic right now, do you understand?'

'I'm busy, Dr Mehta. I'm in a meeting,' Mantra glibly lied.

'Well, you'll have to excuse yourself then, Mantra. Tell them it's a matter of life and death. Which it may well be. I expect you here by 4 p.m. latest.'

Mantra gave in reluctantly and called for a taxi—she wasn't in the mood to drive. Makarand still hadn't shown up since that fateful day and she hoped he was in jail somewhere, subsisting on a diet of stale bread and water.

When she returned much later that evening, she didn't really care if any of the placement companies she'd written to would reply. She had found her way out of this mess called life. Of course, the tumour could be benign. The results of the fine needle aspiration test she'd just been subjected to would come in only a few days later. But she could hope in the meanwhile and pray for herself for a change too. As she tucked herself into bed that night, flashes of lightning lit up her room, heralding the first rains of the season. A good omen, as far as she was concerned. She dragged her bed to the window and slept like a baby with fat rain drops splashing her face, and woke up to the delicious fragrance of freshly washed earth, with a James Brown song playing in her head. *The* James Brown song—*I feel good.*

The rains continued for the rest of the day, soothing the parched earth and magically turning bronze into green.

Reshma's wasteland, too, got a new beginning. She'd cleared the exam with flying colours. Tears and cheers were exchanged with Mantra.

'Call bhaiyya and tell him the good news,' Reshma urged. 'I promised him I'd let him know the *moment* I found out.'

Mantra paused. Then she dialled the number and handed the phone to Reshma at the very first ring, retiring to her bedroom.

'Didi! Bhaiyya wants to talk to you.'

'Tell him I'll call back later. I'm busy.'

Like hell she'd call back. There was nothing left to say to him. Urgent important day-to-day exchanges were dispensed with in notes stuck on the fridge:

> Happy anniversary, old ball and chain.
> Screw you too.
> Send my special white shirt to the dry cleaners today—need it on Friday.
> Please do not feed the cockroaches—I noticed crumbs on the sofa last night.

Who knew that the fridge magnets given to them by friends as mementos of their holidays would be put to such good use?

29

Anjali was perhaps the only person in Mumbai who was using words that are not permitted in family newspapers or Parliament when it came to the monsoon. For two long days it unleashed its fury relentlessly, flooding the streets and forcing her to remain housebound. It was most unfair because Karan was in Singapore and she'd so been looking forward to spending quality time with Shiv without inventing excuses and fretting about deadlines. She and Rohan, not the best of friends still, were left moping at home, fighting over the right to use the laptop, arguing over the music, everything.

'Hello, you're supposed to be on study leave, this is not a holiday,' was her constant rebuke.

Rohan toyed with the idea of returning to his motherless room at the hostel. The only thing that held him back was the rising mercury in Delhi: his motherless room was also air-conditionerless.

Perhaps Anjali was crabbier because the regular bread man's replacement had addressed her as 'Mummy'. The cheek, considering that he looks like he isn't a day under sixty! she'd fumed inwardly. Even worse, she had to miss two whole days at the gym—exercise was such a fantastic stress-buster. The cleaner had been shocked to find her doing the sweeping and swabbing—well, she had to do *something* to keep her body shipshape. When the watery sun sank on the evening of the third day, it took the rain-soaked clouds with it too, and both Anjali and Rohan slammed the front door shut within minutes of each other. One to meet a girlfriend who had become an ex, and the other to meet an ex who'd become a boyfriend. Sort of.

The phone woke Mantra up with a start. She saw that it was still pitch dark and her heart started pounding in her chest. The digital alarm clock glowed 12.30 a.m. in an eerie sci fi green light that intensified her alarm. Phone calls in the middle of the night usually meant dreadful news. As she tentatively lifted the receiver, the words 'Mum? Dad?' were racing in her head, and her heart was hammering to the menacing beat of the theme music from *Jaws*.

'Vir?' came to her head too a split second later—a note on the fridge had stated that he was going to Delhi for an emergency board meeting. Heck, she still cared about him despite the fact that she hated him.

'Hello? Anjali!' she squawked. 'What's the matter?'

'I need to talk to you right now. Can I come over?' Anjali said urgently.

'Tell me what's happened now! Right now!' Mantra beseeched anxiously.

'Oh nothing. Well, something, but nothing for you to get excited about personally. It's about Karan and Shiv. I'm in the neighbourhood, so I thought I'd drop by and get some advice,' Anjali continued. She sounded hysterical.

By the time Anjali arrived, Mantra had splashed her eyes wide awake and fixed two steaming mugs of hot chocolate—the most comforting drink she could think of. She'd just laid them out on the coffee table when Anjali let herself in.

'I'm considering walking out of my marriage,' she said baldly.

'What? The bastard asked you to leave Karan for him?' Mantra wasn't prepared for this. It was too much, too soon.

Anjali didn't nod her head—she bit her lip instead. Shiv hadn't exactly asked her—why, he was too much of a gentleman to break up a marriage. All he'd said was that he was grateful for the scraps of affection she threw his way. Was she reading too much into his often flirtatious and occasionally earnest remarks? More importantly, was this deep and meaningful relationship just happening in her head? Would he eagerly and lovingly accept her if she offered to move into his life full time? *Very* difficult to tell with him. A shudder crept down her spine at the memory of Shiv recoiling when she'd presumptuously mentioned the word marriage thirty years ago. She wasn't certain any more. But something disturbing had happened. She had to act fast and act now.

Mantra silently handed a mug of hot chocolate to Anjali.

'Yuck. I don't want this rubbish—I'll get myself a glass of wine.'

'Oh no, I'm not having a conversation with you when you're drinking alcohol. If you've woken me up to discuss something serious, please do it while you're sober,' Mantra said coldly.

Anjali took one look at her icy demeanour and burst into tears. Mantra flipped through a magazine disinterestedly. She wasn't in the mood for nonsense.

'Say something, Mantra. Please, tell me what to do,' Anjali pleaded between sobs, wringing her hands dramatically.

'What can I say? If you love Shiv enough to leave Karan, go to him. Far be it from me to stand in the way of true love.'

'Oh drop the sarcasm and please help me decide. Please, Mantra. Please! Karan's got a job offer in Singapore and he's very keen on it. I *have* to decide soon!'

Mantra chucked the magazine on the floor and looked directly at Anjali for the first time that night. 'Okay. I'm going to interrogate you now, to get to the heart of the matter. I want precise answers—you have fifteen seconds to answer each question. Ready?'

Anjali nodded.

'Till Shiv came along, were you happy with Karan—yes or no?'

'Yes,' Anjali whispered, and then added, 'a bit bored, but sort of happy. Actually, more passive happy than active happy.'

'I'm not going to ask you if you love Karan. My question is, do you still like him?'

'Oh *yes*,' Anjali moaned, 'very, very much. That's what makes it so difficult, Mantra! I love both of them!'

Mantra's eyes widened with shock and her hands flew involuntarily to her lips. 'You love *both* at the same time? Oh my God, you've become just like a man! Your menopause must have begun—I've read somewhere that testosterone levels rise.'

Anjali snapped. 'Leave my hormones out of this, okay? I still have my periods so I'm fine! The thing with Karan is, you know, if he beat me or cheated on me or was an alcoholic or a junkie, I'd feel justified about walking out. But he's always been so nice and warm and understanding and I still do care deeply about him besides.' Anjali's voice broke and a spate of fresh tears followed, but Mantra continued her questioning regardless.

'Apart from making your blood circulate energetically, is Shiv nicer, warmer and more understanding than Karan?'

'No!' Anjali shouted involuntarily, and then glared at Mantra for luring her to an admission. 'He's different,' she added defiantly.

'Hmm, different from Karan. By which you're saying you have more in common with Shiv than with Karan, right?'

'No! Yes! I mean, God, I don't know. Stop asking difficult questions, for heaven's sake!'

'Then stop asking me to give you advice on difficult situations, Anjali,' Mantra retorted, the edge back in her voice.

The room was silent while Anjali gathered her thoughts together. 'Shiv makes me feel better about myself. I feel younger, more carefree, almost like I'm a teenager again, Mantra. He makes me forget that I'm wrinkly and middle-aged and have nothing to look forward to in the twilight of my life. I thought everything was over for me at my age—that I had nothing to look forward to but death. But Shiv brought me back to life. I feel special, really, really special, and so gloriously alive when I'm with him. He laughs at all my jokes and I'm not even a funny person! Mantra, I feel that this is my one last chance to live again. I do so want to take it—and I want it so bad.'

Mantra secretly understood Anjali's desperate fear of living without any more expectations or excitement in her life. She'd experienced it herself. But this was not the moment to sympathetically squeeze Anjali's hand with a wistful, 'I know *exactly* what you mean.' That may have encouraged her. This was the time to play the devil's advocate to save a family. So she chose her words carefully.

'You know, when you say that,' Mantra said quietly, 'you sound like practically every other married middle-aged person I know—male and female alike. You live with a person for so many years, you're bound to feel this over-the-top excitement for someone new. The truth is, I'm sure Vir and I and Karan, too, would dearly love to do what you're doing—get into a fresh relationship, have someone to flatter us and make us feel good about ourselves—that's why new relationships are fun, isn't it? The new love interest says such nice things. Hey, what do you know, you've inspired me to leave Vir, thank you for making me see the light,' she added sarcastically.

Anjali's jaw dropped. 'Goodness! You're going to leave my brother? For whom? Are you crazy?' Then she shot Mantra a filthy look. 'You're putting me on, aren't you?'

'Well, yes and no. There's our divorced neighbour in 8B who always gives me the once over. He's quite attractive and witty too actually, even though we've only exchanged pleasantries in the elevator. He'd make a pretty decent bore-buster. Six and a quarter on ten, to be precise. But the no part is, I'll never leave Vir for anyone because I'm not stupid. When I *do* leave your precious brother, it won't be because of another man in my life. Period.'

'Gosh, that means you really do love him,' Anjali exclaimed.

'No, all it means is, I'm way too smart to get into another relationship even with a decent guy because they all end up more or less the same. What a bore. And from this stems my advice to you, Anjali: Leave Karan by all means if you want to. Go to your sexy Shiv. But do not marry him. Please *do not* marry him even if he begs!'

'But why?' Anjali questioned, looking bewildered.

'Because, after a few months of living together, your scintillating conversations will become a distant memory. You'll have exactly the same dull and boring conversations you've had with Karan; you know, about bills and groceries and plumbers and carpenters. These are the only things Vir and I discuss too. You may find yourself interested in someone else again to, as you so nicely put it, make you feel like a teenager again. My God, you may become a serial divorcee! So, in the interests of less paperwork in family courts and saving the environment, live in—but don't marry! Get it?'

'You're just being downright nasty.' Anjali shot up in a huff, picking up her car keys to leave.

'I'm merely telling it like it is,' Mantra said in a hard voice. 'Grow up and get real, dammit. If you have to leave Karan, leave him for a man you can imagine growing older with. Someone who is warm and kind and steadfast enough to not let your wrinkles and chicken neck get in the way of affection. Someone you can count on to help you to the loo when you have arthritis, not someone who's merely in love with the idea of being in love. Those people invariably fall out of love too and who is the loser then? Fucking you, that's who!'

'I should have known that you'd be the wrong person to ask—foolish of me to expect you to be impartial. Heck, you've always made it clear that you disliked Shiv!' Anjali yelled.

'And for many years you hated him too, if I remember right,' Mantra said dryly to an empty room. The front door had been slammed shut mid-sentence.

Mantra burst into tears. Ragged tears that made her body shake and shudder uncontrollably. It was killing her to watch hopelessly as someone she cared about was being swept away by powerful destructive currents, wilfully ignoring her outstretched hand. Anjali did not want to be rescued and Mantra would have to accept that, difficult though it was. She missed the comfort of Vir—she'd have given anything to have his body to hug that night. Sure, it would have been rigid but at least it was warm. She picked up a cushion instead and crushed it to her face to muffle her sobs.

When the tears gradually subsided to a trickle, she brushed them aside with the back of her hand and noticed a lurid red smear. A fresh wave of alarm swept through her until she realized that she wasn't bleeding—the bloody cushion was! So much for these chic, ultra-expensive Indian handicraft stores, she thought and started giggling. Hysteria had taken over. And anyway, she reasoned, hopefully the tumour is malignant and cancer will kill me soon, way, way before Anjali realizes the enormity of the mistake she may make.

Still giggling, she dashed off a text message to Anjali: 'If you're honest with yourself, you'll realize that Karan is like fine wine and Shiv has the personality of plonk! These are my very last words on the subject.'

There was no response, she hadn't expected one. But at least she had said what had to be said. She went to bed that night with a fervent plea: I hope I don't wake up ever again. Suicide was briefly contemplated and dismissed. What held her back was the standard little paragraph that would appear in the papers, of which the most mortifying sentence would be: 'Middle-aged housewife commits suicide'. Better to be a never-mentioned nobody than to be described in such a shabby, dismissive way.

30

It was Reshma who first read the report on Mantra's tumour a week later. She'd answered the door to the courier boy and while she wasn't the sort to sneak a peek at other people's mail, this was too tempting to resist. It seemed like a laboratory report, after all. She re-read it four times to make sure. Vir was the second person to find out. A sombre Reshma handed him the envelope the second he entered the house.

'What, Reshma? No hello?' he cheerily inquired. Vir was in a great mood—he was finally in the clear as Uday Handa's shady goings-on had been exposed.

Reshma mutely placed the envelope in his hand and Vir settled down on the sofa, loosening his tie and making himself comfortable. His mind was at peace and his body yearned to follow suit.

He reached for the television remote control and was astonished when Reshma snatched it up and out of his way. 'Read this first, bhaiyya,' she urgently implored.

He read it. Then re-read it. When he finally looked up, he couldn't focus clearly. His vision was blurred. He got up and made for Mantra's bedroom—the door was shut as always.

'Didi's not home,' Reshma said softly. 'She told me she won't be home for dinner tonight.'

'Did she say where she was going?'

Reshma shook her head.

Vir nodded and dialled Mantra's number. It rang unanswered.

Anjali was clueless about Mantra's whereabouts too. 'I haven't spoken to her for the last few days,' she curtly told Vir. She was still sulking over her last fiery exchange with Mantra.

When Mantra returned that night, she was slightly tipsy. Zaheer was a heavy drinker and she had followed his example for a change. Besides she finally had something to celebrate—her column was through and the monthly retainer deal had been inked too; she was ready to go flat hunting as soon as she found a broker. She'd make do with a one-bedroom flat in the distant suburbs, she decided. That was all she could afford anyway.

She was humming to herself, happy to be alive for a change, when she let herself into the flat and then screamed. A harrowed-looking Vir was lurking menacingly on the other side.

'Why don't you ever answer your damned phone?' he snarled.

'Maybe because I have no interest in communicating with certain people,' was her cool rejoinder.

'Cut the crap Mantra—we have to talk.'

Mantra ignored him and strode into her bedroom, relishing the idea of slamming the door in his face. Her plans were foiled because he followed swiftly at her heels. She swung around to face him with a sneer. 'Sorry, but I'm not in the mood for a chat. We, no, make that *you*, have already established that this is my room—so get out!'

To her astonishment Vir enveloped her in a bear hug. 'I'm sorry, Mantra. Really sorry,' he whispered contritely. 'I'll explain—it's a long story. But first, why didn't you tell me about the tumour?'

'How did you know—' Mantra began, and then stopped short. She'd given instructions to the lab to courier her report to her residence. She'd wanted to see it first, before Dr Mehta got her interfering hands on it. That way, she was in charge of her own life or death.

'How dare you read my mail!' she screamed as she struggled to extricate herself from his tight embrace. 'I hate you, Vir, really and truly hate you! You want to talk? Then get this—I want a divorce! And I want it now!'

It took Vir over an hour to calm Mantra down. There was a more pressing matter to discuss, but he wearily conceded to himself that his apologies and explanations for abruptly shutting her out had to come first. When he got to the part where Uday had been unceremoniously thrown out of the organization, Mantra slapped him. Hard. While he was nursing the stinging blow on his cheek, she burst into tears.

'You're an ass, Vir—a total ass! If you'd only told me what you were going through, if I'd known that Uday had implicated you in his money-siphoning scam and that you were in danger of losing your job, you'd have spared me months of agony wondering why you behaved like you did. I thought you hated me all along. We could have dealt with it as a team, dammit!'

'Yes, I was an ass,' he agreed and held her tight again. He was relieved to note that she didn't struggle this time round. 'But I needed time to think and work out my exposé plan and the only free time I had was at home. I *needed* to be alone. Also, have you ever considered that I was trying to spare you the pain?'

'Spare me the pain? You gave me more pain over the last few months than I've ever experienced in my entire life! I thought you were put off by me because I can't—I mean, I don't have a libido any more,' she continued to wail.

'I was frustrated yes, but not frustrated enough to leave you for that! That's something I can deal with. Besides, Mantra, I discovered something during my nights in the spare bedroom that may interest you. I don't have much of a libido either.'

Mantra's tears subsided instantly. 'What? *Cosmo* doesn't turn you on any more?' she gasped.

'Not even *Playboy*,' Vir said wryly, and kissed the top of Mantra's head.

'Not even if I wear a negligee with tiger stripes?'

'Well, perhaps. I'm game to try it. But I can't promise.'

Mantra ruffled his hair sympathetically and was astonished to discover that he had a fringe. She held him back to examine his new hairstyle better.

'Good heavens, you've changed your hairstyle? Why? I liked the close-cropped look.'

Vir looked sheepish. 'Yes, well, the barber thought that, well, you know, receding hairline and all that.'

Mantra had a good laugh—the best she'd had in ages. She couldn't resist reciting one of Rohan's favourite childhood poems as she mussed up his hair again:

Fuzzy Wuzzy wuz a bear,
Fuzzy Wuzzy had no hair,
Fuzzy Wuzzy wuzn't fuzzy,
Wuz he?

Vir grinned. 'Hey, I'm ready to sing that sweet old-fashioned song to you in return—the one that starts with, "Darling, I am growing old, silver threads among the gold." Do you remember it? There was also a line about life fading fast away, I think?'

'Tsk, Vir, you always think of depressing things. It had some very reassuring lines too. "But, my darling, you will be, will be, always young and fair to me,"' Mantra sang with a broad grin.

'Ageing is no big deal,' she continued. 'According to my parents, growing old is very liberating. Dad frequently quotes one of Albert Einstein's lines these days: "I have reached an age when, if somebody tells me to wear socks, I don't have to."'

Vir laughed and nodded in empathy. 'Right, now that we've accepted the fact that we're old and decrepit, we're going to need to lean on each other more heavily. We'll share our problems, okay?'

That's when Vir seized the opportunity to tenderly settle Mantra on the bed and gently break the news that her tumour was malignant. He'd had a long chat with Dr Mehta and had fixed an appointment for the next evening with the surgeon she had warmly recommended.

They spent the night wide awake in each other's arms but wrapped in their own sombre thoughts. Mantra had discovered that there was perhaps a God after all, now that her fervent prayers for a shortened stay on earth had finally been answered. Not a very nice chap this God, granting wishes after you stopped wanting them. She resolved to switch back to atheism. It was easier to accept the fact that life was just plain shit and it wasn't because of some sadistic higher power's whims.

'It will mean a mastectomy, I assume,' Mantra mumbled after a long, long while.

'It may, according to Dr Mehta,' Vir reluctantly revealed, hugging her closer as silent tears dampened his T-shirt.

'That means that in 2011, when I can finally have sex again, I'll be disfigured and you'll be put off!' The silent tears had become wails.

'If I wanted a *Playboy* bunny type, I'd have married one!' Vir shushed. 'I've never been a breast person. I'm leg man—always was.'

'You're a liar!'

'Nope! You were in shorts when I first met you—it was your dead sexy legs I fell in love with first, if you recall. I never bothered to check out your breasts before I ventured a nervous hello.'

'And if I'm a victim of a terrorist attack and one of my legs have to be amputated will I still turn you on then?' Mantra argued reasonably.

'Yes, because your legs were just a shallow attraction. It's your brain that turns me on the most. Even when you ask me ridiculous questions like you're doing now!' he retorted.

'One more question—if my brain was damaged or I had Alzheimer's would you still love me?'

Vir sighed wearily. 'I think you've asked me this idiotic question before, and my answer remains the same. If you have Alzheimer's how will it make a difference whether I still love you or not? You won't even know who I am, dammit!'

'You're a bleeding unromantic sod!' Mantra muttered and snuggled closer.

'And you're like bleeding God—your mind works in bloody mysterious ways.'

It was a puzzled Vir who broke the silence a while later. 'Mantra, why did you say you can have sex in 2011?'

'I'd read this article in the papers the other day. They're working on a sort of Viagra pill for women called LibiGel—at least I think that's what it's called. Anyway, if it's a success, they're planning to launch it in 2011. I've cut the article out—I'll show it to you later. And, by the way, those porn DVDs at home? Those weren't Rohan's. I'd got them to try and find my mojo.'

Vir turned the bedside lamp on to get a better look at Mantra's face. 'Goodness, Mantra! You watched porn because you cared about me?'

Mantra blushed deeply in response and Vir shouted with laughter. 'And would you have been willing to swallow lizard poop and all those other vile concoctions they have for flagging libidos to keep me happy in bed?' he teased.

'Not lizard poop, never! I don't love you *that* much!' she asserted firmly.

'You know what, I may have done that just for you. See, I need you more than you need me.'

He really did feel deep affection for Mantra—she was deliciously insane. He was certain now that they would win her fight against cancer armed with their customary laughter—not helpless, wimpish tears.

Mantra tugged Vir's sleeve for attention. 'I've just had another depressing thought—if I have to have surgery and other things, I may not be able to write that column for Zaheer now.'

'And why not?' was Vir's challenging response. 'It's just your right breast that may go, not your right hand! Seriously, Mantra, I want you to keep yourself busy. Everybody needs to keep busy to distract themselves from the day to day miseries of life. I honestly believe that if you had done something, hell anything, during these last few months, you wouldn't have lost your marbles. Even selling Tupperware may have saved you from harbouring ridiculous thoughts of leaving me. An idle mind honestly is a devil's workshop.'

Mantra gasped with horror. 'What! You want me to organize Tupperware parties?'

'Oh, rest assured I'd go to any lengths to keep you by my side! But I have to concede that a column is a better idea.'

'Hmm. Hey, what do you think of an article advising a boss-type person on how to drink with the boys? See, this is a highly refined art and the trick is to maintain a fine balance. If you get smashed out of your skull and do an Elvis imitation on a table top they'll laugh at you behind your back. If you nurse your drinks and get starchy with riotous drunk subordinates, they'll trash you behind your back. The article would sort of tell the boss-type how to fit in without making an ass of himself.'

'Not bad,' Vir sleepily mumbled. He hadn't actually registered a word of what Mantra was saying.

31

After a series of further tests, a mastectomy was what the surgeon ordered. Reshma was acting the most difficult over it. She was expected to move into the hostel in a few days to start her term at college, but she resisted.

'I'll stay home with you, didi, till you recover. I'm sure it's okay if I start college a month later.'

'It's absolutely not okay!' Mantra growled. 'Now don't be a silly girl. We adore you but we'll manage just as well without you.'

Acrimonious arguments and tears followed. 'And who will cook for bhaiyya when you're in hospital?' Reshma finally played what she thought was her winning card.

'Our ex-cook from Dubai, that's who,' Mantra assured her with a gleeful smile.

Kaushalya was rejoining the family in a week's time. It was so unbearably hot in Dubai, she had hot-footed it back to Mumbai, money be damned. Besides, she disliked her employers there—Mantra didi was a goddess in comparison. Her only disappointment was Makarand—it seemed that he'd vanished. There was some gossip going around that he was in jail for something or the other. Even worse, the security guard had informed her that he'd finally had a son—too bad, because he'd promised to make Kaushalya his second wife. Ah well.

Over the next few weeks, Mantra bravely prepared herself for the surgery, trying to come to terms with losing a part of her body. It must be said that Kaushalya's delicious cooking helped considerably in increasing her dopamine levels. Strict instructions were given to Vir that her parents must not get wind of her condition.

'I absolutely agree. Apart from getting terribly upset, they'd probably insist on some very wacky quacky cures for you. You'd be cruelly tortured in the name of parental love.'

Mantra giggled. 'Now that you mention it, Mum *did* say that she'd met a very good witch doctor from Arkansas at the ashram.'

Vir snorted.

Meanwhile, Anjali was still struggling to decide which person in her life she'd prefer to lose: Karan? Or Shiv? Karan was returning from yet another trip to Singapore that evening—the deal was practically in the bag, he'd said, he just had to study the written offer in detail before signing up—and she promised herself that she'd decide one way or the other by the next morning. Eventually, it was Rohan who solved her nerve-wracking dilemma.

Mother and son had kissed and made up, and their relationship was warm and cosy again. While Anjali was indulgently organizing sinful deep-fried rainy day snacks for him in the kitchen, he was sprawled on her bed idly playing games on her cell phone when it beeped. Oddly enough, while teenagers may place frightening 'Keep out or else' signs on their bedroom doors and throw terrific tantrums if their parents so much as accidentally overhear their telephone conversations, they fail to understand that their parents' lives are private too. As if on auto pilot, Rohan casually read her message. He was shell-shocked. With shaking hands he opened her message inbox and swiftly speed read a few of her saved messages. It was with dread that he opened her sent messages too—a one-sided longing was his last hope.

That hope was cruelly dashed in quite the same manner as the rocks that were being viciously pummelled by the sea outside his window.

Fuck! Fuck! Fuck!

The confrontation took place when Anjali lovingly handed him a plate of sizzling hot sesame prawn toasts. He flung it violently against the wall.

'Give those to your boyfriend, you slut!' he snarled, and strode out of the house slamming the door behind him.

A second later, he rang the doorbell insistently. He wasn't finished yet. He marched into the bedroom to find Anjali slumped on the edge of the bed, her face buried in her hands. Her cheeks were burning with shame as she imagined Rohan reading those text messages. Oh God! She was scum in his eyes.

'Go to that bastard—my father's too good for you!'

'I'm not going anywhere. I'm staying here,' she whispered in as steady a voice as she could manage, and then broke down. Poor Anjali. Once again her family had got in the way of what she thought was her true love, but this time she gave in of her own free will. She'd just had a revelation: Rohan was the only person she really loved—she'd willingly kill for him, die for him, go to jail for him, be tortured for him. All her strongest emotions were reserved for him alone. How could she have let this one person down?

The sight of his unrecognizable mother weeping copious tears made Rohan break down too.

It was raining cats and dogs and elephants too. Rohan was soaked to the skin. His shirt clung to him like cling film, his jeans were getting heavier by the second and his shoes squelched as he walked down Marine Drive, pausing occasionally to gaze reflectively at the turbulent Arabian Sea. He loved it when the waves rose up in revolt to give passers-by a stinging slap, leaving a gritty, salty reminder in their wake. Salty like the tears that wouldn't stop streaming from his mother's eyes. He wished she would stop weeping. He wished he knew how to comfort her. He wished he hadn't found out. Fuck, he wished that it had just been a bad dream.

He glanced obligingly at his watch when a passer-by asked him the time—it was 8.45 p.m. Father must be back home by now, he thought. Either he was cheerfully unpacking or packing to leave for a long, cold spell. Maybe forever. Fuck!

'I have to tell Karan, I absolutely must,' Anjali had sobbed. 'I can't live with this guilt any more.'

'For God's sake, don't do it, Mother!' he had shouted. Then, when she visibly flinched at the harshness of his tone, he had flinched too—seeing his mother broken, defeated and piteously human made him feel physically ill.

'Don't worry, your secret is safe with me,' he had added gently. He should have given her a reassuring hug, but he couldn't bring himself to touch her. Who is this person? he wondered. Do I know her? Not really. Not at all, in fact.

'But I—'

Rohan had cut her guilt-wracked protests short. 'It will break him. Don't. Please.' After a long pause, he added, 'Look, whatever you decide to do, please don't tell him that I know, okay?' He'd be damned if he let his relationship with his father be strained too.

Thereafter, he had left the house, leaving it to her to make the final choice.

Sitting on a rain-soaked bench with his head between his hands, he retched. He remembered the story Aunty M had told him about the time she'd whisked her maid off to a police station to register a complaint against her husband for domestic violence. The maid was battered and bruised, but never opened her mouth to speak. It was Aunty M who did all the raving and ranting, but the cops never took her statement.

'Why are you coming in the middle,' they'd told her indifferently. 'Leave these people alone, it's between them. *Aapas ki baat hai*.'

The maid had turned and resolutely walked out of the police station. A stunned Aunty M had had no choice but to follow.

I must drop the guilt, there's nothing I can do, thought Rohan. It's between them. I just have to make sure I divide the comfort and support in equal measure. How did that poem go? Ah, yes—'They fuck you up, your mum and dad, they don't mean to but they do'. Brilliant poem. That man really knew what he was talking about.

Rohan felt he'd become older and wiser. Not wiser actually, but sadder, he corrected himself. The correct expression should be older and sadder. Damn, I feel horribly pseudo and profound.

He wasn't going home that night. Perhaps he'd spend it here by the sea, or at a friend's place. He couldn't burden Aunty M and Uncle Vir with this terrible problem. It was his mother's awful secret, for starters, and he was determined to shove that skeleton into a cupboard and lock the door firmly. Besides, Aunty M's mastectomy was scheduled for the next day. She had problems of her own. Fortunately, he had the foresight to send a text message to his mother telling her he wouldn't be back that night. It was the least he could do to save her from more worries.

It was when he watched the sun rise from the window in a strange bedroom that he experienced a weak ray of hope. His mother had feverishly repeated over and over again that she hadn't gone all the way with the creep, like that was some redeeming feature. Such hypocrital bullshit—a bit like Bill Clinton declaring that he hadn't inhaled dope. Cheating was cheating, whether it was emotional or physical. Rohan wasn't sure if he believed her, but he hoped like hell that his father did. After he showered, he made his way to the hospital where the surgery was scheduled.

Another text message was sent to his mother: Don't come to the hospital—I'm standing in for both of you.

Waiting at the reception area for Aunty M and Uncle Vir to arrive, he gloomily wondered if the fact that his mother had not replied was a bad sign.

Fuck! Fuck! Fuck!

32

As a sombre Vir was driving to the hospital for the surgery, Mantra experienced an overpowering urge for a smoke. 'Just one cigarette, please,' she begged Vir in a shaky voice. 'I promise it's the very last.'

Vir's lips tightened and the car screeched to a halt at a cigarette stall they encountered on the way. He nimbly stepped out and returned with a pack of tens and a match box. The air conditioner was switched off and windows were rolled down.

'We still have half an hour to spare. I'll drive around aimlessly till you finish that lot off if you wish,' he gruffly offered.

Of all the tender gestures Vir had ever made in their lifetime together, this one touched Mantra the most. She also greatly appreciated the fact that he didn't wave the smoke away with his usual disgusted expression or fake offended coughs. Mantra exercised restraint though, and smoked only half a cigarette; mainly because her hands were shaking uncontrollably.

'Sure you're done?' Vir asked as Mantra ground it into the ashtray. When Mantra dumbly nodded her head, he crushed the pack in his bare hands and flung it on to the back seat.

'Like, wow! As Rohan and Reshma would say,' Mantra qualified her exclamation. 'You're a strong man!'

'Hmm. This is nothing. See what I'll do to you if I ever catch you smoking from this second onwards!'

A relatively calm Mantra was wheeled into the operation theatre, with a visibly nervous Vir rushing along at her side. She'd made a special effort to be cheerful to keep his spirits up. He looked like the proverbial lamb being led to slaughter.

'Tell me, from where you're standing, do I look like a bit character in *ER*?'

'The heroine, not a bit character!' he gallantly responded with a fleeting smile.

'That's better.' Mantra applauded. 'Come on, chin up, Vir! I'm relieved this surgery is finally happening. I feel like I have an evil gremlin or alien or something inside me, ready to tear out of my tummy oozing slime, like in that ghastly movie. I'm longing to evict it ASAP!'

'A few hours from now, that gremlin will be out,' Vir grimly promised with a conviction he did not feel. Mantra wasn't aware of the warning the surgeon had given him in an aside. The tissues would have to be sent to a lab to ascertain whether the cancer had spread to the lymph nodes. If it had, this was just the first battle in the war of gremlin eviction.

It was Mantra's turn to look ashen-faced when the anaesthetist began to swab a throbbing vein in her arm. Needles terrified her, and three nursing attendants were called in to hold her shuddering body down while Vir tried to distract her with engaging conversation.

'I'm going to start looking for a house of our own while you recover,' he cleverly said.

'*You're* going to look? Never! I'm going to choose it or else we'll be living in a bleeding tree house in leopard-infested Sanjay Gandhi National Park!'

'Now, that's an idea,' Vir grinned.

'Don't you even think of it!'

'Hey, you brought it up, I didn't.'

And the needle was out. As the countdown began, Vir started looking grim again, while Mantra was experiencing the best high she'd ever had in her life.

'Hey, Vir,' she beckoned him closer and whispered. 'I don't need to wait for female Viagra after all. Just pinch some of this incredible anaesthesia stuff, okay? I'm totally turned on.'

He nodded with a faint smile.

'By the way, in case anything happens to me, I have the grand sum of Rs 4.3 lakhs in my bank account,' she added drowsily with a giggle. Her words were getting slurred.

'Mantra! Don't say things like that!' Vir rebuked her, and then he laughed. She was teasing him by throwing an old remark he'd made in his face. 'Bitch!' he said affectionately, but she didn't hear. She was out.

Vir and Rohan sat side by side outside the operation theatre during the surgery. Both were tense and silent, lost in their thoughts, when Rohan's cell phone beeped. It was a message from his father and he opened it with trepidation. 'Am at reception. Get me a pass to join you.'

Fifteen minutes later, three grim and silent men were seated side by side. Karan, by far, looked the most drawn. Not a good sign, Rohan noted, with an inward groan.

33

Later that evening, when Anjali joined them during visiting hours, Rohan knew that she had indeed told his father. Their body language said it all. They sat far apart from each other without exchanging a single word. Maybe Rohan imagined it, but he thought he saw his father flinch when Anjali entered the room.

Vir was lost in Mantra, holding her hand as she wavered in and out of consciousness. The looks he cast at her were so tender, even Rohan was surprised. He'd never seen his uncle so absorbed in his wife in his entire life. Now, that was a sturdy marriage playing out before his eyes. When one partner was down and out, the other was ready and waiting to do the picking up. If only his parents cared about each other like that. His aunt and uncle would never ever have experienced marital problems, the lucky things.

The three silent spectators got up slowly and very reluctantly when an urgent bell rang the end of visiting hours. A desperate Rohan suddenly had an inspiration.

'I'm staying with Uncle Vir till Aunty M gets back home,' he eagerly offered. His father, he noted, looked relieved. Thereafter, Rohan took great care to meet his aunt after visiting hours. He'd borrow Vir's twenty-four-hour pass to sneak in at times when he was certain the coast would be clear of his parents. Just as well that I'm old enough to live independently, he thought with a twinge of self-pity, or else my parents may have completely destroyed my life.

On the last day of Mantra's hospital confinement, Great Revolutionary Leader's wife deigned to pay her a visit.

'You may never have got cancer if you had babies. Breast feeding reduces the chances,' Mrs Sharma declaimed in her usual regal way.

'Oh really?' Vir sprang to Mantra's rescue with a charming smile. 'I wasn't aware you'd studied medicine. Now, Reshma here is studying medicine. Resh, is she right?'

'That's just a theory!' Reshma scoffed.

Mrs Sharma was made of sterner stuff. 'You don't have to study medicine to know these things,' she said in a supercilious way while studying Reshma's face suspiciously.

Her parting words to Mantra were delivered in an urgent hiss: 'Listen, Mamta, I don't know if you've noticed this, but that girl has Vir's nose. Oh yes, that's his nose—definitely his nose!'

Mantra gasped as Mrs Sharma nodded significantly and then sailed out of the room.

'That bitch implied that Reshma is your love child with some other woman!' she complained to Vir in an outraged manner after Reshma left.

He wrinkled the very nose Reshma was alleged to have inherited. 'She's an ass—just like her husband. But worry not, that's the last we'll see of them. Sanjay is off to head a branch somewhere in Eastern Europe.'

'What? You mean he's got a promotion after being blind to Uday's slimy act?' Mantra was disgusted.

'Not a promotion—he's just been kicked upstairs. That's the worst branch in the company's global network and it's rumoured that it may be shut down in the near future,' Vir smirked. 'I'm willing to bet he's frantically meeting headhunters as I speak.'

Rohan did not go back to his parents' home when Mantra

was discharged. The coward returned to college in Delhi to complete his study leave there. He did pop back home briefly to pick up his things and congratulated himself on making the right choice. Delhi may have been sizzling hot but the atmosphere at home made him sweat even more. However, the fact that his parents were still living under the same roof was an encouraging sign. What gave him more hope was the fact that his mother's cell phone was parked on the dining table. Nobody who has secrets does that. Maybe they'd work things out eventually.

If only Rohan had known that his father would pack his bags and move out a few hours after him, not slamming the door behind him but pulling it gently shut as was his wont. Perhaps that may have made him stay in Mumbai longer.

34

Anjali did not want to burden Mantra and Vir at a time like this but what choice did she have? They were the only people she had left who perhaps still cared about her. She arrived at their door with an overnight case and a bald statement: 'Karan and I are through.'

Vir was livid. His reaction was the usual 'Let me at him' brotherly rant.

Anjali put up a restraining hand and gave Mantra a significant look. 'If there's anyone to be punished, it's me.'

'She's right, Vir. Now I don't think you should be part of this girlie discussion, so leave us alone to talk, will you? Go watch TV, or play your stupid computer games. Just leave us in peace.'

Vir left the bedroom looking puzzled. Ah, it's probably some silly woman thingy blown out of proportion, as usual, he thought dismissively. If it's dead serious stuff, Mantra will tell me about it later. But it can't be serious—Anjali looks calm and collected, not frazzled.

Au contraire. Anjali was sobbing her heart out behind the locked bedroom door while revealing the secret that Rohan badly wanted buried forever.

'Be nice to my baby. He finds me so repulsive he didn't even hug me when he left. He hugged Karan, though. A long hug that lingered,' she said enviously.

'Of course I'll be nice to him. I'm *always* nice to him.'

'Yes, but be extra special nice. Please! Call him now—casually find out what he's up to,' Anjali urged between sobs.

Mantra called him, but neither of them could hear each other clearly. Rohan was at a pub with his buddies and the music was deafening. Fuck, it's such a relief to hang out with normal people again, he exhaled, relaxed for the first time in days.

Later that night, Mantra gave Vir a brief gist of Anjali's problem. He let out a low whistle. 'My sister cheated on him? My propah tight-arsed sister?' he said in awestruck tones.

When the enormity of the situation finally got to him, the awe was buried under mounds of despair. 'He'll never take her back. Never. Hell, I have no idea what I'd do if I were in his shoes. Thank God my parents aren't alive to see this. My mother would have been hysterical.'

'You be nice to her, okay? She needs us now,' Mantra said sternly and punched him on the shoulder. Her punch was followed by a sharp yelp of pain. She shouldn't have lifted her right arm—the area was still sore.

Anjali spent the night in the guest bedroom, but Mantra and Vir found her asleep on the living room sofa the next morning. Mantra looked on approvingly as Vir covered her with a blanket without any prodding. He was a nice chap when he wasn't stressed out—cool and caring. A fantastic combination.

When Anjali finally woke up around noon, she shuddered as she recounted the horrors of the night before. 'That room is haunted—I swear to you, Mantra, it's haunted. Every time I drifted off, the bed started shaking violently. Gosh, it was scary. That knock-out tablet you gave me just didn't work in that room.'

'Rot! That room is not haunted,' Vir scoffed. 'Every time I've been there, I've slept like a baby.'

'So you would,' Mantra softly muttered to herself shaking her head, 'so you would.' Indian mothers—really!

It was Mantra that Karan first made contact with a few days later. He did not ask for a divorce—he merely implied a separation. Anjali was free to live in his house in Mumbai while he moved to Singapore.

'The talks have been on for a long time—I'd been dithering since Anjali wasn't keen on the idea. It's all worked out nicely now, hasn't it?' he couldn't resist adding bitterly.

Karan was a bloody decent sort, Vir and Mantra agreed. He'd offered to transfer a very comfortable monthly sum into Anjali's bank account, and a touched Mantra had accepted on her behalf.

'How dare you? Tell him I don't want his money—I don't deserve a penny!' was Anjali's distraught reaction.

'Then you tell him yourself,' Mantra said firmly. 'If I have to play the go-between, I will only negotiate arrangements that I believe are fair.'

Anjali didn't call him. Not because she accepted that the arrangement was fair but because she was too frightened to speak to him. She wouldn't touch his money, she promised herself. The house, though, she would live in—what choice did she have? Mantra's spare bedroom gave her the shivers.

Rohan flew in to Mumbai to wish his father goodbye. The farewell was more cheerful than tearful—both made a concerted effort to achieve that. Uncle Vir had a great surprise waiting for him when he returned from the airport to spend the night at their place; he couldn't bear the idea of spending time with his mother—not yet. They were going to camp at a tiger sanctuary the next morning—a male bonding session.

'Fantastic! Oh shit, I'm not carrying any shorts and things.' He needn't have worried. His mother had thoughtfully sent a tote bag with the things he'd need. Amazing. Even when he didn't take her for granted, she delivered. Rohan soon discovered that Uncle Vir wasn't as considerate as his mother, however. He was being shaken awake at 4.30 a.m. for the third morning in a row.

'Oh give me a break,' he sleepily whined, 'we never saw any tigers the last two days, what makes you think we'll see one now?'

Vir callously poured a mug of icy cold water on his face and growled. 'Get out of bed. Now! Jump to it!'

No tiger was spotted that morning either. It was on their next trip into the forest in the evening that they saw one at a watering hole. It was fortunate that Rohan and the guide had well-developed muscles because it took all their strength to hold an overjoyed Vir from leaping out of the jeep. For a brief moment, the tiger turned its piercing gaze on them.

Rohan gasped and felt a thrill running through his body. The lines of a William Blake poem he'd never appreciated at school tumbled involuntarily into his head:

Tiger, tiger, burning bright
In the forests of the night,
What immortal hand or eye
Could frame thy fearful symmetry?

Aunty M was right. Poetry wasn't all that wet.

35

Mantra and Vir moved into their new house on their wedding anniversary. They were having a house-warming party—just the two of them since Anjali and Rohan the Graduate were spending a week in Singapore with Karan. That was Rohan's idea, taking Anjali along. His father had disinterestedly agreed with a flat 'If that's what you want, it's okay by me'. Rohan was too realistic to hope that his parents would get back together again; his father's lacklustre response had squashed his hopes. But they could perhaps be friends at least?

His mother was stubbornly unwilling, initially.

'Oh come on, Mother,' he cajoled. 'This may be my last holiday together with the family. I may not return after my MBA in the US for years—I'll have to work there and earn in dollars to pay off my massive student loan.'

'Oh well, I can pick up a few interesting ingredients in Singapore, I guess.' She finally gave in when Mantra enthusiastically added her bit to Rohan's unrelenting cajoling.

She'd changed, his mother. She was quieter and more introspective than before. So introspective, in fact, that she'd stopped playing the brisk, bustling, interfering mother hen. It was Rohan who had to initiate the hugs these days, despite the fact that she willingly returned them with an intensity that never failed to make him experience a twinge of sadness.

Fuck, she responded with gratitude—how sad was that? Over time and, of course, counselling sessions with Aunty M and Uncle Vir, he had forgiven her, absolutely and unconditionally. All he wanted was to see her eyes light up and sparkle when she smiled—just like they used to. It was a blessing that her catering business had taken off in a big way. That, at least, must give her something to feel good about.

Shiv had caught a brief glimpse of mother and son at Mumbai airport. He immediately darted out of sight, dutifully following the terse text message he'd received on his cell phone about a year ago: 'Never call me again. Stay away. Please, I beg you.'

He'd wondered about it for a bit, then let it go. She was a *lovely* girl—he was fond of her and wished her happiness and all that. A warm glow spread over him when he recalled that he was solely responsible for identifying a career for her and launching it too. That more than made up for his shabby treatment of her when they were teenagers, didn't it? His dues were paid—he was the good guy now, someone she'd think of with deep affection for the rest of her life. It all worked out okay really, considering that he'd started feeling a little claustrophobic in her company. Her intensity frightened him. Ah, just as well.

Vir uncorked the champagne, and they took a sip and cheered the new house. After which Mantra grimaced and switched to her regular vodka. That tasted so much better, really. When Vir ventured into the kitchen to fix dinner (it was his idea and Mantra was determined to appreciate the food even if it killed her), she settled herself in a comfortable armchair and browsed through the papers.

It was reported that a good monsoon was predicted for the year. A municipal corporation official was quoted as being overjoyed. He'd faced the ire of Mumbai's residents after the relatively dismal show the year before. The rains had been heavy, but too few and far between to fill the lakes that filled the buildings' overhead tanks. Air currents had abducted the rain-filled clouds and swept them away to shower joy on another country.

A wry thought stole into Mantra's head as she put the papers down with a sigh. Last year could have been a very wet year. If, of course, I'd had the good sense to collect my tears in buckets and shower them over the country. I could have even sold them to water tankers and made a bit of money on the side. Damn. When I'm upset, I never think of useful things.

The cancer had spread to the lymph nodes, after all. Mantra had shed more tears over the loss of her hair than she had over the loss of her flesh. 'I'm like a bloody dog, shedding hair wherever I go,' she wailed.

She had no idea what she looked like, however—Vir had thoughtfully removed all the mirrors at home, and for that she was grateful. She was certain that if she saw herself hairless, she'd have a heart attack and die on the spot.

She refused to believe the oncologist when he warmly assured her that it would grow back—thicker and more lustrous than before. 'Just like in those shampoo ads,' he said encouragingly.

Vir gave her some pretty scarves which she churlishly tossed into the bin. 'No way! I refuse to go around looking like a dowdy old Mother Goose,' she whined. 'I'd much rather pretend I'm an ageing but exciting sci-fi chick.'

'That's exactly it!' Vir thumped the dining table in a Eureka moment way. 'That's exactly what you remind me of! In fact I think that you should always have this style—it suits you, Mantra. It gives you an interesting elfin look.'

He got a glare in response.

The chemotherapy sessions left her nauseous for days, too nauseous to appreciate Kaushalya's fabulous cooking—that was the unkindest cut in her opinion. Fear loomed again—the lump in her breast hadn't made her feel this sick so she must definitely be dying, she reasoned. Once again the oncologist, who now featured on her speed dial, assured her that chemotherapy made people feel much, much, much sicker than they really were. 'You're actually getting better with every passing second, my dear,' he said.

Vir was more bracing, though a little less sympathetic. 'You're absolutely fine, Mantra. You're like a bloody rat or a roach—you'll even survive a nuclear explosion.'

'Are you aware that you suffer from terminal rudeness?' she asked with a grin. She was relieved that Vir had got back to being his old self. His uncustomary tenderness had begun to grate on her nerves. They were *meant* to be rude to each other. Affectionate insults—the glue that held their marriage together.

All she did during those days was lie in bed feeling sorry for herself. Samira rarely dropped by, thankfully; she was too busy leading a hectic life creating tacky art in the mornings and partying at night. She'd made it to page 3 eventually. Mantra had laughed out loud when she saw a picture of Samira with half of her husband's face in the frame. The caption read: 'Artist Samira Mirchandani with a friend.' The tables had certainly turned in that relationship. Smart woman, Mantra grudgingly conceded, and to think I had her tagged as a bimbo! Presents were still delivered at Mantra's door, however. The Botox gift coupons were replaced by a Cleopatra wig (which Mantra never wore) and coupons for massages at spas (which Mantra never used). As time slowly passed, the oncologist was proved right—Mantra's hair did start growing again, a few months after the last chemotherapy session.

Vir arrived and ceremoniously offered her a plate of burnt toast masquerading as bruschetta. 'Voila! Try this.'

It wasn't *that* bad, Mantra mentally conceded. Better than Reshma's cooking, for sure.

'Oh, there's something in here you really must read—it's apparently an interesting new trend in the UK,' he said, picking the newspaper off her lap. He turned to the science page and jabbed a finger at an article. Mantra gave it a cursory glance.

'Why on earth are you making me read an article on people in their fifties who make out like rabbits?' she grimaced.

'Just to let you know that we have lots to look forward to,' Vir said wisely. Or was it hopefully?

Acknowledgements

My Girl Friday, Kushalrani Gulab aka Bunny: What would *you* do if you'd written a book and had a sister whom you regard as one of the finest editors in the country? Ask her to help you with it, right? Heck, I had to beg. My knees are still sore and as red as the ink she cruelly ravaged my manuscript with. Thanks Bun, all that prostration has kept me (and my book) in great shape.

My official editors, Avanija Sundaramurti and Mekhala Moorthy: Thank you very, very much for your enthusiasm, objectivity and the fine finishing touches. Editors like you help authors sleep well at night. Now, if only you were a little less stubborn about the house style, you'd be perfect!

My cover designer, Viraj Rohan Circar: I've always wanted my talented nephew (nepotism again, damn) to design my book covers and, fortunately, when the terrific design team at Penguin saw his concept and design, I got the go-ahead. Thanks boyo, I love your style!

My supporters, Roma Circar, Salil Sadanandan, Ranjona Banerji and Gia Goyal: All of them read the book at the manuscript stage and offered invaluable bits of advice. All except Gia, because I absolutely refused to lend it to her. Only because her baby likes to chew paper and I have a frighteningly moody printer. However, she really, really, really wanted to read it and I thank her for that.